Running with Horses

KAT CANFIELD

CHAMPAGNE BOOK GROUP

Running With Horses

Published by Champagne Book Group
2373 NE Evergreen Avenue, Albany OR 97321 U.S.A.

~~~

First Edition 2022

pISBN: 978-1-957228-70-9

Cover Art by Robyn Hart

www.champagnebooks.com

Version_1

Excerpt

Dee took a hot shower and fell into bed. About midnight, her grumbling stomach woke her. Maybe she should have eaten something before going to bed. Now wide awake, she padded to the kitchen, flipping on the television as she walked by. The late local news popped up on the screen.

She fixed a bowl of cereal and sat down. The reporter talked about a second body found in the sugarcane fields in the western area of the county. The police were investigating it in connection to one found the week before. The reporter speculated there could be a serial murderer working in Palm Beach County.

Picking up the remote, she changed the channel. *Not exactly a topic to hear about when you've found a way to evade the stalker.* She continued flipping the channels until finding an old movie. The news of two murders kept rolling through her mind.

She took another bite of cereal. Her thoughts strayed back to the news story. *Forget about what you heard.* But she couldn't. Both victims were Hispanic men in their twenties, strangled by an unknown assailant. At least the victims were men; a sense of relief flowed over her. Yet it sent a shiver up her spine to know a murderer lurked somewhere in the shadows of a place she wanted to call home.

It couldn't be the stalker. Cop blood permeated on her mother's side of the family tree. And cop thinking came along with it. Chances were the men knew the murderer personally, which gave the murderer access. Hispanics made up a large part of the transient horse community. *Could I have seen or spoken to such a person?*

She could sense eyes spying on her when the stalker did his surveillance. An unsettling feeling came over her. There were no windows in her apartment so it must be her imagination brought on by the news story. Focusing back to the Bogart movie she'd found, she hoped for distraction. Her hands began to shake. Slipping them under her thighs helped calm them.

Maybe I should ask the community security patrol to make a run past the house. No, it's only my overactive imagination. Time to get over it.

"You'll never have a life if you don't take a stand," she said, loudly, to make herself believe it. But she fell to her knees in prayer for protection and peace of mind.

And we know that to them that love God all things work together for good, even to them that are called according to his purpose.
Romans 8:28 ASV

Chapter One

Dee Collins scanned the farm where she boarded her horse in Wellington, Florida. At nine PM, the farm should be devoid of humans. She routinely checked the horses one last time for the day. After she drove through the squeaky electronic security gate, the tension left her shoulders. Hiding in the winter capital of the horse world, she planned to get lost among the many migrating equestrians. No one would recognize her here; she planned to keep it that way.

A year ago, in her old home in Hialeah, she'd found the security camera she had installed smashed to bits. The message written on the wall next to it had chilled her to the bone. It read, "I'll use this bat on your skull next."

Running seemed the only option. Running and hiding. She'd spent the past year hiding at racetracks from New York to Florida with her horse, Roscoe. She'd lived in the on-track housing in a small one-room area no bigger than the tack stalls used to store hay and feed. She prayed the man who stalked her had given up. She wanted her life back. A few months ago, she'd found this farm, moved into an apartment, and determined to build a new life. However, she still took precautions by taking an extra glance around before climbing out of her truck.

The sound of horses pawing at their stall doors captured her attention. She'd taken the job of groom and stable hand a week ago when the regular groom, Miguel, failed to show up one morning. Rocket Man, one of the horses, recognized the sound of her truck anytime she drove in. He kicked the stall door at feeding times as her arrival meant food. Sadly, he'd taught the obnoxious trick to her horse, Roscoe, who stood in the next stall over. She would forgive Rocket Man the disgusting habit—the glistening black stallion looked like a muscular equine god—but her plain-looking brown horse, not so much.

This evening, the banging sounded louder than normal. Much louder. She doled out the hay which they all munched—except Chanel.

The toffee-colored mare stood in the corner of her stall, pounding the floor and the wall with her hoof. Judging from the size of the hole, the digging had begun a while ago. Picking up a halter, Dee entered the stall. Chanel continued her pounding, hitting the wall. When Dee touched the horse's neck, a clammy heat radiated through her hand.

"You're colicky, aren't you, girl?"

Chanel pressed her head against Dee's chest. She'd spent every day since childhood around horses and had learned their subtle language. The hole in the floor and the sweat on the mare's neck told her this horse needed attention.

"I need to get you moving." She led Chanel out of the stall and around the barn. She walked the mare—or more like the mare walked her—at a quick pace. Relieving a horse's pain was no easy thing.

"I've got to call a vet, Chanel. Slow down. I'll make the call."

Scrolling through the numbers on her phone, she tapped the trainer's name. The call connected to voicemail. "Magda, Chanel is colicking. She needs a vet now. Call me immediately. I don't know which vet you use." She hung up. Magda hadn't posted emergency contact numbers in the stable like the other trainers on the farm. *How am I supposed to know which vet to use?*

Waiting for a return call was not an option. This horse needed a vet as soon as possible. She walked with Chanel to the barn next to hers. The trainer in this barn, Dee's new friend Silva Martin, posted emergency numbers so Dee called the veterinarian listed. The call went to an answering service and the lady who answered said she'd take her phone number, notify the vet, and he would call back immediately.

The return call came five minutes later. "I hate to bother you so late. My name is Dee Collins, and I work for Magda Jovanovich. One of the horses is colicking. I called Magda, but she didn't answer, and Chanel needs a vet now. My friend, Silva, has you listed as her emergency call vet. Can you please come help?"

"Are you at Everglades Farm like Silva?" The man's deep voice sounded calming after the quick pace she'd maintained.

"I'm in the barn next door."

"You sound like you're running. Are you okay?"

"Chanel is keeping a quick tempo me. She doesn't want to roll but is pacing as fast as I can maintain my steps beside her."

"I'm leaving now. I'll be there shortly."

Dee stopped in front of the tack room long enough to grab a thermometer. Chanel paused, seeming to understand the need, while Dee took her temperature. One hundred and two; elevated from the normal ninety-nine. The marching continued.

Time ticked by while Dee kept pace with Chanel. The other horses in her barn surveyed them over the stall doors. They tossed their heads, and soft, sympathetic nickers came from each as they passed. Dee silently prayed for the horse's safety. She never considered it wrong to ask God to protect horses like she would a human.

After what seemed like hours, a truck pulled up to the front gate. Dee had selected this farm not only because it had a security gate, but because the gate squealed so loudly. She always took note of who drove through. It gave her reassurance to be aware of who came onto the property. She took comfort from the safety of that gate even though her stalker had never contacted her face to face. His calling card had been to leave black roses for her when he vandalized her property.

She recognized the form of a veterinarian's mobile unit as the driver punched in the security code. He drove through the gate and parked in front of her barn. A tall man with dark hair got out and strode into the stable. His wide shoulders and slim waist looked rather good in blue plaid shirt and khaki trousers. If Chanel hadn't been so sick, Dee might have sighed at the sight of such a handsome man.

Her heartbeat quickened. The man moved with an air of strength and confidence.

"Hi, I'm Dr. Marcus Helton," he said, extending his hand. "Is this the horse in trouble?"

What a calm and soothing voice. "I'm Dee. It's been close to an hour now since I found her pawing in the stall." Dee told him about Chanel's raised temperature and her other odd behaviors, and as she did she had a hard time focusing on anything other than Dr. Helton.

Their hands touched when he ran his over the horse's abdomen. A jolt of electricity came out of the blue. Dee's breath caught in her throat. Had he noticed it? His silence gave no clue. Then he looked up; their eyes met. He glanced away. Ah, so he had been aware of it also.

"You caught this in time," he said. "Any longer and we'd be taking her to my clinic. You did an excellent job keeping her moving. I'll give her a shot to ease her pain."

"Magda still isn't answering her phone. I hope we don't have to take her to the hospital. I'd hate to make that decision. I don't even know if Magda owns her or not."

"Magda isn't a client. I met her when I was here for one of Silva's horses. I don't know who her regular vet is. What kind of trainer doesn't provide emergency information to the people who care for her horses? I can't imagine any of my clients being that irresponsible."

"I know, right? She has nothing posted that is visible. I thought about looking in her tack boxes but I'm not going through them without permission. She has strange ways when it comes to horses. I'm chalking it up to cultural differences. She's Russian so maybe they do things differently."

"You recognized the signs of colic, which is more than most stable help I come across. How is it you're working with Magda?" Dr. Helton gave her a lingering look. "She isn't popular with the other trainers at this farm."

"The groom who worked here before me didn't show up one morning. I was here, and she offered me the job. I already had a stall for my horse in this barn before she moved her horses in. Right place at the right time, I guess." She gave a slight shrug.

"Well, lucky for this horse, you understood something was wrong. She needs fluids. Can you hold her?"

"Sure. I've helped the vets at the racetrack."

Together they treated the horse. A smoldering warmth coursed through her each time Dr. Helton stood close beside her. She tried hard not to look at him when it happened because she didn't want to make him uncomfortable.

When the IV was finished, she brought Dr. Helton a chair. She turned a bucket upside down a few feet away and sat upon it, keeping an eye on the horse as well as the doc.

"Which track did you work at?" Dr. Helton asked after a few minutes.

"I worked at Hialeah many years ago and recently up in Kentucky."

"Did you work for any trainers I'd know?"

"Probably not." She pressed her lips together. She couldn't risk giving out any personal information. Doing so might lead to the stalker discovering her new location.

"It's been many years since I interned at the tracks in Dade County," he continued.

That's good, Dee thought, relaxing a bit.

"What brings you to Wellington?" he asked.

So he's not giving up. "I love dressage, and there are many horses here who need good grooms."

"There's always a need for grooms," he said. "It's nice to have one who speaks English. For late night emergencies, I often get one who doesn't."

She glared at him. "Just because most stable help is of Hispanic descent is no reason to be prejudicial."

"I'm—I'm not." His eyes widened, and a blush bloomed on his cheeks. "I'm sorry it sounded that way. I meant it's nice to have someone who can tell me what I need to know and say it so I understand. It's also nice to have someone who can assist me as you have. If you didn't have a job, I'd hire you myself. A good assistant is hard to find."

That was a nice apology. She liked the compliment. Plus, what he said about Hispanics working in horse barns was true.

"*Gracias, amigo,*" she answered in perfectly accented Spanish. "*Estoy feliz de ayudar.*"

"You speak Spanish? I'm not sure what you said, but I'm sorry I sounded insensitive. What was I thinking? Of course, you can speak Spanish. You said you worked the racetrack in Hialeah. That's like Little Havana."

She leaned back on the bucket with her hands clasped around one knee. "Yes, I *hablo español*. My grandparents came from Cuba, and I grew up in the shadow of Hialeah Racetrack. I watched the flamingos fly over the track every day after the eighth race. My grandfather helped fight against Castro. They immigrated to the U.S. when my father was six months old." She hadn't shared her story with anyone since coming there and certainly hadn't intended to give him so much information.

"Again, I'm sorry if I offended you. I heard the last name of Collins and didn't expect such perfect Spanish."

"I'm not offended. I've worked hard at getting rid of the accent. I like to pretend I don't understand when people speak Spanish. I can learn a lot eavesdropping."

"Hmm, when I need a translator, I'll call you."

"I'd like that." Dee smiled. Perhaps it hadn't hurt to share some of her personal information.

"Your horse is starting to look for food in the shavings. She's feeling much better. I think she'll be fine tonight. What time do you feed in the morning?"

"Six," she answered.

"You feed at six? It's close to two now. Hardly time to get home before you come back. You don't have someone else who could feed in the morning?"

"No, it's late to get someone else. Besides, Chanel is my responsibility."

"Okay. I'm sure you know this but offer her only a handful of hay in the morning. Call me if anything is amiss. I'll come by to check on her tomorrow. Here's my business card. My cell number is on the back. You can call me direct without going through the answering service."

"Thanks, Doc. I can't believe Magda hasn't called. I'm going to watch Chanel for a bit longer. I can't thank you enough for your help."

"You're welcome. I'll see you tomorrow morning," he said as he walked toward his truck. Before getting in he called back to her. "And please call me Marcus."

Marcus. She liked his name. It fit him: tall, handsome, manly. He looked as good from behind away as he had when he arrived. Surely, she hadn't imagined the magnetism passing between them, yet he didn't seem fazed by their close contact. She put it out of her mind for now.

Chanel stood in the corner of the stall. Dee looked at her watch. By the time she got home, she would get only a few hours' sleep before it was time to get up and come back.

"Chanel, if I go home I won't sleep for worrying about you. How would you like a roommate tonight?"

The horse snorted.

"You get comfortable, and I'll be back with some bedding for me. Shavings make me itch."

In the tack room she found several horse blankets to spread out on the floor of the stall. If Chanel took a turn for the worse during the night, she'd know it. Once her makeshift bed lay under the manger, she turned out the barn lights. Considering the terror that possessed her after finding her car vandalized or her house broken into, she believed herself a lot safer with the horses. Her nerves tingled under the skin at the thoughts of those terrorizing moments. *Will these horrible sensations ever go away?*

Dear Lord, thank you for sending a caring vet to help this horse. Thank you for watching out for me this past year. While I don't understand the reasons for this trial, I know You have a plan in mind. And I pray for Your continued protection. Amen.

~ * ~

Marcus looked at the dashboard clock after filling out the paperwork on Chanel—after 2 A.M. He left the farm and drove home. He'd put his daughter to bed before getting the emergency call. What a blessing it had been when his mother suggested moving into his house after his ex-wife left.

He sent a prayer heavenward, thanking Him for her decision. After his father died, his mother didn't like living alone. The arrangement worked for her and provided care for Kaitlyn when he received emergency calls. God did answer small needs.

His thoughts turned back to the lovely, blonde-haired, blue-eyed Dee. Those eyes were a contrast to her olive skin tone. Usually, he didn't think a lot about the people who cared for the animals he vetted. He considered the horses his clients; people were personalities he dealt with. But Dee captured his attention. It was more than her beauty. Something about her pulled from deep within and drew him to her.

"You're an enigma, Miss Dee," he said, and smiled.

Perhaps her evasive nature triggered his curiosity. She'd shied away when he asked too many questions. And that blonde hair wasn't natural—that was one of the things a man picked up from living around women. Her thick, dark eyebrows and long black lashes gave her away. As for her horsemanship, that trainer didn't appreciate what a gem she had in Dee, going the extra mile for those horses.

He'd worked the racetracks down in Miami when he first got out of veterinary college. Something about her seemed familiar, yet he couldn't place her. Taller than most jockeys, petite, and fit, she may have been an exercise rider. Perhaps he'd seen her in passing. She knew her horses and veterinary procedures, proving she did more than clean stalls and feed. She definitely interested him.

No, she didn't. He reminded himself he had an aversion to all dateable women. His divorce had been finalized only six months ago. It hadn't been pretty. His ex-wife had destroyed his faith in women. After he received full custody of his eight-year-old daughter, the only women he had faith in were her and his mother.

He chuckled. *What woman in her right mind would want to take on that package?*

Reaching home, he fell into his bed after another long day, but sleep didn't come easy. He couldn't wait to check on the colicky horse in the morning—and to see Dee.

Chapter Two

Sleeping came sporadically. When Chanel lay down, Dee watched to make sure the mare didn't roll. She waited a few minutes, but the horse was resting, a good sign. It seemed as if only a few minutes passed when the other horses let her know it was time to wake up and feed them. They had internal alarm clocks. The door banging began a few minutes before six.

Dee fed everyone else first, then gave Chanel a handful of hay. The mare went at it hungrily. The colic symptoms appeared to be gone. After feeding, Dee went to the small restroom located off the tack room. A quick wash of her face, a swish of mouthwash, and she began her work day.

Magda still hadn't called. As Dee folded the horse blankets she'd slept on, the squeal of the gate alerted her to someone about to enter. She peeped out of the tack room to see who had arrived so early. Doctor Helton's veterinary truck came through the gate. She slipped the blanket into the tack box as he walked in.

"Horse blankets?" Marcus asked. "It's a bit warm for those, isn't it?" He paused when he saw a stack of them on the floor. "You slept here last night?"

"You're quick," she said. "I couldn't leave Chanel in case something happened. She's doing well this morning, by the way."

"That should've been my first question. Chanel rested well?"

"Yes, she did. She's munching hay as we speak. Thanks for coming out last night to care for her."

"No problem, that's what I do. If you were here all night, then you haven't had breakfast. I could run out and get you something."

"I didn't even think about that. I have some fruit in the refrigerator."

"Do you drink coffee? I came by here before getting a cup for myself. I'll bring you one and something else to eat if you'd like."

"Well, a black coffee would be nice, but don't go out of your way. If Magda ever calls, I'll ask her to bring me one."

"She hasn't checked on her horse yet? Dee, that's negligence. She put a lot of responsibility on you. What if that horse needed transport to the clinic, and I needed to do surgery? I'd need permission from the owner or the owner's representative. Even if you said to go ahead, the cost could have come back on you if the owner decided not to pay."

"And I'd have said go ahead and paid the bill myself. I wouldn't let an animal suffer."

"Well, still, Magda should be here now, as they are her responsibility. She should be doing your work so you can get some sleep. I'm sure you didn't get much last night."

His concern warmed through Dee. Everything he said about Magda was right. "I'm fine, Dr. Helton. I've done with a lot less sleep. It's part of the job. You needn't worry about me."

"Please, Dee, call me Marcus. No need for formality. I'll bring you a cup of coffee." He strode back to his truck.

Dee tried not to smile as she cleaned stalls. Her thoughts were all about Marcus. A good-looking guy like him showing interest in her like that—well, it had been a long time. Warmth flowed through. This past year she'd never been comfortable letting anyone get close. But here she'd made a few friends. Something about *here* eased her anxieties. Perhaps God had answered prayers, and her nightmare could be over.

Still, she couldn't afford getting involved romantically if she might need to run again. *If only I could figure out who this stalker is.* The one person she thought it could be had been in prison when the first incident occurred. But the warmth radiating throughout her body as she thought about Marcus running out to get her a cup of coffee, drove all the negative energy out of her.

"He's only being nice to me because I helped him last night," she murmured. She smiled, lost in thought.

"Here you go, Dee."

She flinched and faced the open stall door. Marcus grinned at her. His outstretched hand offered her a cup. *Did he hear what I said?*

"Black coffee, as ordered." He placed the large to-go cup in her hand. "I also brought you a biscotti."

Her heartbeat elevated when their hands touched. "Thanks." She took the cup and napkin containing the biscotti. "How did you know I liked biscotti?"

"Lucky guess." He smiled. "If you don't, I'll eat it. I like them enough to eat two." He walked to Chanel's stall and opened the door.

The horse ambled over to him, poking her nose into his hands, hoping for more food.

"You appear much better," he said as he ran his hand over her neck. He took her temperature. "A perfect ninety-nine degrees." He patted her on the rump. Closing the stall door, he moved back to where Dee was cleaning Rocket Man's stall. "Chanel can have a small amount of grain for lunch, then her normal feed this evening. No work today. If all goes well, she can go back to work tomorrow."

Rocket Man, her favorite of Magda's horses, nuzzled Dee's back. The glistening black stallion gently rubbed a stiffened upper lip over the sore back muscles caused by her night on the floor. He rubbed all the right spots.

"I'll tell Magda when she comes in. I'm sure Chanel appreciates your help." She let Rocket Man continue massaging her back as she dunked the biscotti. "Thanks again for the coffee. I appreciate it."

"You're welcome." Marcus stood watching the horse rub Dee's back. "Amazing. It's like he knows how to do massage," he muttered. Louder he said, "I need to get to the office. If you need anything, call me."

"Thanks again, Doc, hmm...Marcus," she called after him. She couldn't help eyeing the play of muscles through the fabric of his shirt and pants.

The stallion pressed his lip harder against her stiff muscles. "Are you jealous, Rocket Man? How about hitting this spot?" She pointed to her left shoulder blade. He happily worked his lip over that spot. She sighed.

"Is that horse giving you a massage?" asked her friend Silva.

Dee jumped. She'd been so preoccupied by Rocket Man's ministrations and Marcus's leaving that she hadn't heard Silva arrive. Silva, with her long, slim legs, treaded in near silence on the cement aisleway. She stood a good eight inches taller than Dee's five-foot-one.

"Yeah, and it feels good." She pointed to her lumbar section and the stallion moved there. "Chanel colicked last night."

"What? Did you need to call a vet? Who did you call?"

"Magda didn't return my call and she has nothing posted so I checked your bulletin board and called your vet."

"Dr. Helton is the best. How bad was it?"

"Fluids, pain killers, lots of walking."

"That's good. How late were you here?"

"He left about two. He wanted to be sure she wouldn't go down again."

"He's a good vet. You could do worse than hanging out in a barn all night with a guy like that."

"We were watching a sick horse. It's not like it was a date."

"Yeah, but weren't you *hoping* for him to ask you out? If I weren't married and was hanging out with him, well, I'd have made the best of it."

"Well, you are married. He's a nice guy, but I'm not looking. We were working. Speaking of which, I need to get back to it. Thanks, Rocket Man. I'm ready for the next stall." Dee kissed his nose before closing the stall door. The horse tossed his head and snorted. She couldn't contain her grin as she shuffled off to the next stall.

"I think he likes you," Silva said as she ducked into the tack room. "Hey, why are the blankets out of the tack box?" She paused a few seconds. "Wait, don't tell me. You slept in the barn last night. You should've texted me this morning. I'd have brought you something for breakfast. No wonder you were enjoying that horse rubbing your back."

"I slept on the blankets last night. I hope it was okay I used some of yours too. I thought about texting you about coffee but someone else brought me some."

"Gee, was that person a certain handsome doctor? I thought I saw him driving down Sycamore Road this morning. Who says chivalry is dead?"

"He was here checking on the horse. It's nothing more than that."

"I wish I'd hired you before Magda did. You went above and beyond staying here. Weren't you concerned being here alone at night?"

"Staying made more sense than going home. Besides, I'd have been anxious that she didn't relapse. And that security gate out front makes enough noise to wake the dead."

"That's true. It's critters scurrying down the aisle that would frighten me."

"I didn't even consider that."

"Like I said, I wish you were taking care of my horses," Silva repeated as she left.

Dee finished her last stall as Magda breezed in. Magda usually rode Chanel first every morning. But since the mare wasn't working today, Dee had haltered Rocket Man instead.

"Why him and not Chanel?" Magda asked in her thick Russian accent.

"I called you last night. Chanel colicked yesterday and needed a vet. I called Dr. Helton at Wellington Equine. He took care of her. He said she shouldn't work today."

"He is good. I don't have vet. I could get interested in fine doctor though. He looks good." Magda licked her lips, then stalked off toward the tack room without another word.

With Rocket Man saddled, Magda took the reins from Dee. She mounted and rode off toward the riding arena. Dee frowned. The woman acted like nothing had happened. She didn't even go look at Chanel or ask about what the vet did or had to say about her.

The rest of the day progressed as normal. When Magda got off the last horse, she threw the reins to Dee and left the barn. Dee stopped her work to watch as Magda sauntered toward one of the other barns on the farm. A half hour later she left, again without checking on Chanel.

Silva breezed into the tack room while Dee cleaned bridles. "What did Magda have to say about you calling out Dr. Helton? She only shrugged when I asked how the horse was."

"She didn't say a thing and never went to look at Chanel."

"She doesn't seem to have much feeling for anyone but herself."

"No, she doesn't. It's like she has something more important going on."

"I'd say she has a love interest somewhere. She's been in a good mood the last few days. She's spending a lot of her free time over in barn four."

"Well, if it keeps her happy, I hope it lasts a while. She's been good to work for the last few days. Except—"Dee lowered her voice— "for last night. If someone had called to tell me my horse was colicking, there's nothing that would keep me from getting here to care for it."

"Yeah, I know, me too. If you worked for me and had to be here because I couldn't, then I'd have taken the evening feeding and sent you home early. Did Magda even offer?"

"No. She didn't even ask what time the horse colicked. She doesn't know I spent the night here."

"I'm sure she never gave it a thought," Silva scoffed. "She doesn't think about anyone but herself. If you set up the feed for your horses, I'll drop it for you. You go home. Swapping feedings helps us both. It's the least I can do for you."

"Thanks, I'll take you up on that. I'd love a long hot bath. Are you sure it's not an imposition?"

"Oh, please. Much as I love hanging out with you, you deserve to get out of here early tonight. Don't worry about the 'children.' I'll look in on them when I come back for my night check. If I notice any problems I'll call you, not Magda, I promise."

"Thanks, Silva, you're a good friend." She hugged her. "I'll see you in the morning."

Twenty minutes later Dee arrived in the driveway of her small apartment. She surveyed the area, always on the lookout for signs of the stalker. It had become a habit. But nothing suspicious had happened since moving here.

She lived in a remodeled garage, a one-room apartment with a tiny bath. It, like the stables, gave her peace of mind. Surely, God had brought her here for a reason. Perhaps the reason was a stable of talented horses whose trainer didn't seem to care much for them.

Having a family next to her in the main house gave comfort and security too. The community had a guarded security gate and high walls. The stalker would find it difficult to make his way through to her new fortress. Changing her name and appearance and moving to a new town seemed the best way to make sure he never bothered her again.

She purchased the house with her winnings from different horses she had trained the year before the stalking started. It had been in foreclosure and a great deal. Since her sister had married and moved to England with her husband, Dee could safely use her sister's name as her own. That's how Ileana Garcia could easily become Dee Collins. No one asked questions and so far the ruse worked.

Then she converted the garage into an apartment and rented out the main house. Since she spent so much time at the stables, it didn't make sense to use the entire house. Plus, if the stalker found her, she could pick up and leave; the rental income would come in handy while she was on the run.

Wellington had become as close to a home as she'd had since hitting the road. But still, she took precautions.

She'd done well as an assistant trainer in her father's racing stable. But her heart preferred dressage. She hadn't planned to groom for Magda but took the position when the previous groom failed to show up one morning. The assignment might prove more of a challenge than Dee originally thought. A new job, a new home, and a new goal would heal her spirit and confidence.

~ * ~

Later in the evening, Marcus drove up in front of Dee's barn. Silva sat on the bench out front.

"What brings you back to the stable, Dr. Helton?" she asked. "I don't believe any of our horses are sick tonight."

"I'm checking on the mare from last night. Is Dee still here?" He looked down the barn aisle.

"I owe her several feedings, so I paid her back this evening. She went home a couple hours ago. Are you here to check on the horse or the horse's groom?" Silva asked with a bit of mischief in her eyes.

"Ahh, the horse." He drew out the words. "How is Chanel?"

"She was ready to knock me down for her feed, so I think she's fine."

"That's good. I'm glad Dee called me as early as she did. Any longer and the horse would've needed surgery."

"Dee's an excellent groom. I'd trust her with my horses anytime. Magda doesn't deserve her. She didn't even thank Dee for calling you or staying with the horse all night."

"If I'd known she would spend the night in the barn, I'd have stayed with her."

"And you planned to see her this evening."

"I don't know what you're talking about." *Did Silva think he had a crush on Dee? Well, did he? No, I'm only interested in the horse.* "She's a nice person. I found her to be a very competent horsewoman. As a vet, I appreciate that. It makes my job much easier."

"Marcus, I've known you for several years. You are all about your patients. I am only kidding. I know you're here to check Chanel. But I also know you came to see her this morning. Then you left and brought coffee back for Dee. I've never known you to do that for anyone else—not even me. I saw the disappointment on your face when I said she wasn't here. You're interested in Dee and not only because she's competent with horses. And for the record, I think it's nice, for both of you."

Marcus opened his mouth to deny what Silva said but stopped. Instead, he toddled over to Chanel's stall. Sometimes it was better not to engage in an argument he couldn't win.

He closed the stall door and went back to where Silva was sitting. "I could use a vet tech. Dee seems competent for the job. She's clearly more knowledgeable than a simple groom. What do you know about her?"

"She came to the farm about six weeks ago looking for a stall for her horse. She said she'd worked the racetracks. I've watched her with the horses and watched her ride. She's exceptionally talented. You're right. She's more than the average groom. I'd take her on as my assistant trainer, she's that talented. I'm glad she chose this farm. We've become close friends. You should see the things she's taught her own horse. He's not much of a dressage horse but he's well trained. I think her heart is set on learning to train dressage horses. But you keep coming around to visit. I like having a concierge vet."

"With that old nag of yours still on the circuit, I can see why you want one. I've worked on him enough over the years." He appreciated Silva's candor and the information about Dee.

"Yes, you have. You keep coming around to check on him and see Dee."

Marcus shook his head as he returned to his truck. "Good night, Silva," he said as he left. "Matchmaking women," he muttered under his breath.

Nonetheless, he thought about what Silva said. She hadn't given him much more information about Dee. She kept her personal life to herself unlike many women he'd run across. His interest in Dee didn't fit into his life. Yet, perhaps, she'd crossed his path for a reason.

~ * ~

Dee took a hot shower and fell into bed. About midnight, her grumbling stomach woke her. Maybe she should have eaten something before going to bed. Now wide awake, she padded to the kitchen, flipping on the television as she walked by. The late local news popped up on the screen.

She fixed a bowl of cereal and sat down. The reporter talked about a second body found in the sugarcane fields in the western area of the county. The police were investigating it in connection to one found the week before. The reporter speculated there could be a serial murderer working in Palm Beach County.

Picking up the remote, she changed the channel. *Not exactly a topic to hear about when you've found a way to evade the stalker.* She continued flipping the channels until finding an old movie. The news of two murders kept rolling through her mind.

She took another bite of cereal. Her thoughts strayed back to the news story. *Forget about what you heard.* But she couldn't. Both victims were Hispanic men in their twenties, strangled by an unknown assailant. At least the victims were men; a sense of relief flowed over her. Yet it sent a shiver up her spine to know a murderer lurked somewhere in the shadows of a place she wanted to call home.

It couldn't be the stalker. Cop blood permeated on her mother's side of the family tree. And cop thinking came along with it. Chances were the men knew the murderer personally, which gave the murderer access. Hispanics made up a large part of the transient horse community. *Could I have seen or spoken to such a person?*

She could sense eyes spying on her when the stalker did his surveillance. An unsettling feeling came over her. There were no windows in her apartment so it must be her imagination brought on by the news story. Focusing back to the Bogart movie she'd found, she hoped for distraction. Her hands began to shake. Slipping them under her thighs helped calm them.

Maybe I should ask the community security patrol to make a run past the house. No, it's only my overactive imagination. Time to get over it.

"You'll never have a life if you don't take a stand," she said, loudly, to make herself believe it. But she fell to her knees in prayer for protection and peace of mind.

Chapter Three

Marcus marched the short block from his office to the Welli Deli. After the phone call from his ex-wife, Lauren, he needed to walk off the negative energy it generated. She demanded to take their daughter, Kaitlyn, on a ski trip to Vail over Christmas vacation. That would happen over his dead body.

"How wonderful would it be for Kaitlyn to spend time in the snow on Christmas?" she had implored him.

While she had a point about the snow, it would mean he wouldn't see Kaitlyn on Christmas morning. He enjoyed hearing her squeals of joy while opening her Christmas presents. Why should he give up his entire holiday with his daughter?

Last year, during their separation, they'd shared Kaitlyn during the holidays. It had worked well for the family. But taking Kaitlyn for an entire week? Sure, she would enjoy sled riding and snowball fights, but those were activities he wanted to experience with his daughter. It might be selfish but it was Lauren who left him and Kaitlyn.

He'd love to vacation with Kaitlyn that week, but Christmas and New Year were especially busy for his practice. Horses often got sick more during this time of year; probably because their routines were changed by the humans who cared for them.

Plus, she would probably spend most of the time alone. He knew from experience that Lauren would be busy with her friends to spend any quality time with Kaitlyn. In fact, since the divorce, Lauren had only spent two afternoons with Kaitlyn, and neither was on her birthday.

He took his regular seat at the counter in the deli. The cook waved at him from behind a grill full of bacon. The usual crowd sat at their tables, the waitresses busily taking orders.

"Good morning, Doc." Lori, the waitress, stood across the counter. "You want your usual?" She set a steaming cup in front of him.

"Good morning, Lori. Yes, that would be good."

"Hey, Doc." Brad Tyler, a county sheriff's deputy and a close friend since high school, slid onto the stool next to him. "Good morning, Lori, how about a cup of that java?"

"Hello, Brad. What's happening today?" Marcus asked.

Lori set a hot coffee in front of Brad. "Good morning, Deputy. You're chipper this morning."

"It's another wonderful day in paradise." Brad grinned.

"Not at this hour of the morning it isn't." She laughed. "You having the usual also?"

"You know me better than my ex-wife, Lori. What's with the scowl on your face this morning?" Brad asked Marcus.

"I'm not scowling." He took a sip of coffee.

"Yes, you are. It's the same scowl I have when dealing with one of my ex-wives."

"Oh, yeah, you have experience in that area, don't you?"

"A lot of experience. Plus, I'm a detective."

"Rookie detective."

"Not a rookie when I'm put on a murder task force my sixth month on the job. An FBI profiler gave us a briefing this morning."

"I heard on the news about a second body."

"Yes, with so many similarities to be a coincidence." Brad lowered his voice to almost a whisper. "Both killed the same way, strangulation, with a sexual component."

"Are you telling me something you haven't released to the public?" Marcus whispered back. "And why are you sharing it?"

"Both victims were men. One worked as a stable hand on the showgrounds, the other as a deliveryman for one of the local feed stores. You're in the same community these guys frequent. You may have seen them or our perp. We are friends, and I'm using your knowledge to help find this person. Is there anyone you can think of who is possibly new to the area?"

"It's winter show season. Two-thirds of the population isn't from here," he reminded Brad. Marcus thought of Dee and her evasiveness.

"I know. But you're still a good person to have keeping your eyes and ears open for me. If you think of someone, let me know."

Lori placed the plates of eggs over medium, bacon strips, and hash browns in front of each of them. They dug in with gusto. She returned with the coffee pot to refill their cups. When she strolled away to wait on new customers, Marcus stopped eating and said, "What other information can you give me? Should I worry, since as you say, I'm in that community?"

"Both victims were men, small in stature. You don't fit the profile. Still, keep on your guard."

Lori came back. "What are you two whispering about over here?" She beamed a smile at Brad. "You're as bad as two little girls."

"Doc here is having woman problems," Brad enlightened her.

"What?" Marcus looked quizzically at Brad.

"What kind of problems?" Lori placed her head on her hand.

"I'm not, not really." Marcus shot Brad a dirty look. "I had a call from my ex-wife this morning. It put a damper on the entire day."

"Oh, is that all?" She leaned in closer. "Well, as soon as you get to the first farm this morning, the horsewomen will hit on you, brightening your whole day. I've heard women talk about you when they're in here. You should hear what they say."

"Wonderful. I didn't know I was a topic of conversation."

"Oh, yeah. The two most-asked questions are 'Is he gay?' and 'Is he married?' They all hope you'll be interested in them and not attached." A mischievous look accompanied her gossip.

"See, Doc? I told you, you have nothing to worry about. The next ex-wife is right around the corner, waiting for you to find her." Brad laughed.

"I learned from the first one, thank you. I think I'll work harder to keep the women guessing."

"You keep eating breakfast with me every morning and the women will give up on you," Brad warned.

"You tell them you know the truth, Lori. 'No, he's not gay' and 'No, he's not married.' But you can also add, 'No, he's not interested.'"

When they finished eating, she gave them both a to-go cup of coffee with the check. Brad stopped Marcus. "I wanted you to know that stuff, so you'll be careful when you're on those farms. I would also appreciate any information you can give me on the people you meet."

"I'll keep an eye out. Any other information you come up with, let me know when you can."

"When I get something else, I will. See ya later." Brad sauntered to his unmarked car.

Marcus walked back to his office in a lighter mood. He was on those farms every day. Thinking about Brad's warning, perhaps he'd met or seen the killer. However, the killer may have picked his victims based on opportunity. A killer might select a woman as easily as a man. His thoughts turned to Dee spending the night in the stable. Opportunity.

His daughter occasionally accompanied him on calls when she wasn't in school. Maybe her going out of town for a week when danger lurked posed an alternative. But it was Christmas.

He sighed. He'd come right back to where he started before the deli.

His first appointment of the morning was a check on a leg injury to Lili Stoneman's bay stallion, an Olympic hopeful. The horse was recovering from a suspensory ligament strain. Today would show if it could go back to training or remain on stall rest. Lili stabled a few barns down from Dee's.

Once he flexed the leg in question, he watched the horse as its groom trotted it on the pavement. The horse's gait looked good. Lili would be happy to have her horse back in work. He said goodbye to her and her staff, then climbed into his truck. What made the truck stop in front of Dee's barn mystified him. But once it did, he got out and went to look for her.

He found her mucking out Rocket Man's stall. "Hey, how's Chanel doing?" he asked.

She looked up and smiled. Leaning on her pitchfork, she wiped her brow with the back of one gloved hand. "She's eating fine, Doc. No more signs of the colic bout from the other night."

"That's good, but it sounds like you think there's another problem?"

"Nothing major. She's nippy when I tighten her girth. It could be bad training or psychological."

"Or she could have ulcers, which could be what triggered the colic."

"Exactly. I'm still learning her habits. Since you asked how she was doing, and I could find no reason for the colic, I thought it might be important information."

"She'd need an appointment to have her scoped. It will have to happen at the clinic, though."

"I'll run it by Magda—again. She didn't seem to believe me when I mentioned it before. Perhaps she'll listen if I tell her it's your suggestion."

Was she trying to manipulate a conversation between himself and Magda? Grooms usually did comprehend more about a horse's habits than the trainer. They should be able to discern normal from abnormal behavior by watching the horse; at least, a good groom did. Marcus wasn't familiar with Magda as a trainer as this was her first winter in Wellington. But from what he'd observed so far, he wasn't impressed.

"I'll mention it to her if I see her," he offered. "Will she come in today? It's Monday, and most trainers take the day off."

"I don't expect her, thankfully, as these horses need the day to be horses. She drills them when she rides. Aside from getting on and off, she pays them no attention. But I'm only the 'stable help'." Dee bracketed the words in air quotes. "Or so she keeps telling me. She enjoys berating me and criticizing any advice I give about the horses."

"Dee, from what I've seen, you're more educated than she gives you credit. Many other trainers would hire you. Why do you stay when she gives you no more appreciation than that?"

"Because if I leave, these horses will suffer. Every one of them is a potential champion if properly handled. Someone must advocate for them. Magda's old groom, Miguel, did what he could. However, he'd never go the extra mile for their welfare."

"If the trainers like Magda didn't have conscientious grooms, I'd have more injured horses to take care of. I prefer not to have job security at the expense of the horses. Do what you can for them, and when the season is over, I'll hire you for an assistant."

"Why thanks, Doc. But that's months away. And yours is not the only offer on the table."

"Yeah, Silva told me she wants you to work with her. I heard a similar comment from Lili Stoneman while I was there this morning. It's nice you have options."

"Options are good."

"I have more appointments to get to before lunch. Keep my offer in mind if the going gets tough with Magda."

"Thanks, Doc, I will."

"I told you call me Marcus."

"When you're working, 'doc' is appropriate. Marcus works when it's well—when you're not at work."

He returned to his truck, thinking how Dee made his day brighter as Lori had predicted.

~ * ~

About noon, an emergency call came in for a farm off Seminole-Pratt Whitney Road. In this section of the county, there were mostly large acreages containing cattle, horses, citrus groves, and sugarcane fields. Marcus crossed the cattle guard on the dirt lane just off the main road. Most of the horses out here worked the cattle.

He steered the truck up to an old single-wide trailer, where the ranch hands stayed, and a dilapidated wooden barn. He'd been taking care of this rancher's horses for years. Today, a horse that had cut itself on something became the priority.

Marcus walked around the old barn looking for the injured horse. Up ahead an older man working on a pump next to the canal waved at Marcus.

"I'm looking for John. Is he around?" he asked.

"Mr. John not here," the old man answered in a heavy Hispanic accent.

"Could you tell me where the horse is that needs stitches?"

"Mr. John not here," the man repeated.

"*Dónde caballo enfermo?*" Marcus fumbled over the Spanish. He'd picked up a few pertinent Spanish words, more importantly the ones that meant "sick horse."

"*Sí, caballo enfermo.*" The old man pointed toward the dirt road beside the canal.

Marcus figured the gesture meant he needed to drive west along the canal road. He hoped when he found the horse there was someone who spoke passable English. After about a half mile, two men and one horse came into view. Other horses milled around nearby. He stopped next to them. The men watched him as he got out of the truck.

"*Hola, usted el veterinario?*" one man asked.

"*Sí*, is this the *enfermo caballo?*" Marcus asked as best he could in his poor Spanish.

"*Sí, sí,*" the man answered, then started into a conversation in Spanish.

Marcus understood the words *caballo* and *sangre*, horse and blood, but nothing else. Fortunately, the sight of the horse with blood streaming down its front leg told the story. Flies already feasted on the blood. A cut that deep would require a lot of stitches. They were farther away from the barn than a horse in its condition should walk. The language gap would make this case difficult.

Marcus took the lead line held by the younger man and motioned for the men to follow as he led the horse to the rear of his truck. Handing the lead line back, he opened one compartment of the truck to begin the field surgery.

First, he prepared a shot of sedative for the horse and injected it into the neck. While he waited for the sedative to take effect, he unwrapped and laid out the rest of the surgical instruments he would need on the tailgate of the truck. The horse's head hung low, the sign the sedative had taken effect.

He washed the wound with water he carried in a portable tank in the truck in case water was not available in the field. The wound was worse than he first thought. He could use a second pair of hands, but how would he ask these men to help?

He washed his hands and pulled out the cellphone he kept clipped to his belt. He flipped through his contacts to find the number he needed and hit dial.

It took a few rings before Dee answered, "Hello."

"Dee, it's Marcus. Sorry to bother you but I'm on an emergency call, and there's a serious communication gap here. Could you speak to these men and help me out?"

"Yes, of course. Put the phone on speaker."

He selected the speaker button and turned up the volume. Dee began speaking in Spanish. The men realized what Marcus wanted and spoke toward the phone. When they finished explaining the situation, they moved back.

"Did you get all that?" he asked her.

"Yes, you have a mess on your hands. They told me you gave her a shot and washed the leg. What else do you need?"

"I need one of them to help hold the skin while I stitch it. I don't know how to ask them for help."

"Not a problem," she said then switched to Spanish to tell the men what he needed them to do.

The older man took the phone and positioned himself opposite the injured leg. He held the phone so they all could listen and talk. The younger man knelt beside the injured leg.

"Doc, they're ready. Tell me what you need," she said.

Marcus gave the instructions, and Dee translated. The conversation went back and forth until the stitches were in. He took bandages from the truck and rolled them over the injury. This horse needed transport back to his clinic. Marcus hadn't seen a cattle or horse trailer around when he came in.

"Dee, can you ask if there is a trailer here to transport the horse back to my clinic?"

"Already ahead of you. They told me there's no trailer available. The owner took a load of cattle up to Indian River. I have my trailer, and I'm heading your way."

"Well, I don't know what to say."

"I had a horse at the track with a similar cut. He spent two weeks in the clinic. Your helpers there were great at describing the wound, how she injured it, and your stitching job. Raul knew the horse would need to go to the clinic. I should be there in fifteen minutes."

"I guess they gave you the directions?"

"Yes, they did. See you soon."

Marcus took the phone back from the older man. "*Gracias,*

señor." He nodded to the man.

"*De nada.*" The man grinned.

Marcus offered the water to the younger man to wash the blood off his hands then handed him a towel. All in all, the situation had worked out much better than Marcus thought it would. The young man turned out to be a good assistant.

As the horse came out from under the sedation, Marcus gave her a couple more shots for pain and tetanus. It wasn't long before the rumble of a truck and trailer came from down the road. Dee stopped close to the horse, so it wouldn't have far to walk. In no time the horse loaded in.

She followed Marcus back to his clinic. He helped her unload the horse.

"She's a quiet girl," he said as Dee led the horse inside. "You didn't ask them her name, did you?"

"Her name is Yellow, and she's a ten-year-old quarter horse." Her smile melted him.

"That figures since she's a palomino. Why do Cuban cowboys always name their horses for their colors?"

"Honestly, it's probably for simplicity. The owner is a repeat client?"

"Yes, John is a good man, takes excellent care of his livestock. I didn't realize when he called that he wouldn't be there. He doesn't have a stable for his ranch horses. That's my reason for bringing her here. She needs a clean, dry stall and confinement while those stitches are in place. Put her in that stall over there. I'll fill the water bucket for her."

"Where do you keep the standing bandages? I'll wrap her up."

"There should be some in the box in front of the stall."

Dee knelt at each of the horse's front legs. Her fingers coiled each wrap around the leg smooth and the distance of the edges exact. Marcus's gaze traveled from her fingers, up her arm, to her profile as she steadily worked. The woman captured his heart in ways he never expected. They shared an affinity for horses but it went way deeper than that. Standing beside the horse after finishing the second wrap, the way she stroked the horse's neck endeared her to him as no one before.

A rush of sensations like he hadn't experienced in a long time coursed through him. She was beautiful, smart, and truly knowledgeable. Talking to her was easy, unlike Lauren.

"Would you like to go to dinner with me this evening?" The question spilled from his lips on its own volition. He waited for her reply. His heartbeat elevated; he held his breath.

Wide-eyed, she stared at him. *Maybe that was a bit premature?*

"Tonight would be good. It's Magda's day off so I can finish up at a decent time. What time? I still need to do night check," she said.

"Great," he stuttered in surprise. "My day should be done on time, as most trainers are off today. I can only hope I won't get called out on an emergency. You won't mind if I take my work truck, will you?"

"Perhaps it would be best to meet you. Then I have my vehicle if you get an emergency call. Where're we going?"

"Do you like Italian? Aglioli's is one of my favorites," he suggested.

"Yes, I've heard they have great food."

"Let's say seven?"

"Great, I'll see you there,"

He couldn't help but watch as she strolled back to her truck. Her silhouette looked wonderful. He could only grin to himself; wow, he had asked her out. He had a spring in his gait as he went about the rest of his day.

Chapter Four

With the chores done and the horses munching happily, the first butterflies of excitement fluttered in Dee's stomach. After hiding this past year, she needed to go out. Being seen in public had its drawbacks but how else could she test the nightmare being behind her? Besides, the man taking her on this date was Marcus.

She couldn't stop thinking about him. Attractive, yes. Confident, absolutely. Loved horses as much as her, definitely. Simply being with him eased the pent-up anxiety of this last year. They complemented each other, like a half she hadn't realized she needed.

At home she showered, then stood in front of her small closet. What to wear? It had been so long since she wore anything other than riding breeches or blue jeans. She'd brought only a few dressier outfits with her from Hialeah. She lifted a light blue sundress off its hanger and a matching short jacket. Six-inch platform heels in gold metallic completed the look. How wonderful to feel feminine even if only for a few hours. She picked the gold metallic clutch that matched the shoes and walked out to her truck. *If only I had a nice car instead of Dad's old truck to drive.*

She arrived several minutes early. Glancing around the parking lot, she didn't see the vet truck. With her hair down, the blonde tresses fluttered in soft curly rings down her back. Tonight, she wore a hint of makeup and dangly earrings. She opened the door and turned in the seat to slip on the heels she'd removed before driving.

"You clean up nice, Miss Collins."

She flinched. *Will I ever get used to being called by a different name?* Turning, she stared into the softest brown eyes she'd ever seen.

"Doc." She released the breath she didn't realize she held. She slid off the truck's seat, her knees shaking as she stood on the hard ground. "You look different than you do when you come to the barn."

"It's Marcus, don't forget, and I hope that's a good thing. It isn't often I get to wear dress slacks."

She observed the questioning look on his face as if he'd noticed her sudden nervousness. She'd have to be careful letting her emotions show until she was comfortable enough to tell him the truth. Something about him spoke to her inner self that she could trust him with the truth of her situation. "I enjoy getting dressed up occasionally. I didn't see your truck when I parked."

"I brought my car. I'm betting there won't be a call out tonight. If I lose that bet, I'll drive to the clinic and exchange it for the truck."

"I wish I did a car as well as my truck. Driving a truck in a dress and heels isn't right." She laughed.

"You were smart enough to drive in sensible shoes. This truck is an oldie but goodie. How many miles does it have?"

"It's getting up there." She waved her hand to bat the question away. "My father took loving care of it over the years. It pulls my horse trailer and hauls feed and hay. It's much more practical than a car."

"You're right about that." He took her arm and guided her toward the restaurant.

A delicious tingly sensation danced along her skin where his fingers touched her.

Inside, the aroma of garlic wafted through the room. Marcus guided her to the maître d'.

"Hello, Dr. Helton, how are you this evening?" the man said with a welcoming smile.

"Good, thanks, Mario. I see you have a brisk crowd for a Monday night."

"This time of the year, every night is busy. I'm glad you made a reservation. Your table's ready. This way." Mario turned and walked toward a table for two in the back corner.

Out of habit, Dee gravitated to the chair where her back was to the wall. Her cop cousins had trained her well to always face the crowd around her. Marcus slid the chair out for her then sat opposite. At the moment, he was the only person watching her. As a matter of fact, it seemed he couldn't take his eyes off her. Embarrassed, she looked down, taking the napkin to smooth out on her lap.

The waiter handed them menus. "May I bring you cocktails?"

"No cocktails. I'd like a club soda with lime. Dee?" Marcus asked.

"I'll have the same." They had similar tastes.

"Yes, sir." The waiter sped away.

Dee read over the menu. "This is incredible. They have so many combinations of pasta and sauces. How can anyone decide?"

"Pick your favorite. I can recommend the pasta primavera."

The waiter came back with their club sodas and took their orders.

Dee glanced around the busy restaurant. With Marcus by her side, she might beat this stalked feeling, and her life could return to normal. Neither spoke. She smiled to herself when she caught him staring at her. The light gleaming in his eyes sent a thrill straight to her heart

"It's nice to get out of barn clothes and be human," he said.

"Yes, it's nice occasionally." She pressed her lips together to keep from grinning at his discomfort. "This is a delightful place. Silva and Steffen asked me to come here with them but being a third wheel seems awkward."

"It's the heart of dining during the winter horse season. Most of the owners, trainers, and competitors eat dinner here."

The comment caused a chill to run down Dee's spine. *I'm out in public where someone could recognize me.* Though she was a long way from Hialeah, the horse world traveled in small circles. She should have considered that. She did consider that. But she'd wanted to go, to have a normal night out—with Marcus. The changes she'd made to her hair color would hopefully keep anyone from recognizing her. Tonight would be a good test.

"Dee, are you cold? I wish I wore a jacket I could give you."

"No, not at all," she replied, lifting her hand in dismissal. She observed the people around her. "I see Bonnie Stein over there. She keeps her horses in barn three on our farm. That gray stallion of hers is magnificent. Oh, and in that corner is Olympic medalist Stephen Paige. This is a who's who of the equestrian sports world." Her excitement at seeing so many people she'd read about in the magazines dispelled her fears of recognition.

"That rowdy bunch at the bar—" Marcus motioned toward the group— "are riders for the British Stadium Jumping Team. Over in that corner is one of the polo teams."

"Are you the veterinarian for all of them?"

"No, not all, but some. I'm on all the farms around here, so I meet them, or others tell me who they are. Is that what brought you to Wellington? The chance to rub elbows with the famous people in the horse industry?"

"Not to see but to learn from them. Where else can one observe the best horses and trainers?"

"Are you interested in dressage or all the disciplines?"

"I fell in love with dressage watching the Olympics. In college I rode on the equestrian team." Dee halted. Too much personal information. Yet with Marcus the desire to share came naturally. For the first time in months she found comfort in sharing. She decided she would trust him with more. "I love the way dressage allows the rider to become one with the horse, like I'm dancing with it. A clinician I rode with once stated, 'Every horse is a song waiting to be sung.'"

"I saw you riding the other day. You ride as if dancing. What did you study in college?"

Dee sat back and chuckled. "Will it surprise you to learn I was pre-vet?"

"Really? Where did you study? No wonder you know so much about diagnosing horse ailments. Why didn't you finish, or did you?"

"I went to the University of Kentucky, but I left before entering vet school."

"That's when it gets interesting. Why did you leave?"

"A few incidents that happened at home while I was on spring break made me decide not to make it my vocation." Of course, as a vet, her statement would pique his curiosity. She decided to go with a watered-down version. "I assisted in euthanizing a superb horse of my father's. I found it difficult, especially since it should never have happened. I helped raise it from birth and it hurt a lot."

Marcus reached across the table and took her hand in his. Her gaze landed on their joined hands. Warmth radiated up her arm. "I understand completely. It's traumatic to put down an animal."

Her gaze left their joined hands and locked onto his soft brown eyes. A bolt of electricity shot through her.

The moment broke when the waiter brought their meals. Marcus let go of her hand and they both sat back. They thanked the waiter and began eating.

"How's your pasta?" Marcus asked between bites of his own.

"It's wonderful," she answered, diving into the enticing scent of garlic shrimp in a basil pesto.

"I told you it would be." He spiraled his spaghetti on his fork. "If you don't mind my asking, what happened to that horse you put down?"

She ate a few more bites before answering. "It fractured a leg in a freak accident on the track. It started when another horse stumbled and collapsed after coming out of the starting gate. Our horse jumped over the downed horse, but they got tangled. A third horse plummeted over them, and all the jockeys were thrown. It was a terrible mess. I arrived at the track hospital as the ambulance brought the horses in." She paused and put down her fork. "My father bred that stallion. We had high hopes for him in the Flamingo Stakes coming up in a few weeks. He suffered two major fractures to the legs, one being a compound fracture. It was the most humane thing to put him down. The horse that caused the accident also shattered a leg, but the owner wanted to save him. They put a cast on him and strapped him up in a stall. He colicked and they euthanized him a week later."

Dee picked up her fork, took a bite, then continued, "One jockey crushed several vertebrae in his back and never rode again. The jockey on my father's horse cracked his collar bone and was out for a year." She took a few more bites of food while biting back tears. "I helped birth that horse. I witnessed his first staggering footsteps. I watched him grow up into a potential champion. I even rode him the first time. His suffering as they pulled him out of the ambulance took away my desire to be a vet. He should have been euthanized out on the track, but they never let the public see such tragedy." She hoped Marcus wouldn't look up the information on the internet and figure out her real name. *Why does he make it so easy to tell him personal things?*

"I understand. It's hard to do no matter what the circumstances. It's even harder when it's your own animal. I've never had to do that— euthanize my animal. It's the worst part of the job. At least, we have good drugs that make it more humane."

"I finished out the semester. I volunteered that summer at the Kentucky Horse Park. It gave me a chance to see other equestrian disciplines and experience other breeds of horses. My father talked me into coming back to the track to help him. But my love of dressage kept calling me, so I left and came here."

"You decided to leave the track for the dressage ring? That's quite a switch."

"I enjoy the show ring. Plus, in dressage, I can show the same horse I'm training. I plan to show some this winter."

"With your horse Roscoe?" he asked.

Dee laughed. "Roscoe is the sweetest, kindest horse ever, but not overly talented. He's a good horse to learn on. I hope to find a more talented mount while I'm here. Enough about me. Where did you go to vet school?"

"Auburn University. I received a scholarship there. A baseball scholarship. I was good enough for college but not for the pros. I worked an internship at the university vet school my freshman year and decided then I wanted to become a vet. So, when baseball didn't pan out, I went to grad school."

"What position did you play?" Dee asked.

"Catcher."

"I can see that. You have the build for it."

"I do?"

Dee grinned. She'd caught him off guard. "You wouldn't understand because you can't watch yourself. Silva, Gale, Julie—all the women around the barn talk about it."

"Yeah, I've heard that all the women talk. I'm not sure I like being the topic of everyone's conversations."

She couldn't help it, a giggle erupted from her throat. Taking a deep breath, she put down her fork and pushed back the plate. Half the meal remained but she couldn't take another bite.

"You eat like a jockey. Are you finished already?" Marcus twirled his pasta.

"I am. I'm taking the rest home, though. It'll make a great lunch tomorrow."

"As hard as I've seen you labor in that barn, you need every bite of that to stay alive. You have a jockey's build; did you ride at the track?"

"Exercise rider, yes, I did. I wanted to be a jockey when I was young, but I watched too many of them struggle with making weight. That didn't look like fun. Plus, I enjoyed handling the horses more. I've done every job there is at the track. My father said I should learn how to do everything, so I learned from the ground up."

"Your father has a job at the track also?"

She realized she should stop herself, but she enjoyed the story-sharing with him. He'd made her feel like a member of his family. "Yes, he's a trainer. He started cleaning stalls and moved his way up to assistant trainer then on to his own stable. He's done well. He also keeps a few mares and dabbles in breeding but mostly he trains for others."

"Who's your father? Perhaps I've met him."

Okay, now they were getting close to the truth. She'd never remain out of sight if she revealed her real name. Marcus would recognize her father's name. He said he'd worked the tracks in Miami. He must have been there while she was in college. She would have noticed him otherwise.

Fortunately, the waiter returned to take their plates, saving her from further revelations.

Marcus paid the check, and they strolled to Dee's vehicle. He took her hand as they walked. The gesture connected her to him in a way that drove all her stalker issues out of her mind. Opening the door of the truck for her, he helped her climb up. She bent to remove the high heels as he patiently waited.

"Dee, it's been a nice evening. I'm glad I didn't have to leave on a call. Next time, whether or not I'm on call, I'll drive."

"Thank you, Marcus, I've enjoyed this evening also."

"I'd rather be taking you home instead of saying goodbye like this."

She looked into eyes that smoldered with a need that matched her own.

Marcus encircled her waist with both arms, drawing her closer. She wrapped her arms around his neck. His kiss radiated warmth from her lips straight to her heart. He kissed her again. Fireworks were going off in her mind, filling her with wonder. This must be what writers meant when they said, "toe curling". *I've kissed guys before but this feels different. Wonderfully different. I want more like this.*

He shut the truck's door. *Okay, he's a gentleman, and we've only known each other a short time. But does he feel the same?* She started the truck and put the window down. "I'd like to do this again soon," she said. She almost didn't recognize her own voice as it came out a husky whisper.

"We will, I promise."

She heard the same longing in his voice that stirred through her heart.

Neither moved. She lost herself in the warm gaze emanating from his eyes. After a long minute he broke the contact, turned, and ambled back to his car. Never-before-experienced emotions washed over her. She didn't want to put a name on the emotion; she only hoped he shared the same sensation.

Driving out of the parking lot, she checked the rearview mirror for signs of being followed, a habit developed since the stalker. Spotting a car cutting around the traffic, her breathing nearly stopped. *It couldn't be, could it?* Her palms started sweating. In a few seconds she went from euphoria to dread. The car was right behind her at a traffic light.

Dee stared into the rearview mirror. Had he found her? Would his identity finally be revealed? The person driving the car waved at her. She blew her bangs upward and waved back to Marcus.

He continued behind her until she turned into her gated community. As she stopped at the guard gate, Marcus honked his horn and drove on. *He's a man who cares enough to see me safely home.* The fear of the last months evaporated. The happiness of meeting Marcus, of having a date with him, of his kiss, replaced it.

Chapter Five

The next morning Dee smiled at the sound of the squeaky gate opening for Marcus. She leaned against the doorpost of the tack room and continued rolling polo wraps. *Thump, thump, thump*, her heart rate picked up. He presented her with a large cup of coffee.

"Why, Doctor Helton, how nice to see you this morning. I wasn't aware of any sick horses on the farm." *I hope he knows I'm flirting and not being sarcastic. I'm not particularly good at this.*

"No, I'm making a farm call, bringing a cup of coffee to the hardest-working groom I've ever met. How are you this morning?"

"I'm great." She took the cup. A tingly, heartbeat-raising electricity moved along her skin where their fingers touched.

"This is a peace offering. I didn't want you to think I was stalking you last night. I wanted to ensure you made it home safely since I didn't drive you there."

Dee's ears and brain stuck to the word *stalking*. The coffee cup shook and almost slipped through her hand.

Marcus set down his cup and grasped her hand. "Dee, wow, what is it?"

The panic ebbed with the warmth of his hands on hers. A vibrant excitement spread through her. The shaking stopped. She smiled at him. "It's nothing. I recognized you behind me and understood you were being a gentleman. Thank you for caring. I'm glad chivalry is not dead."

She hadn't meant to distress him, but sometimes words evoked emotion she couldn't hide. Pulling her hand out of his, she placed it on his cheek. He leaned into it. "Thank you for being so wonderful. You didn't have to bring me coffee. I appreciate it."

"I didn't have to," he said. "I wanted to. It gave me an excuse to see you again." He tugged the brim of her baseball cap. "I'm not sure if I like your hair down and curling over your shoulders or all business-like in a braid and ball cap."

Dee laughed. *Now who's flirting?* "A braid or ponytail is much more practical at the stable. I'll be happy to wear it down next time we go out." She twisted the coffee cup around with both hands, while she built up some courage. "Hopefully soon."

"Would tonight be too soon?" He picked up his coffee to take a sip. His eyes gleamed invitingly.

She hoped the disappointment didn't show in her eyes. After all, she had a job she'd committed to. "Tonight I promised Silva I'd help her out since her groom, Gale, has the day off. Magda comes in late on Tuesdays, which gives me time to do the extra chores."

"When do you get a day off? Maybe I can be off that day."

"I don't have a day when I'm completely off. Wednesdays might be good. Gale feeds for me on Thursday mornings so I can come in late that day. And I can always get out of here early on Mondays."

"It's no joke when I called you the hardest working groom in town."

"Every groom works hard. Some more than others."

"I understand you want to become a dressage trainer, but I'd hire you as my assistant right now. Any chance I could convince you..."

"Wouldn't that be like mixing work with pleasure? I'm not sure I'm ready for that, but I'll remember your offer if I fall flat as a trainer. Speaking of work, I'd rather stay here and sip coffee, but there's not enough time left before I need to get Magda's first horse saddled. I have to keep moving."

"That's fine, I'll watch."

"Just like a man, sitting around while the woman labors. I can work circles around you." She lifted her brow in challenge.

"Oh, really? Well, while you muck those stalls, I'll drive around doing nothing but look at horses."

She could stay here flirting with Marcus, but the stalls wouldn't clean themselves and she surmised he had farm calls to attend to. Magda demanded a lot of Dee during the day. After Magda left, there would be time to race over to Silva's barn for a lesson. The few hours with Silva were worth all the extra work and sweat.

Marcus kept his gaze on Dee a few minutes more before he said, "I'll see you later. I need to get to the clinic. Maybe we can get together later?"

For the first time in almost a year, she hadn't minded someone's scrutiny. Perhaps God had turned life around in her favor. "I'd like that, Marcus. Call me."

"Will do." He strode back to his truck.

Dee peeped out of the stall and gazed at him moving away. If she ever made a list of what her perfect man would be, he checked every box.

~ * ~

An hour later Silva came into the stable. Dee hummed along to a tune playing on her smartphone.

"Good mood this morning?" Silva asked.

"Who wouldn't be on such a beautiful morning? Your horses are ready for their workday."

"You're quick and efficient."

"Comes from years of practice. You're the second person today to tell me I work too hard."

"Who else said that? It can't be Magda."

"Oh, no one," Dee said.

"No one, huh? So, who's that smile for? Let me guess—a certain veterinarian came by the stable this morning."

"Maybe." Dee laughed.

"I think you should ask Gale or Julie to groom and saddle the horses for Magda one day a week. You need to take a full day off. Then you could spend an entire day with the doc."

"A day off would be nice, but I need to do other things that don't include an entire day with the doc. You wouldn't do that to your girls, either. Magda would eat them up and spit them out. Then you wouldn't have a stall cleaner or groom. Feeding for me one morning a week is all I need. I'll manage the rest."

"I wish I hadn't leased my stalls in this barn to her. She's the most inconsiderate, thoughtless person I ever met. You and I work well together, and I hope we continue to."

"I hope so as well. But while Magda is here, let me handle her. We need to keep your girls out of it."

"You're right. Still doesn't mean I like it. Here comes Magda now. Thanks for feeding for me this morning. I'll feed for you next time you want to go on a date or something."

"Thanks, I'll remember that."

Magda breezed in and hurried down the aisle. "You don't have first horse saddled yet?" she asked in her clipped English.

"Chanel is ready for the saddle. You're early this morning," Dee answered.

"Yes, but horse should be ready. Does not hurt to stand saddled."

"Yes, ma'am." Dee hurried down the aisle for the saddle.

"Where is your groom?" Magda asked Silva.

"Today is her day off. I can groom and ride my horses without help for one day," Silva said with a sardonic edge in her voice.

"Grooms don't need days off. Horses need care seven days a week. A groom gets easy day when the trainer takes off. That's enough."

"Grooms are people. Even horses have a day off occasionally."

"A day off from riding maybe but not from care. That's what groom does, care for horses. You in America too long. You are soft now. In Russia, grooms no days off. They are with horse every day."

"Yes, well," said Silva.

Dee walked back with the saddle and finished getting Chanel ready. Magda took the reins and led the horse toward the arena.

Silva waited until Magda was out of earshot. "She's a piece of work," she said. "No wonder Miguel left."

"I know, but getting to work with these horses is worth putting up with Magda."

Silva headed back to her barn, turning to say, "You might change your mind if you become serious about Marcus."

Dee had the barn to herself for the next forty minutes. She groomed and saddled Rocket Man, ready for when Magda returned with Chanel. Someday Dee would have her own horses in training.

No time to think about that now with Magda on a tear. She didn't say a word when Dee handed her the next horse. She jumped off one and mounted the next. Finally, she slid down off the last horse, tossed the reins to Dee, and stalked off toward the other barn. Someone over there held Magda's attention. *I wonder who it could be?* At last, the day was done. Twenty minutes later, Magda left the farm.

Dee finished washing the last horse. Her phone rang while she scraped the excess water off.

"Hello," she answered.

"Hey, it's Marcus. Are you busy or can you talk?"

"Magda finally left for the day. I can talk," she replied.

"Good, but I didn't call to chat. I need a translator again. I'm in the field next door with some polo ponies. I need to learn more Spanish, I guess. Do you mind coming over and acting as an interpreter again?"

"No problem. I'll head right over." She hung up.

Dee climbed over the board fence between the two farms. Up ahead Marcus stood with two horses and several men. She'd never approach these men on her own. They'd waved at her when she brought the horses in from the paddocks. She would wave back, in a wary-of-strangers way. This afternoon, she walked straight toward them.

"Dee, this is Juan Fernandez," Marcus said. "He owns these horses. It appears they've eaten something poisonous. He speaks some English but not enough to help me identify the poisonous plant. I thought you could help."

"*Hola*," Dee said to the men.

They exchanged pleasantries. Juan told her what he thought poisoned his horses.

"Juan said there's a plant he doesn't recognize growing in the wooded area in the back of this field," Dee told Marcus. "All the horses have been grazing there. When you said it was poison, he thought of those particular plants. He's not sure of the right English word for it. His description sounds like nightshade."

"It could be nightshade, but I would think all the horses would show signs. Can Juan show us where it is?"

"*Sí, sí*, I show you, Doc," Juan said.

Juan led the way while the other men kept the sick horses standing still. No one spoke as they entered the woods. There were several well-worn trails. Juan picked one and went in. The temperature dropped noticeably under the canopy of trees. No wonder the horses liked it back here. A small patch of green grass next to the fence marked the property boundary. Marcus knelt over the patch of grass and picked through it.

Dee strode to the fence, leaning through the rails. She pulled up several weeds and brought them back to Marcus. "Could these be what you're looking for?" she asked him.

"Yes. The weeds in the patch I'm looking at wouldn't cause the symptoms the horses are exhibiting, but what you have would." Marcus followed her back where the weeds were found. "Juan, there's evidence your horses are munching through the fence. It's not nightshade, but what you call 'locoweed.' It produces a mild narcotic effect, which is consistent with the symptoms your horses are showing. Basically, they're *stoned*, which is why they're staggering. If you move them to another field, I think you'll find they'll go back to normal."

Dee translated the information to Juan before throwing the locoweed back over the perimeter fence. Marcus returned with the others across the field.

"If they get worse, call me," Marcus told Juan. "But I think they'll be fine."

"*Gracias*, Doctor, *muchas gracias*." Juan waved.

Dee rode back to the farm with Marcus. "You know, I have a few more calls. I'd enjoy the company," Marcus said.

"I would, but it's feeding time."

"They can eat a bit late, can't they?"

Dee laughed. "Do you hear that incessant door kicking? Rocket Man can't be fed one minute late."

"I hear him. Then this will have to do." He leaned over the seat and gave her a quick kiss. The endorphin spike almost drowned out Rocket Man's whinny. She hopped out of the truck and sighed.

Up ahead Silva stood watching from her barn. Dee missed having a close confidante. When her sister married and moved to England, she lost her best friend. Maybe Silva could fill some of that void.

"Where were you and the good doctor?" she asked. Her mock disciplinarian tone came with a sly smile.

"Assisting with Spanish translation on the farm next door."

"Oh, wow. I'd heard you exchange a few words of Spanish with Miguel before he disappeared. You speak Spanish well enough to translate?"

"You can't live in Hialeah without speaking some Spanish. It's my second language. You speak German as a second language, right?"

"German is my first language. I didn't think about you speaking Spanish. Collins is an Anglo name and you don't have an accent."

"Names are not an example of what languages people speak. There are lots of German-sounding names, but they speak English. Besides, you don't have a German accent."

"You're right. How did we get off topic? What's going on with you and the doc?"

Dee laughed. "Well, as you guessed, Marcus came by this morning. He brought me coffee."

"Marcus, is it? I'd say there's more to it than coffee."

"Okay, okay, yes, there is. He took me to dinner last night."

"I knew it! So, where'd you go? Are you going out again?"

"Slow down. You remind me of my sister, asking so many questions."

"You told your sister? I wanted to be the first to hear about it."

"You *are* the first person I've told. My sister lives in England. I haven't talked to her recently. But she'll ask the same questions when I talk to her. I miss her. We went to Aglioli's, and we had a great time. The food was exquisite. Will there be a second date? I hope so. You're right. He's a nice guy."

"I'm delighted for you. It's been a tough time for Marcus this past year. I'm happy he's going out again."

This made Dee's ears perk. He didn't seem to be a guy who's having a tough time. "What happened to him last year?"

"You two didn't talk about it? I think he's still bitter. He and his wife divorced last year. I'm not privy to all the details. But he received full custody of his daughter. He and my husband, Steffen, go to spring training ball games together, and the three of us have gone to dinner a few times. He brings his daughter to the barn to play with the horses."

"He told me he played baseball in college, so it makes sense he watches the game." *He's divorced and has a kid? He should have told me. Not that it matters if he's divorced but still. Yet, I can't fault him, it's not like I told him about my stalker.*

"Steffen will be happy Marcus took you out. All I'm aware of about the divorce is what Steffen told me." Silva stopped speaking. Her eyes locked on to Dee's. "I never had a sister. You are as close to one as I've ever wanted. I'm glad you came to this farm and we became friends."

"Thanks, Silva, I feel the same way."

Dee wasn't ready when Silva scooped her up in a big hug.

Chapter Six

As Dee busily cleaned stalls the next morning, her thoughts focused on Marcus. She had to admit she half expected him to appear with that to-go cup in his hands. It was disappointing when he didn't. No doubt he was busy attending sick horses. She couldn't expect him to come by every morning. When the nightmare was over, she could see herself getting serious about him. But would he still be interested in her after she told him someone stalked her?

"Dee?"

She snapped out of her reverie at the sound of Silva's voice. She looked out of Roscoe's stall. "I'm here, Silva."

"You're done with stalls already?"

"Yeah, how did you know?"

"Because you always do your own stall last. Do you want a lesson today when you're done toiling for Magda?"

"Sure, that works for me."

"I guess the good doctor didn't make a coffee run this morning."

"No, no coffee. He has better things to do than bring me coffee."

"But you wish he did, right?"

"Well, yes, but I can't expect him to show up every day." Dee kissed Roscoe's nose before closing the door. Even talking didn't keep her from her tasks.

Silva walked beside Dee on the way to dump the wheelbarrow in the muck pit between their two barns. "Has he asked for another date yet?"

"No specific date, only that he'd try to work around my time off. Why?"

"Just wondering. You'll ask me to cover your chores so you can go, right?"

"Yes, if I need to. You're making sure I tell you if he asks me out again."

"Isn't that what big sisters do?"

"My sister is my twin, and we're thirty-three. But since you said big sister, I guess I'd like one of those also."

"Glad to fill the void." Silva laughed as she headed back to her barn.

The day flew by. For some unknown reason, Magda shortened her rides by several minutes each. Dee barely had time to cool out one horse and tack up the next. Magda had to wait approximately one minute for Dee to get the next horse ready, and she complained. Then she rode it for about ten minutes before dismounting and handing it over to Dee. After bringing the last horse in, Magda hurried out to her car and sped out the farm gate.

Dee breathed a sigh of relief. However, one look around the barn showed a total mess with polo wraps and wet saddle pads piled up. All the time before feeding would be spent getting the aisle and tack room back to its orderly state. She thought about sending Marcus a text, then decided against it. He didn't need her distracting him while handling calls and possible emergencies.

~ * ~

Marcus knelt, removing the bandage on the horse in the clinic. The stitches looked good—no infection. He applied antibiotic and replaced the bandage.

"You're looking good, old girl," he told the horse as he stood and patted her rump. "Sorry I can't wrap your legs as nice as Dee did. You'll have to put up with it." He took a peppermint from his pocket.

The horse nuzzled in close at the sound of plastic being removed from her treat. She nibbled his palm. With another pat, he exited the stall.

Unfortunately, none of the day's calls took him past Dee's farm. He'd wanted an excuse to see her—and that surprised him. He'd sworn after the divorce he'd never be involved with another woman. Yet something about Dee made him want to be involved. The frightened looks she occasionally displayed and the evasive tone she sometimes used piqued his interest. He saw a strong, independent woman on the surface.

But those vulnerable moments attracted him. Removing that anguished look from her eyes and quieting the uncontrolled shivering became a worthy goal if he could discover the cause. Asking for an explanation would be the easy way, yet he knew gaining her trust would go further toward getting an answer. Spending time with her could be the best way to do that. He'd considered texting Dee several times but decided against it. Neither one really needed the distraction during a busy day.

His daughter, Kaitlyn, ran through the clinic door to the stabling area. "Daddy, Daddy, Daddy," she yelled.

He knelt, catching her in his arms for a big hug. "Hey, sweetness, how was your day?"

"Fine, Daddy. Whose horse is this? What's her name? Can I pet her? What happened to her legs?"

Kaitlyn's rapid-fire questions elicited a chuckle. "Her name is Yellow. She belongs to Mr. Weekley. She cut her leg, and I put lots of stitches in it."

He gave the horse a couple flakes of hay while Kaitlyn recited a play-by-play of her day. They walked to the office together.

"Hi, Doc, how was it out there?" asked Margo, his office assistant.

"Good. No serious problems came up," he answered.

"Your mother dropped Kaitlyn off. She said she had a meeting to go to, and you probably forgot."

"I didn't forget. My last farm call took longer than expected. Kaitlyn didn't give you any problems, did she?"

"I sat right next to Miss Margo," Kaitlyn said with offense. "She took me out to see the horse before you drove in."

"She's an angel. I never mind her being here. You know that," Margo said.

"Can we go visit Miss Silva? She said I could ride one of her horses the next time you took me there. Can I go ride before dinner?"

A trip to Everglades Equestrian Center ranked high on his list. Silva might not have time for a ride right now, but he could still visit Dee.

"I need to water the horse out in the stall before we go," he told Kaitlyn.

"Don't worry, Doc, I'll take care of the horse before I leave so you and Kaitlyn can take off. I'll see you tomorrow."

"Thanks, Margo. I appreciate it. Let's go, sweetness."

~ * ~

Dee left the tack room in a mess; it would still be there after her lesson.

Marcus pulled into the drive before the lesson finished. She looked his way as he got out of the truck with a little girl, no doubt his daughter.

"Hi, Kaitlyn." Silva knelt to the girl's level. "How are you today?"

"I'm good, thank you. Would you have a horse I could ride today?" Kaitlyn asked.

"Well, I think they're eating dinner. If I'd known you were coming, I'd have saved one for you."

"Sorry, Silva, I should have called. She can ride another day. My mother had an appointment this evening and Kaitlyn wanted to come visit."

"I told her the next time you two came by I'd let her ride. I'm sorry, Kaitlyn."

Dee rode Roscoe over to where Marcus, Silva, and Kaitlyn stood. "I heard you didn't have a horse for this young lady to ride. Would you like to cool Roscoe for me?" Dee asked Kaitlyn.

The little girl's eyes were wide with excitement. "Can I?" she asked Silva.

"If Dee wants you to cool her horse down, I think that's a good idea," Silva said. "We can do a short lesson if that's all right with your father."

"Please, Daddy?" Kaitlyn implored.

"Of course," Marcus said. "I know better than to get between girls and their horses."

"Smart man," Dee and Silva said together. They looked at each other and laughed. Dee swung down from her horse.

"Kaitlyn, this is my friend, Dee, and this is her horse, Roscoe," Silva introduced them. She turned around and whispered to Marcus, "Since her father forgot to do that."

"Sorry," he said.

Dee dropped to both knees in the dirt before Kaitlyn. "I'm glad to meet you. So, are you ready to take a riding lesson?"

"Oh, yes. Miss Silva lets me ride when Daddy brings me with him on calls. But I really would like to take regular lessons and maybe show someday."

Dee laughed. "You sound like all young girls." She stood up and dusted her breeches. "Roscoe is a special horse. He knows how to count. Tell me a number, and he'll count it out for you."

"Really?" Kaitlyn asked. "How about counting to eight, since that's how old I am."

"Roscoe, count to eight."

The horse raised his right hoof and pawed the ground eight times.

"Wow, he's a smart horse. Can he count to three?" Kaitlyn

asked.

"Roscoe, count to three," Dee commanded.

Again, the horse pawed three times.

"I love this horse!" Kaitlyn exclaimed.

"He's fun to ride too. Come here, and I'll show you," Dee said.

Kaitlyn tottered into the arena with Dee.

"Roscoe, down," Dee commanded. Roscoe bent both front legs, settling on his knees. "Now you can put your foot in the stirrup," she said.

Kaitlyn slipped her left foot into the stirrup while Dee helped her swing her other leg over the saddle.

"Roscoe, stand," she commanded.

He stood back up on all four legs.

"Daddy, did you see that? He let me get on by myself."

"I saw it, Kaitlyn. Dee's right, he's a very smart horse."

"I'm at a loss for words," Silva said. "He may not be the perfect dressage horse, but he's an awesome trick horse. What else does he do?"

"I'll show you another time," Dee said to Silva. "Right now, Kaitlyn needs to pick up the reins 'cause we're going for a walk."

Kaitlyn did as instructed. Dee stepped around the arena, and Roscoe followed. The three paced the arena several times both directions.

"Do you think you can trot?" she asked.

"Yes, I've trotted before."

"Okay, let's go."

Dee jogged, and Roscoe picked up a slow trot next to her. Kaitlyn bounced around but stayed on the horse. After a small circle they came back to the walk. "Good riding, Kaitlyn. Your dad should consider letting you take lessons."

"Oh, I want to. Maybe you can teach me."

"Maybe I can. Tell you what, take Roscoe around the arena yourself." Dee moved out of the arena. She passed Roscoe an imperceptible sign. He moved off, taking Kaitlyn all the way around. He really was a smart horse.

Marcus moved up behind Dee and whispered in her ear. "That's an incredible horse. I think he hijacked my daughter. That's all I'll hear about for the next week."

His whisper tickled her ear and sent a shockwave straight to her heart. She took a minute to regain her composure. "Bring her out once a week, and I'll give her a lesson. I've taught kids before—simple basics—but they have to start somewhere."

"I will. If for no other reason than to watch Roscoe do tricks.

Sorry to interrupt your lesson. What I saw looked good."

"We were finishing. Roscoe would rather play with Kaitlyn."

Roscoe brought Kaitlyn back to where the group stood. He nuzzled Dee's arm with a sigh.

"Will he bow down like before, so I can get off?" she asked Dee.

"Yes. Roscoe, down," she commanded.

The horse knelt as before.

Dee helped Kaitlyn swing her leg over and jump off. "You tell him to stand up, Kaitlyn."

"Roscoe, stand up," Kaitlyn said.

The horse stood back up on all four feet.

"Daddy, he listened to me!"

"I see that, Kaitlyn. He's amazing. You need to tell Dee and Roscoe thank you."

"Thank you, Dee." She turned to the horse. "Thank you, Roscoe."

Roscoe snorted and nodded. Then he lowered his head, placing his forehead on Kaitlyn's chest.

Dee stole a glance at Marcus who stood in awe.

Everyone strolled with the horse back to Dee's barn. She unsaddled Roscoe and led him to the wash rack. Kaitlyn followed asking lots of questions while Dee rinsed off the horse. She patiently answered all of them.

~ * ~

Marcus and Silva left Dee and Kaitlyn behind to sit on the bench in front of the barn.

"You weren't aware the horse did tricks?" he asked Silva.

"I didn't. She said he didn't like racing so she bought him to see if he had other talents. She didn't tell me he could do tricks. I guess she found his talent."

"She did that. I'm impressed. If she can do that with him, what else can she do? She'll make a good trainer."

"I told you that. I'm glad I'll have the chance to develop her talent."

"Magda doesn't work with her?"

"Not at all. I don't think she's even seen Dee ride."

"By this time next year, Dee will be a better trainer than Magda is," he predicted.

"She already is. For a woman who's supposed to be on the Russian Olympic Team, Magda's not a rider. She has rough hands, and her training methods are horrible. Her people skills are atrocious. Today, she pushed Dee to the limit. Magda barely exercised each horse and cursed at Dee when the horses weren't ready. Thank goodness Magda left early so Dee could take a lesson. I saw the tack room before we started; things were everywhere. It wasn't the organized room Dee keeps. I sent Gale over to clean the tack while Dee took her lesson."

Dee and Kaitlyn joined him and Silva.

"Kaitlyn, do you think you and I can help Dee feed her horses, then we'll take her out for pizza?" Marcus asked his daughter.

"Of course, we can," Kaitlyn answered enthusiastically. "Can I feed Roscoe, Miss Dee?"

"Sure, sweetie, if you'd like. But you don't have to do that. I have work to do in the tack room before I can leave for the day."

"No, you don't," Silva said. "Look."

Dee ran to the tack room. "Silva, what did you do?"

"I sent Gale over while you took your lesson. I could see and hear how your day went. Feed and get out of here. Tomorrow is your morning to come in late, so I don't want to see you till then."

Dee glared at Silva before shaking her head. To Kaitlyn she said, "Come on, let's feed."

Even after a bad day, she took the time to thrill my daughter with horse tricks. Marcus felt gratitude and his heart warmed. *Why does she groom for Magda who doesn't appreciate her?* The pleasant rattling of feed buckets and his daughter's laughter comforted him through and through, offsetting his disdain for Magda.

"Dee's care for those horses is the only reason you're not here on more emergency calls. Miguel didn't show up one morning and Magda didn't care. Dee jumped in to care for them. You know, Magda never called Dee back when Chanel colicked. Training is where her heart lies."

"Are you two done talking about me?" Dee asked as she and Kaitlyn came out.

"Daddy, Dee let me feed the horses by myself. She said I'll be a good rider someday. I want to be a good rider," said Kaitlyn.

"You can be, if your dad brings you around more often," Silva told her.

"Quit ganging up on me, you three." He turned to Kaitlyn and said, "We'll see. Between school, piano lessons, and my job, Grandma has enough to do without adding something else."

"I'd rather ride than take piano lessons. I hate them."

"We'll talk about it. How about pizza for dinner? Dee, you will join us, won't you?"

"Oh please, Dee, come with us." Kaitlyn clutched Dee's hand in a death grip. "You're my new best friend."

"Thanks, Kaitlyn, I think you're my new best friend as well. Since you both asked, sure, I'll come with you."

"Let's go, Daddy," Kaitlyn grasped his hand, tugging them both toward the truck.

"You're not to be here early tomorrow," Silva reminded Dee. "You have a fun time tonight."

"Thanks, Silva," Dee shouted over her shoulder. "I'll see you in the morning. but not too early."

~ * ~

In her truck, Dee followed Marcus in his to the parking area behind the vet clinic.

"What do you like on pizza, Dee?" he asked as she climbed out.

"I only like cheese," Kaitlyn interjected before Dee could respond.

"I know what you like. I'm asking Dee," Marcus said to Kaitlyn.

"I like everything except the tiny fish," Dee answered.

"They put fish on pizza? Yuck!" Kaitlyn squealed.

"Not on ours they won't," he said. "I'll order two pizzas, one for kiddo, and one for us." He unlocked the back door and held it open. "You two go on in. The pizza place is over in the plaza next door." As Dee passed by, he gently grasped her hand. He whispered, "I have an ulterior motive for bringing you here. You wrap legs much better than I do. Would you mind replacing them for me?"

With an imperceptible giggle and a nod she continued inside.

"There's a horse in the clinic my dad is taking care of. Warna see?" Kaitlyn asked.

"I helped bring her here. How's she doing?" They walked through the heavy metal door that separated the main office of the clinic from the stalls and operating area.

"She has bandages on her legs," Kaitlyn said.

"She has stitches in one of her legs. Your dad must have done this wrapping job when he checked the stitches. He puts in excellent stitches but needs lessons on standing bandages."

Dee haltered the horse. "Will you hold her for me?" She handed the lead rope to Kaitlyn, then removed the wraps, careful not to disturb the white elastic over the stitches. She wrapped both legs back up to keep the circulation even in both.

She stood and patted the mare. The horse put its head down at Kaitlyn's level while she rubbed the animal's ears.

"She likes you," Dee said.

"I like her. Do you think she could do tricks like Roscoe?"

"Probably, if someone trained her. She's a roping horse. Her owner probably doesn't care about tricks."

"I want a horse of my own, so I can teach it tricks. Then I can ride like you and Silva."

"Owning a horse is a big responsibility. You have to feed, groom, and clean up after it. And you need a place to keep it."

"Daddy says the same thing, but Mommy said you get other people to do that for you. I don't know who's right."

Dee had learned the responsibility of horse ownership before receiving her first pony. She'd been about the same age as Kaitlyn when she got that pony. It sounded like mother and father had different ideas on the subject. *Better not get involved in their family issues.*

The two were talking about horses when the back door opened and the amazing smell of fresh pizza wafted in. Marcus entered bearing two boxes, one large and one small.

"Dinner is here. Sorry but the pizza place doesn't have a dining area so we have to eat it here. Kaitlyn, go wash your hands," Marcus said. "We'll meet you in the break room."

"I'll go supervise," Dee said. "This horse needs a bath." She held up her dirty hands.

"Well, she isn't getting one until the stitches come out."

Dee followed Kaitlyn to the restroom. Both scrubbed off the black dirt and dried their hands.

Kaitlyn's hand snagged the corner of Dee's shirt, drawing her back from the door. "Will you talk my dad into letting me have a horse?"

"That's between you and your dad. I'll mention it, but you need to show him you're ready for the responsibility. Get good grades in school, do your homework without being told, and it'll go a long way to show you're ready."

"Okay," she said with a disgruntled frown.

Dee remembered when her mother gave her and her sister the same speech. She hadn't liked it, but now she knew her mother was right. Kaitlyn bounded off to the break room. Dee followed.

"Let me see those hands," her father said.

"I inspected them," Dee replied. "They were perfect the first time. You should be proud of her."

"I am. Here's your very own pizza, sweetness." He passed her the smaller box.

"Thank you." Kaitlyn sat with the box open in front of her.

"Miss Dee, here are a couple pieces for you." Marcus offered her a paper plate.

"Thank you, kind sir." Dee winked at him.

Marcus winked back.

For the next few minutes no one spoke, just munched on the food.

When he finished a slice, Marcus asked Kaitlyn, "Do you have homework tonight?"

"I did it earlier while I was waiting on you to come in from work. It's all done."

"Fantastic. I'm proud of you. Did you practice your piano before Grandma brought you over?"

"Yes," she said between bites.

"Did she have to ask you over three times?"

Kaitlyn chewed and swallowed before answering, "Only twice."

"Wow, what made you so good this evening?"

She gazed up at him. "I was hoping you would take me to ride, and you did."

"I'm impressed." He scooped another slice out of the big box.

"I watched Dee wrap the horse's legs while you were getting pizza. I think I could do that and be your assistant."

"You might, one day." He laid down the slice he'd been munching. "Thanks, Dee. I have to admit, you do a much better job wrapping legs than I do."

"The bandaging over the stitches is more important. You did that superbly. I've had more practice than you since I do multiple ones every day." She finished her last bite.

"Perhaps tomorrow she can go for a walk around the building. She's healing fast. I'll know better after I check the wound in the morning. All done?" Marcus asked his daughter.

"I ate all but one piece. Can I keep it for breakfast in the morning?" Kaitlyn asked.

"Pizza for breakfast?" Dee asked.

"It's a guilty pleasure she learned from me. There's more here. Do you want another piece, Dee?"

"No, I've had plenty."

"You want a slice for your breakfast in the morning?" he asked. His eyes twinkled with amusement.

"No, I'm good."

"Your loss, right, Kaitlyn?" He closed both boxes.

"Yep, her loss." She stuffed the last bite into her mouth.

"Hey, Kaitlyn, why don't you go out and say good night to Yellow?" Marcus asked.

"Okay." She threw her paper plate in the trash then skipped out of the room.

"Thank you for giving her an evening I'll hear about all week."

Marcus gathered up his and Dee's plates.

"You're welcome. I enjoyed it." She wiped the crumbs off the table into her hand with a napkin before depositing it in the trash. "By the way, she asked me to talk you into getting her a horse. I gave her the same speech my mother gave me at her age about first proving that I could handle the responsibility. I hated it then but understand it now."

"How old were you when you got your first horse?"

"Christmas when I was eight. I cleaned the stall and groomed it after school."

"I knew eventually this day would come." He leaned against the counter. "But lessons might prove better until I see if she continues the interest. Do you mind giving her lessons?"

"Of course not. Roscoe is great for that."

"I'll see how she does this week, then we'll set it up." He let out a heavy sigh. "I hate to cut this short, but I need to get her home and ready for bed. It's a school night." His eyes locked onto hers. Did she see the same feelings reflected back? "I'd like to spend more time with you."

"I'd like that too, but I understand; your daughter is your priority. I'm enjoying the time spent with both of you."

"We should share more evenings like this."

He moved around the table, drew her to her feet, then kissed her tenderly. Dee melted into him. He deepened the kiss. At the pitter patter of small feet, they parted seconds before Kaitlyn breezed in.

"Pick up your pizza box, Kaitlyn. It's time to get home," Marcus said.

"Dee told me Yellow likes me. I think she's right."

"She did? She's probably right." Marcus locked the clinic while Dee helped Kaitlyn into her dad's truck.

"Thank you, Kaitlyn, for a fun evening. You're welcome to come ride Roscoe next week."

"Thanks, Dee." Kaitlyn hugged Dee. "I'll work hard this week, so I can have lessons. And my own horse to teach tricks to."

"You do that."

Dee hopped into her own truck and waved to Marcus and Kaitlyn as she drove toward home. His kiss lingered on her lips, leaving a tingling sense of contentment in its wake.

Lord, thank you for bringing me to this place. I'm beginning to understand Your will. Bless that child and her dad. Amen.

Chapter Seven

Silva waved as Marcus drove past her barn. He waved back. Curiosity about his evening with Dee must be killing her. He stopped at her barn after finishing with his call. Silva kneaded her hands and fingers over the back of her Olympic hopeful. The lovely gray rolled his eyes back in pure ecstasy of the massage.

"Dee comes in late this morning. She's not here yet," she said.

"I'm ahead of you this morning," he replied. "In fact, she's on her way and will be here shortly."

"You talked to her this morning?"

"No, we texted in between calls. Marvelous invention, texting—short, quick, and to the point."

"I hope you're not texting and driving."

"I'd never do that. How's Loxley doing? I hear you qualified for the freestyles Friday night. Congratulations."

"Thanks. Are you coming to watch?"

"I'm not on call this weekend, so you may see me around."

"That's good. I was afraid that, like Dee, you never took time off."

"The wonderful thing about winter season is it's busy. Vets from up north follow their clients to Florida for the winter so I have two working out of my clinic this season."

"So, did you stop to check on Loxley and congratulate me on making the freestyles?"

"I'm passing the time until Dee gets here. I didn't want to be so obvious in case Magda already arrived."

"Ah, I get it. Well, you're in luck, Doc. I'd say that squeaky gate opening means Dee has arrived. Magda rarely appears before ten. Your timing is perfect."

"Good luck tomorrow night. He looks fit and ready." He gestured toward the horse.

"Thanks. See you."

He made his way to Dee's barn. She stood in front of the tack room, unlocking the door as he strolled in. He embraced her and danced her into a corner. Since he didn't have to worry about a little girl coming in to disturb them, he kissed her.

"I've waited all night for that," he said.

"So have I." She wound her arms around his neck. Standing on tiptoe, she returned the kiss.

He tightened his arms around her. Something about her in his embrace seemed so right. He might not have wanted another relationship, but Dee melted his cold, hard heart. It would be nice for this moment to never end, but the phone vibrating in his pocket told him he had other responsibilities to get to. Lettering her go proved difficult, but pressing engagements waited for him.

"Okay, that's enough for this morning. I have to go back to work." He sighed.

"Well, talk about quickies."

"That's simply a warmup. How about a real date on Friday night?"

"I promised Silva I'd help her at the freestyles."

"I'm not on call this weekend." He bent to whisper, "I can do a late night. I thought we'd go to the freestyles together then maybe catch a late movie."

"Who watches Kaitlyn when you go out? She could come with us."

"Killjoy. My mother babysits. I must tell you, though, I haven't been on a movie date in a long time. Do you like sci-fi? I haven't seen anything except cartoon movies in the past few years. There's a new action flick playing."

"I'd like that. But I'm making you aware. I like the cartoon types too."

"I'll let you take Kaitlyn to the next one." The things a man did when raising a little girl on his own.

Dee laughed. He could listen to her all day. He kissed her again, parting her lips to dip a tongue inside. He could stand here kissing her all day. The phone vibrated again.

"I've got to get going. I've got a call holding and Magda will be here soon," Marcus said. "I'll text you later."

No matter what Magda threw at Dee today, it wouldn't matter. She had a date with Marcus tomorrow night. Magda, never punctual, came in late. Whenever she rushed to get out of the stable early she always came in late the next morning.

You must have a guy out there you go rushing to and don't want to leave the next morning. Dee smiled to herself. She'd never stayed out all night with a guy so could only imagine what it would be like. She wondered how she'd handle it if Marcus expected more.

As a baseball player, he'd understand her analogy of only getting to first base with guys in the past. She hoped he'd understand. Her faith meant a great deal to her. Other guys had walked away when she said no. But something about Marcus told her he would respect her enough to understand. *I've managed to stay virginal for thirty-three years.* She chuckled. Not many women could say that.

This morning, Magda didn't show up until eleven. Chanel stood in the aisleway with saddle and bridle on, waiting. Magda jumped on without checking the girth and left for the arena. She said nothing to Dee, not even hello. So it would be another one of those days.

There was no lunch break—getting one horse ready and cooling out a hot one, like an assembly line, until all five horses were ridden. Because they started late, they finished late. Rocket Man banged the door, letting everyone know feeding was *late*. As Dee tossed the last flake of hay and closed the stall door, Silva strode over with two cold sodas. They went outside and sat on the bench.

"It was much quieter over here today," Silva said.

"Voice-wise, yes. Work-wise, no." Dee sat with her head tilted back against the side of the barn. "I'm beat."

"Are you meeting Marcus tonight?"

"No, tomorrow night. After the freestyles we're going to a movie."

"That's wonderful. And you don't have to come help me at the freestyles, I've got plenty. You and Marcus should go have an enjoyable time."

"I *want* to help you. I want to be in the warm-up paddock as part of your team."

"Then I'm feeding for you Saturday morning. Have the feed ready, and I'll dump it. As you said, we're a team."

"Sounds like a plan."

They clinked their bottles.

~ * ~

Friday morning Magda came in on time, and the day went

smoothly. After feeding the horses, Dee ran home to shower and change before the freestyles.

Upon arrival at the showgrounds, she parked behind Silva's horse trailer. She jumped right in grooming and saddling Silva's horse, Loxley. Silva, in her white breeches and the long tail jacket, known as a Shadbelly, looked stunning. She directed her team the way a conductor did a symphony. Dee gave Silva a leg up and all headed toward the warm-up area.

Beautiful horses practiced their moves in the warm-up. They appeared to dance with their rider partner, gliding through pirouettes in a delicate ballet. Riders seemed to communicate telepathically while the horse moved under them, so elegantly choreographed. One day soon Dee would own a talented horse like these.

Marcus joined the entourage. He wore blue jeans and a crisply ironed polo shirt. She'd always like how he looked in work clothes, but dressed like this, handsome didn't begin to describe him. As he approached, she made a point to close her gaping mouth and reminded herself to act normal.

"Lox is looking good." Marcus whispered the words close to her ear.

The sounds tickled the minute hairs inside. Fireworks shot through her insides causing her to shiver.

"Are you cold?" he asked.

"No, I'm fine. It's warm for this time of year."

"That's because you're working."

She wondered if she had the same effect on him.

They watched the warm-up. Horse and rider worked perfectly together. Loxley, seeming to understand that all eyes were on him, kicked up his heels. Silva steadied him. The entourage stood near the entrance of the large international stadium. Having finished her warm-up, Silva circled Loxley on a loose rein.

"Silva, you're on deck," the ring steward yelled.

"Thank you, Walter. Time to remove the wraps and boots," she said to her grooms.

Dee and the other girls ran to Loxley's side. They worked in unison preparing the horse for his trip down centerline. Dee wiped the foam from Loxley's mouth and bridle formed when the horse worked the bit. She slipped him a few sugar cubes.

"Here goes nothing," Silva said. Horse and rider moved toward the entrance.

Dee and Marcus found Silva's husband, Steffen, sitting in the stands. He'd saved a group of seats earlier for the entourage. She took a seat between Marcus and Steffen.

Silva motioned for the music to start and rode down centerline. Dee admired Loxley's strut in complete harmony with the music. A perfect halt at X and Silva saluted the judge. Dee realized she moved her hands and hips as if she were riding Loxley through the movements. She stilled her hands. She saw a few minor flaws, things Silva worked to perfect on her daily training sessions. Her score would depend on how the five-judge panel viewed the ride.

The final pass down centerline in *passage,* a trot with a high floating pace, ended on the last note of the music. Dee watched the final salute. The group in the stands stood and cheered. Silva waved as she exited the arena.

Dee hopped out of her seat. "I've got to get down there to help with Loxley's cool down," she said to Marcus. She jogged down the stairs and trotted to the warm-up area. "Great job. You two really knocked it out of the arena," she said. Silva dismounted then hugged her.

They waited for the scores to come in from the judges. Steffen and Marcus joined them in the warm-up area. Dee stood with her arm around Silva in anticipation of the marks. Finally, the results came up on the huge scoreboard at the end of the arena. The average of the five scores was 69.7%. A huge cheer went up from everyone in the stadium. The number put Silva in first place.

"It won't hold up," Silva said. "I needed more precision in those transitions."

"Silva, the bobble on the last change I hardly noticed." Dee encouraged her friend. "Only the judge on that side could see it."

"There are four more riders to go," Silva said. "All of them are Olympic veterans."

Marcus took Dee's hand as they strolled inside the venue to sit. The next two riders had major mistakes. Silva remained in first place with two rides to go.

He wrapped his arm around Dee and whispered in her ear, "Breathe, Dee, I don't want you to pass out from oxygen deprivation."

She leaned into the embrace. "I didn't even realize I was holding my breath. I'm so excited." She wasn't sure if the butterflies inside her were from Marcus holding her close or the anticipation of Silva's win.

They waited for the last ride. It was flawless and beautiful. Dee realized before the last salute it was the winning ride. But second place still got her friend the points needed for the Olympics.

Dee grabbed Silva by the shoulders, and they jumped up and down. "Olympics bound, Silva!"

"I can't believe it! I'm qualified for the Olympics! You two have to come to the stable to celebrate tonight, won't you?" Silva asked.

"Dee, we can see the movie another night. Let's go to the victory celebration," Marcus said.

"Do you mind? I know you wanted to go to the movie."

"We can do a movie any time. Nights like this don't come along every day. Someday I'll watch you take a victory ride." He bent to give her a kiss.

She tugged him closer. The crowd disappeared while they stood there kissing. Dee missed part of Silva's victory ride because she didn't want the kiss to end. Dee and Marcus strolled hand in hand back to the trailer. She didn't even look behind her. With him beside her, her confidence soared.

~ * ~

The celebration continued at the stable. Dee set a bag of carrots with a blue ribbon attached outside Loxley's stall. Marcus maneuvered her through the people celebrating inside the barn. They found a quiet place on the bench outside her barn.

"What did you think of the Friday night freestyles here in Wellington?" he asked.

"It was exciting, rhapsodic. I've never seen anything like this outside of the Olympics. The Winter Equestrian Festival is so exciting. I'm so happy I found this farm and made friends with Silva. Someday I hope to be as good a rider and maybe even ride on the Olympic team. It will take some serious work, but I'm willing to do it."

"I think you'll succeed. And I'm glad you found this farm also."

He kissed her. Dee slid her fingers through his hair. She didn't want the evening to end, but soon she'd have to tell him about the stalker. As comfortable as Marcus made her, she still feared his reaction when she told him.

Could she share with him what brought her here to hide? Would he still enjoy being with her? He had a daughter also, whom she might be putting in danger if the stalker found her. Dee couldn't bear for either of them to be hurt. And if the stalker found her, would she run again? Should she tell Marcus and let him decide if he wanted to shoulder her problem?

Silva and Steffen ambled hand in hand around the side of the barn.

"Hey, we wondered where you two went. Would you like more champagne?" she asked.

"No, thank you," Dee said. "I'm going to check my horses and give them some hay. Don't worry about feeding for me in the morning. I'll come in at my usual time and take care of yours for you. Everyone over there can celebrate longer tonight and not worry about getting here in the morning."

"Dee, you don't have to do that. You should get to stay out late with us!"

"No, you celebrate. You deserve it." Dee stood. "Besides, I'll want another morning off sometime soon." She grasped Marcus's hand and tugged him up. "Would you like to help me throw hay to my horses?"

"Love to."

"Congratulations again, Silva," Dee said, hugging her friend.

"Thanks, girlfriend." Silva hugged Dee in closer and whispered in her ear, "I'm happy for you. Enjoy the rest of the evening with the doc here. Even if it's all night long."

Dee's cheeks heated as if she stood in front of a hot oven. Good thing it was dark, so no one saw her blush. The champagne must have gone to Silva's head for her to speak that out loud even if it was only for Dee's ears.

"Hush," she whispered back.

They both giggled.

"Come on, Steffen, Let's go back to the party and leave the lovebirds alone." Silva took his hand, and they stumbled back to their barn.

Dee flipped the lights on as she tiptoed to the feed room. Rocket Man banged his door and low rumblings came from the other horses. There was no fooling this bunch. She handed a few flakes of hay to Marcus, took several herself, and gave them to the horses. She locked the tack room door and turned off the lights. Silva's timing ruined Dee's chance to explain the truth to Marcus. She'd have to wait for another time.

At the door to her pickup, he pushed her back against the door. He sought her lips and planted more of the sweetest kisses Dee could ever remember receiving. She responded by clasping her hands behind his back. The taste of the carrot he'd snuck out of Loxley's bag augmented the kiss. Smells of horses and leather permeated the air between them. She breathed in the wonderful aroma mixed with the scent of his aftershave.

Her heart hammered in her chest. Her skin tingled from the touch of his lips all the way down to her toes. Time stood still as he slowly kissed his way from her lips to the pulse throbbing at the base of her neck. *I could spend the rest of my life with this man...except I don't want to let us both get hurt.*

With a deep sigh, Dee brought her hands to his chest and separated them, "Marcus, wonderful as this night has been, by the time I get home it'll be time to come back. Silva will be hungover in the morning, so I'll help the girls then."

"You don't want to share a horse blanket on the floor of the tack room? I'd stay with you if you asked." His whispered words tickled the hyper-aware nerve endings along her neck. He nuzzled the hollow below her ear before gently kissing his way back to her mouth. She grasped handfuls of his shirt, pulling him closer. *I never want to let him go. He makes me feel so safe and secure. Please, Lord, don't let him leave me when I tell him the truth.* The deepest sigh escaped her chest. With conflicted emotions, she turned her head away.

"Marcus, I don't want the moment to end, but . . ."

He leaned his forehead against hers. "I know. As much as I want to take you home with me tonight, I have a mother and an eight-year-old daughter there. Those are logistics I need to work out for us." His sigh matched hers.

"There are some logistics I need to work through also. Soon, very soon, everything will work out the way it's supposed to." She cupped his face in both her hands.

She couldn't admire him any more than she did right now as he spoke of his family. A man who cared this much surely would understand her predicament. Finding the right moment would be difficult and it definitely wasn't now.

"In the very near future, Dee, the time will be right. But that's not tonight." He pressed one last lingering kiss against her lips before assisting her into the truck. Her pulse hammering, she wished for nothing more than to be with Marcus.

As she drove home she couldn't help thanking God for bringing her to this farm and finding wonderful new friends. Soon the burden she so much wanted to put behind her would be alleviated.

Chapter Eight

Dee's arrival at the stable a few minutes early didn't fool the horses. Roscoe and Chanel nickered while Rocket Man hammered the stall door.

She hummed to herself while she absently scooped feed into each bucket. Her mind centered on Marcus. As she concentrated on him, she felt—what? All warm fuzzy. Sure, she'd experienced desire before, but this seemed magnetic. The more time she spent with Marcus, a handsome magnet, the harder it pulled her, the metal object, into his life. *Am I imagining this? Is it only me or does he experience the same magnetism?*

A rustling sound came from inside the tack room, drawing her attention back from where it had wandered. The stalker? Had he found her? Would the life she had found here come crashing down? Her hands shook. She gulped for air. *Get ahold of yourself.*

"It's probably a small animal in there." She sucked in a lungful of air. "Check the door, dummy."

Saying the words out loud grounded her but she almost couldn't turn the knob for the quiver of her hand. The door was still locked. *Backbone, girl, backbone. God, give me strength.* She pulled her key out of her pocket. Having the smooth metal in her hand quieted the shaking.

Unlocking the door, she opened it an inch at a time. Inside, deep breathing came from a lump by the tack boxes. When the lump moved, she jumped six inches. Her hand reached back for the wall in search of the light switch. Then she recognized the red hair and freckled skin of the face atop the lump snuggled up in the horse blankets. Silva's groom, Gale, turned over with a hand over her eyes.

"You scared me!" Dee exhaled a breath that took all the tension out with it.

"Is it morning already?" Gale rubbed her bloodshot eyes, then sat up. "It was so late last night with the party still going on in our barn. I didn't think I could drive home so I came in here. I hope you don't mind that I used Silva's key."

"That's good," Dee said. The slow drain of the adrenaline moved out of her system. "I mean about not driving home. Go on back to sleep for an hour. I'd planned on feeding for you this morning. Silva should have told you."

Gale lay back down. "Thanks, Dee, you're a peach." The words were barely out of her mouth before low snores sounded from the floor.

Dee turned off the light and closed the door. The kid was barely twenty-one, so her tolerance to alcohol was lower.

Dee went over to Silva's barn to feed. She picked up a few stray plastic cups along the way. The horses' heads hung low this morning, more than likely because the lights had been on and people had stuck around until exceedingly early in the morning.

Back in her own barn, Dee went to work cleaning stalls. It occurred to her she might never get over the uncontrollable shaking the stalker instilled in her. Perhaps it would be better not to tell Marcus about it.

~ * ~

Marcus woke that morning from dreams of Dee. So much for never getting serious with another woman. But he wasn't interested in a casual relationship. The one time he spent the night with a woman he hardly knew produced his daughter. He'd married Lauren because it had been the right thing to do. He tried hard to make it work, but it became a difficult one-sided relationship. Her looks had only been skin deep. He couldn't afford to make that mistake again.

Dee's evasive nature and mixed signals set off warning bells. But the tug to his soul only made him want to figure her out, help her if he could. Underneath the strength he observed on the outside, deep down, he sensed lingered fear and frustration. And while great to look at, her beauty came from the inside out. The way she'd taken to Kaitlyn warmed him through and through. His senses told him they belonged together. There was no way he'd say it out loud or to Dee yet, but he was falling in love.

Kaitlyn opened the bedroom door, ran in, then jumped on his bed. Thoughts of Dee vanished.

"Daddy, aren't you up yet?"

"I am now. Why are you up so early when there isn't any school today?"

"Cartoons, silly—it's Saturday!"

"I'm silly, am I?" He hugged Kaitlyn and tickled her.

She wiggled across the bed. Her giggles filled the air. She escaped and ran back out the door.

The smell of frying bacon wafted through the open door. His mother must be making breakfast. That reminded him of his conversation with Dee last night. He could imagine what would happen if an unpredictable eight-year-old ran in and a woman lay in his bed. How embarrassing. How did people handle these situations?

He got up and changed out of his pajama pants into jeans and a T-shirt. He hated pajamas, but if his eight-year-old daughter ran into the bedroom without knocking, well, he preferred to wear them. He stumbled downstairs to the kitchen in search of coffee.

"I told her not to wake you," his mother said. "You were out late."

"I was, and I'm thirty-six years old, Mom."

Judy Helton looked up from scrambling the eggs. "I meant I wanted her to let you sleep longer. You can stay out all night. I'm glad you were out for reasons other than a sick horse."

"No, not a sick horse this time." Was he ready to tell her about Dee? "I went to the freestyles last night. Several of my clients were performing."

"Good, I'm glad you're getting out some. It's time."

"What's that supposed to mean?"

"It means you should consider dating again."

"How do I do that when a munchkin runs into my bedroom without knocking?"

"It's time she learned to knock. It was cute when she was five, but now it's rude. And I know you well enough to understand you won't be bringing women around to sleep with."

"You're right, that's not me. I meant it in jest. And it's not as cute as it used to be."

"I'm glad we agree on that. Did you go by yourself or with friends?"

"I was with friends—one friend, since you're fishing for information."

"I was not," she said with a scoff. She handed him a plate of eggs and bacon.

"Thanks for breakfast. What would I do without you?"

"Starve, live in a dirty house, and let a little girl run roughshod over you."

That statement held a grain of truth. "If I bring home a date, I'll tell you. I'm not sure I'm ready for that yet."

"Who's this girl 'Dee' Kaitlyn can't quit talking about? Whoever she is, she left quite an impression on her."

She left quite an impression on me. "Dee works for a trainer whose horse I treated. She let Kaitlyn ride her horse the other evening and offered to give her lessons. Dee taught tricks to her horse which impressed Kaitlyn. It impressed me too."

"Is that who you had a pizza with at the clinic? Kaitlyn told me all about the horse with stitches."

"I see I can't get away with anything with a tattletale around. Yes, we shared a pizza at the clinic together. And before you ask, I went to the freestyles with her."

"When am I going to meet her?"

Marcus said nothing, pushing the eggs around on his plate.

His mother sat in the chair next to him. "Marcus, I want to see you happy again. It's been a long time. You've been cheerier these past weeks than you have been in years. I think it's wonderful you've found someone. I'm quite aware of how a woman might react to you living with your mother. Don't let that be an obstacle."

"Thanks. I've told her about our arrangement. I don't think it should be a problem for her." He finished his breakfast and put the plate in the dishwasher. *See, I'm not so messy.* He went to the living room to watch cartoons with his daughter.

At lunch time, he took a chance that Dee might have a free minute and sent her a text.

Good morning how are things going there? Can we get together later?

He didn't expect a reply right away. It surprised him when the phone pinged with an incoming message.

It's not morning now 😊 *crazy here yes on later*

He'd thought about going to see her this afternoon. He could take Kaitlyn but didn't want her around Magda. Something about that woman made him extra cautious. He wished Dee would quit working for her. But he understood she cared for the well-being of the horses and would not leave them.

Besides, it was her life—who was he to tell her to quit? She'd offered to give Kaitlyn lessons; perhaps it was time he let his daughter do that. If she continued to show interest, he'd consider finding her a horse or pony. He understood his daughter's love for horses. He and his sisters had shared a horse for many years. He gravitated toward sports as he grew up, but the love for the horses never left. It caused him to want to specialize in equine medicine and not the more profitable small animals. So, yes, he understood why Dee kept working for Magda.

One thing he could do to pass the time until he could see Dee was take his daughter shopping. He'd rather take a beat-down than shop but getting some riding clothes with Kaitlyn might be fun.

~ * ~

Magda was energetic and worked each of her horses hard. When she brought one of the younger horses back to exchange for the next she asked Dee, "What is going on next door? They look hung over."

"Silva won the silver medal last night at the freestyles. They celebrated till early this morning. I think the horses are tired."

"Well, good for them," Magda said before taking the next horse to the arena.

For Dee, the day moved steadily on. Magda didn't chit chat or make comments on horses—or Dee's work for that matter. That made it a good day. When Magda dismounted the last horse, she hopped into her car and left. Dee breathed a sigh of relief. She would have a few hours before feeding time to ride her own horse.

Silva came into the barn as soon as Magda left.

"I thought she'd never leave," Silva said. "I'm glad she was on good behavior today."

"A better day than most. From the few minutes I had to look your way I noticed a lull to the normal pace in your barn."

"You could say that. It's not a good idea for the entire barn to party that hard. But it was a good celebration. Hopefully, next time it'll be for gold."

"It will be. You're working too hard for that not to happen."

"I have a proposition for you." Silva hesitated, looking Dee in the eye.

Dee nodded her on. "I'm listening."

"Would you like to ride two horses for me today? It'll help me out and would be good training for you. Both are higher level horses than Roscoe."

Dee's thoughts skipped back to the day when her father gave her one of his horses to train. The excitement of obtaining her goal mixed with the angst of failure sent a tremble across her heart. Silva must think Dee rode well enough to make such an offer.

"I'd be honored to ride them. Thank you, Silva." She placed a hand over her chest and took a deep breath before hugging her friend. "I'll come over to tack them up as soon as I grab my boots and helmet."

"Oh, no you won't. You're my assistant trainer, not a groom or stable hand. Gale and Julie will do the grooming work. Get your boots and helmet and let's go."

Dee grabbed Silva by the shoulders. "Oh, Silva, thank you, thank you, thank you!" She released her friend before skipping off to the tack room.

Dee rode a tall gelding named Captain, while Silva coached from the sidelines. They worked on flying changes—a change from one leading hind foot to the other. The first few attempts Dee either signaled early or late. Captain skipped along, giving her a buck. Finally, she found the rhythm and performed two perfectly timed changes. Now she and Captain were dancing to the same music as they crossed the arena.

She patted his silky neck. "Good boy, enough for today. Tomorrow we'll have the timing perfect."

Her second ride was a large pony named Bickel. The stride difference between him and Roscoe was significant. This guy required a lot less effort to perform the movements. "You're a fun ride and quick," she said.

Handing the horse to someone else for untacking and cooling out was a treat when she finished. Unlike Magda, Dee thanked the girls for their work.

She trotted back to her barn; it was feeding time now, and Rocket Man reminded her with multiple front kicks to the stall door. While riding, Dee's phone had been in her tack room. When she finished, she picked it up and discovered a text from Marcus. Unfortunately, two hours had passed since he'd sent it.

Can you feed early and we can catch that movie tonight?

Dee sent a text back. *Sorry, I was riding. I'm done with feeding. Can we still make the movie?*

She held her breath while waiting for a return text. She sat in the tack room, concentrating on the phone. As she willed it to ring with a new text, a shiver ran up her spine. That sensation of being watched came over her. *Where is this coming from? I'm safe here in the stable,* she reasoned. The sensation persisted.

"Oh, quit letting it rule your life," she said out loud.

Covering her mouth with her hand, she stood up. Her gaze landed on Marcus who stood leaning on the doorpost. "Oh, my goodness." On wobbly legs, she crossed the short distance and collapsed into his arms. In his arms the tension dissipated.

"Are you cold? Why're you shivering like that?" Marcus asked.

"I'm fine. How long have you been here?"

"I just arrived. I admit I was admiring your sitting in such rapt concentration. You're beautiful when you meditate. But then you started to tremble."

She released her tight hold. Still in his embrace, he planted a kiss on her lips. In that moment, relief flooded over her since she could let it be over. Here in his arms all the apprehension flowed out of her. Safety and security awaited her if only he didn't leave once she told him about the stalker.

The kiss continued, long and deep. Dee never wanted it to end. When they parted, she continued to gaze into his eyes. She observed only concern in them.

"No, I wasn't cold," she murmured.

"But you were trembling."

She averted her eyes. Her brain scrabbled to find a logical excuse. Finding none, she asked, "Do we have time to make the movie?"

"We can make a later showing. I take it Magda had you running circles? Is that why you didn't text back earlier?"

"Silva had me ride two of her horses. I left the phone here, so I missed your text. I didn't find it until moments before you came in. Didn't you see my reply?"

"I did. I saw it right after I parked the car." He put his hands on her shoulders. His gaze asked questions for answers she wasn't ready to give.

"What were you concentrating on before you looked up and saw me? I've seen you rattled like that before."

"What are you talking about?"

"You were staring at the phone, said something about not letting it rule your life. Then you began shaking like a leaf."

"It's not important. You surprised me is all."

She waited for him to let her go but he continued to delve into her eyes. Fortunately, a kick to a stall wall diverted their attention. She wasn't sure if it came from Roscoe or Rocket Man. Marcus eased back. Grateful for the distraction, she went toward the sound.

Dee checked all the horses. Whatever initiated the kick to the wall had disappeared.

She drove out of the farm with Marcus close behind. The realization hit her that the stalked feeling had melted away. She wished she could keep him around more. She needed to confide her secret, yet she still couldn't tell him. Letting those horrible emotions show in front of Marcus made her left weak and ashamed. She'd let this stalker make her paranoid. Her faith told her that God indeed had a plan and it appeared to include Marcus.

~ * ~

Marcus thought about the incident in the tack room. What scared her so much she could visibly quake like that? He'd wanted to explore it but also didn't want to force her. She would share her troubles when she was ready. The look in her eyes told him to let it go. He'd wait for her to tell him in her own time. Pressure might drive her away. That moment, entwined with her, she'd grasped for a lifeline. Where had the confident, strong woman gone for those few moments?

Dee drove into the security gate of her complex and stopped at the guard gate. After speaking with the guard, she went through the gate, and the guard waved Marcus through. She made a turn off the main street of the complex, then another turn before stopping in her driveway. When he joined her, they walked to the side door of the house, which led into the garage. She unlocked the door, and they went inside.

"I've never had a guest since I moved in." Dee turned on the lights.

"Cute apartment," Marcus said. "It appears to have been the garage at one time, right? The garage door is sealed over. It has so much room."

"I had the back wall taken out, which opened to a fourth bedroom in the house," Dee gestured toward the wall. "I closed off the door that entered from the main house. It gives me all the room I need and privacy to the family that lives in the house."

"They didn't have a problem with that?" he asked.

"No, because I own the house, purchased from the winnings of horses I helped train at the track. I rent the house to them and live in here."

"That's enterprising." He rubbed his chin in contemplation. "Why didn't you live in the house and rent the apartment?"

"I don't need a whole house. This is perfect. I found it in a foreclosure sale, so I got a great deal. Perhaps one day I'll want more room, but for now this is perfect."

"Okay, that makes sense." He paced a circle as he scanned the room. "But you don't mind how dark it is in here?"

"I'm only here in the evenings when it's dark outside, anyway. I spend the bulk of my day at the stable. I get plenty of vitamin D there, I assure you, Doctor."

Marcus laughed at the snide way she corrected him. "You did an excellent job of putting this together. You surely didn't do it yourself?"

"No, I bought the house, wrote up the plans, contracted the work, and when it was done, I moved in. Have a seat on the sofa. You can turn the TV on. I'll get a quick shower and change, and we'll go."

He scanned the tiny apartment. The furniture was new, and neatly spaced shelves held miniature horse statues and a few pictures. A tiny kitchen with a refrigerator, a stove, and sink covered one wall. A single bed with a dresser and nightstand lined the back wall. The sofa, a recliner, and a side table faced away from the kitchen. The television placed within a bookcase occupied the opposite wall. A wall separated the bathroom from the main room. The room suited her.

It wasn't long until Dee opened the door and came out dressed in jeans and a button-up green plaid shirt. "Okay, I'm ready."

Her hair, still damp, flowed over her shoulders. He loved to see her like that. They went out to Marcus's car where he opened the passenger door for her to slide into the Mustang GT.

After he got in, she said, "I like your car. Sporty looks good on you."

"Now you sound like my daughter." He drove out of the complex toward the theater. "She and her friends all think it's fun to ride in. My mother has an SUV to haul them around, but they clamor for me to take them places in this."

"Your daughter has good taste."

He glanced over at her. "Sometimes, yes. Wait until you see the pink riding breeches she talked me into buying today. Also, a pink riding helmet and pink gloves. I made her get a black pair too. She's ready for her next riding lesson."

"Good for her." She chuckled. "There's nothing wrong with pink on a little girl. I guess it would surprise you to know I have a pair of purple breeches."

He couldn't resist rolling his eyes. He hoped she didn't notice. "Don't tell me you have purple gloves and a purple helmet."

"Not a helmet, but I have purple gloves. And Roscoe has a purple saddle pad and matching polo wraps. I have pads and polos in red, blue, green, and of course, pink. It's boring to ride in black and white all the time."

"You come from the racetrack with all the colorful silks. It makes sense you'd like to add color." He sensed her turn toward him in her seat. Somehow he envisioned a snappy comeback.

"There are lots of colors at the track. I should get out one of my royal purple and gold saddle towels, put it over my saddle pad and ride around the farm. Do you think I'd get looks?"

Definitely a snappy commentary. "Yes, I think you would. But somehow, I think it would suit Roscoe. Thoroughbreds look sharp in jockey silks."

They arrived at the theater and went inside. They bought popcorn and headed in to find seats. When the pre-movie request to silence cellphones came on, Dee snickered.

"You don't come to the movies when you're on call, do you?"

she whispered.

"No, I don't. So I don't get to the movies often." He whispered back

The lights went down. Marcus put one arm around her as they munched the popcorn. *Yes, I could spend many an evening like this.* All thoughts of her earlier distress disappeared as he enjoyed her company.

~ * ~

They were holding hands when they came out of the theater. Halting at the top of the stairs, Dee scanned the parking lot. Marcus glanced at her then skimmed through the parking lot. *What is she looking for? Why is she always so cautious?* They skipped down the steps to his car. He opened the passenger door for her to slide in before going to his side.

She put her hand on his arm as he started the car. "Would you mind running past the stable to check the horses?"

"Sure. I almost forgot you do that every night. You're hard on a date night!" He laughed.

"Sorry. When the season is over, I don't plan to be stable help anymore."

They talked about different scenes from the movie they liked or thought were cheesy. Dee appeared the most at ease he'd ever seen her. That made him happy. Whatever bothered her, he perceived his being with her made it easier. Now if she would trust him enough to tell him what it was.

He drove through the gate into the farm. All the barns were dark. As a vet that was a comforting thing. As soon as Dee exited the car, even before the lights came on, several horses nickered, and Rocket Man kicked the door.

"Horses detect by smell more than sight," Marcus said.

"And if you change any scent on your body from the normal, your horse won't recognize you."

"I think neither one of us can beat the other with horse trivia." Marcus took the hay she handed him. She threw a flake to each horse.

"Oh, I think I'd win. Can you name the runners-up of all the Kentucky Derbies?"

"No, can you?"

Her mischievous grin nearly undid him. "The year 2019, the place horse was Code of Honor. The year 2018, the place horse was Good Magic. In 2017, the place horse was—"

Marcus held up his free hand. "Okay, you win. You can beat me in racing trivia. I'm sure there's something I can beat you at regarding horse trivia."

"Yeah, that was unfair. Racing programs are kind of in the blood. You would beat me hands down if it were the bones or muscles of the horse. I'm good with the legs, but the rest of the body, not so much."

"That's good, then we each have our niche."

Once each horse had its hay and settled to munching, Dee turned out the lights. With a hand on her shoulder, Marcus turned her into his arms and found her lips. She tasted of popcorn, butter, and salt. Speaking of butter, she seemed to melt in his arms. He didn't break the kiss until one horse inside whinnied and kicked the wall. Dee laughed.

"What's so funny?" Marcus asked.

"That's Rocket Man. He's jealous. He thinks you're moving in on his property."

"Hey, big man, the human is mine," Marcus yelled down the dark aisle. When he spoke again, he whispered in her ear, "Seems wrong that I'm competing with a horse for the affections of a woman."

They drove to her home, and he walked her to the door. Unlocking it, she turned back to him. He took her in his arms. "There aren't any animals here who will call me out, are there?" he asked.

A soft snort erupted from her throat. "Not that I'm aware of. I've had a wonderful time tonight and would like to do this again. But I have to be back at work early in the morning. I promise the next time we go out, I'll arrange night check and morning feeding. It takes planning."

"I'm fine with that. I'm not a man who expects things. There is a time and a place for more intimate affairs. We can spend our time getting to know each other."

"You're the most wonderful and understanding man I ever met. Thanks for not expecting *more* so soon."

"Sometimes that *more* gets people in trouble. I'm content with holding you in my arms and savoring your sweet kisses." He embraced her and sought her lips. He envisioned them melting together Perhaps he'd been too hasty to think he'd never fall for another woman. When he ended the kiss, he leaned his forehead against hers. A mutual sigh hung in the air.

With one last kiss, he floated back to his car.

Chapter Nine

Dee put the saddle on Chanel as Magda breezed into the stable. "I don't want to start with this horse today. Get the gray horse ready," she demanded.

In all the time Dee had groomed for Magda, Chanel always got ridden first. Dee slid the saddle off Chanel and placed it on the saddle rack. The horse trotted back in her stall, happy to get back to munching hay. Magda never called her horses by their name; she distinguished them by color, age, or sex.

Dee struggled to get the gray, Dancer, ready as fast as possible while listening as Magda rummaged around the tack room. *What is she looking for?* If she'd ask, Dee could probably tell her where it was. Magda wasn't as hands-on with her horses as a trainer like Silva or any of the other trainers on the farm. Neither was she a talented rider. Dee wondered how Magda ever made the Russian Olympic team. Luck and lots of money might make up for the difference in talent, but it took more than that for the Olympics. *She is definitely different from any trainers I've seen.*

Magda grabbed Dancer's reins. "Young horse next," she shouted as she marched away.

"Well, at least she told me so I didn't have to guess," Dee muttered. Whenever she thought she had figured Magda out, she did a one-eighty. Dee went to get the young horse, Rusty.

The assembly line of horses continued into the afternoon. Magda would tell Dee which horse was next as she strode to the arena. Each horse had been worked so hard, it came back white with lather.

Rocket Man became the last horse of the day. He skittered

around on the cross ties while Dee saddled him. "Easy, old boy," she said in a soothing tone. He reminded her of an old saying: "Like a long-tailed cat in a room full of rocking chairs." Even his hair stood on end. He didn't look his normal sleek-coated self.

Magda came back, throwing Chanel's reins to Dee and yanking Rocket Man's out of her hand. The horse balked as Magda jerked on his mouth. He tossed his head and backed up several steps. She turned and smacked Rocket Man on his neck with the end of the reins. She dragged him down the aisle and out toward the arena.

Chanel enjoyed her rinse off on the wash rack with a loud sigh. Suddenly, Dee heard shouting from the arena area. It sounded like a lot of different voices, all of them shouting. Then the words, "Loose horse! Loose horse!" became clear. Those were words that put panic in everyone on a farm with working horses. Injuries to other horses and riders often occurred in these moments.

Dee shoved Chanel back in her stall even though the mare was still wet. That was the safest place for her to be until they captured the loose horse. Dee ran out of the barn and looked toward the arena. Rocket Man was coming down the drive in a flat-out run. He slowed only enough to throw a few bucks into the air. A group of people in the arena were bending over what Dee assumed was Magda on the ground.

Dee sprinted toward the open front gate. It hadn't closed yet behind whoever just drove in. She waved her hands in an effort to get Rocket Man to stop. He swerved away from the gate and bore down on where she stood. At the last second before he crashed into her, she shouted, "Whoa!"

Rocket Man slid to a stop in front of her. He pressed his forehead on her chest and stood still, breathing hard. She hugged his sweat-soaked neck. *What did she do to you, pretty boy?* They stood that way for a several seconds. Finally, she picked up the broken ends of the reins, preparing to lead him back to the barn.

"Dee!" Marcus shouted. She turned at the sound of his voice. He dashed over, clutching her by the shoulders. "Are you crazy? He could have run over you or knocked you down if he didn't stop soon enough."

"He wouldn't run over me. He might veer around me, but he wouldn't run over me," she said.

"You had a lot of faith that he would stop. Thank goodness he didn't hurt you." Marcus hugged her tight.

Dee wiggled out of the bear hug. "I'm okay, Marcus, really I am. I have to take Rocket Man back to the stable. You should go check on whoever is down in the arena. I'm guessing it's Magda. She may need first aid."

"What happened, did you see?" he asked.

"I heard the shouting, and I saw someone down on the ground."

"Okay, I'll go see if there's anything I can do." He sprinted in that direction.

Dee took the sweating, blowing horse into the stable. She walked him up and down the aisle for several minutes to help cool him down. Though she was curious about what had transpired in the arena, she took extra care while hosing the sweat off. Rocket Man gradually calmed his flaring nostril. He expelled a deep breath and lowered his head.

~ * ~

When Marcus arrived in the arena, the other trainers were kneeling around Magda. Marcus knelt beside her and several of the others backed away. She was unconscious. In a few minutes she came to, pushing herself up.

"Lie still, Magda," he said. "Who saw what happened?"

"Rocket Man bucked her off," Silva said. "We've called the paramedics."

"I'm fine." Magda attempted to get up.

"Don't move. You could have a concussion," Silva said.

"No, I'm fine, let me up."

"Magda, you need to stay down until the paramedics can check you out," Marcus said.

"Oh, the beautiful doctor," Magda said. She pressed a hand to his cheek. "I am not horse you have to keep down. People need to get up." This time she stood up. She wobbled and fell back. Silva and Marcus caught her and eased her to the ground.

"You really do need to stay down, Magda. How are you otherwise? Any pain anywhere?" he asked.

"I'm fine, I told you. Unless I could lie with you. We cuddle like lovers."

He back away, letting Silva and one of the other trainers handle Magda. He thought she might have pulled him down to the ground if he stayed near her one minute more. Soon he heard sirens in the distance.

Everyone moved back to let the EMTs do their job upon their arrival. He listened while they asked her a series of questions, attempting to determine the extent of her injuries. As they slid her onto the backboard, she pushed them away.

"I am fine. I need no help. I no going to hospital. Help me stand up and I go home," she said. The paramedics took her hands to pull her to her feet. She wobbled but remained upright.

"You really should go to the hospital and be checked out, miss," said the female paramedic.

"No, I am fine. No hospital. I go home."

"Magda, do you have someone who can come get you and take you home?" Silva asked.

"No, I drive myself." She took a few tentative strides. "See, I am fine, I told you. But if beautiful horse doctor will walk me to my car, I appreciate that."

She put her arm around his waist and leaned into him. He went with Magda out of the arena toward her car.

"Even with a concussion she's flirting with the doc."

Marcus wasn't aware which of the bystanders made the comment but it made him uncomfortable. He helped Magda get into her car.

"Good doctor," she said, smiling, "why don't you drive me home? I could enjoy bedside manner with you."

"You need to go home and go to bed, Magda. We'll get one of the girls to drive you, if necessary."

"You would like to put me to bed, yes?" Magda looked at him all dreamy-eyed.

"After the bump on the head you took, rest is what you need, nothing else. I'll ask Silva or one of the other ladies to take you." Marcus turned away. "She needs a ride," he said as Silva trotted up.

Magda slammed the car door and started the engine. She had it in gear before either one could stop her. Gravel hit them as she sped toward the front gate.

"Well, I guess not." Marcus shook his head.

"She sure latched onto you," Silva said.

"She may have a slight concussion, so I was trying to be nice. Something about her gives me the creeps."

"We all think that. If the stable board hadn't been paid in advance, we'd like to have her evicted. I don't get how Dee does it."

"I don't either. I wish she'd quit."

"I've begun having her ride some of my horses. Her talent's too good for mucking stalls."

"She told me that. You made her day." They went inside where Dee stood with Rocket Man.

"Is Magda okay?" she asked. "I see she drove herself out of here. Is she going to the hospital?"

"She says she's fine," he answered. "The paramedics suggested a possible concussion and recommended she go to the hospital. She was adamant she wasn't going with them. How is my real patient, Rocket Man?"

"He appears fine. Do you want to check him out? Silva, did you see what happened?" Dee asked.

"She asked the horse for one thing but cued him for another. Finally, I think he had enough and dumped her. He has an attitude with her every time she rides him."

"Did you find any cuts or bumps while you washed him off?" he asked.

"Nothing. I massaged his legs, and he didn't show any tenderness."

"Jog him down the aisle for me."

Dee jogged the horse down the aisle and back.

"Nothing is apparent as of yet," he said. "Why don't you jump up on him, so I can see him under saddle?"

Marcus observed Dee's hesitation. With Magda gone, she couldn't ask permission. Also the horse had just bucked its rider off. He'd be reluctant to have anyone climb on after that.

"Dee, if he were my horse, I'd want him checked out. Marcus is here and can give an honest evaluation to stave off any problems," Silva said.

Dee nodded then tacked the horse.

Outside, Dee vaulted into the saddle, landing gracefully. Marcus and Silva looked at each other as Dee trotted the horse toward the arena.

"Well, there's no doubt she was an exercise rider at the racetrack," Marcus said. "She's braver than me."

He observed the foot falls as Dee moved the horse around the arena in both directions. He ascertained no irregularities in the gait. He asked for the trot then canter. She brought Rocket Man back to the walk and returned to where Marcus and Silva stood.

"How does he look?" Dee asked.

"I see no ill effects."

"I'm glad. He's an extremely talented horse who shouldn't be ruined by poor riding." She swung down as nimbly as she had up and trotted the horse back to the barn. Marcus and Silva trailed after her. He took Silva's arm to slow her pace so Dee couldn't hear.

"Did you see Rocket Man when he ran out of the arena?"

"I saw him head toward the barn. Did something happen?"

"He ran straight at Dee. She stood there and didn't move. I thought he would run her down, but he stopped in front of her and put his head on her chest. It was like he was looking for her. They have an affinity for each other."

"H appears to prefer Dee to Magda. He dumped Magda on purpose. With Dee in the irons, his eyes sparkled and his ears tuned to her. I'll make a suggestion to Magda about letting Dee ride him, but she hasn't listened to anything else any of us have told her."

They strode into the barn as Dee finished unsaddling Rocket Man. "Did you still want to ride?" Silva asked. "Feeding time is near, but I saved a horse for you to have a lesson on."

"Let me get Rocket Man put away and I'll come over."

"Okay, we'll get the horse ready. See you in a few." Silva returned to her own barn.

"Marcus, did I miss a text? I wasn't aware you were coming over."

"No, I didn't text. I thought I'd come by and help you with feeding."

"What a delightful surprise. When you helped Magda to her car, I thought you might drive her home."

Did I detect a hint of jealousy in her voice? It made him go gooey inside. "That bump on the head must have made her loopy. She asked me to. I hope she understands I'm not interested."

"I can't believe she didn't go to the hospital. Did she even ask about Rocket Man?"

"No. Did you expect her to?"

"I hoped she would."

Dee settled Rocket Man in his stall, and Marcus and Dee went to the arena.

This time she let him give her a leg up. He watched while Silva coached Dee through the ride. When she finished, she walked the horse around the arena to cool it down.

Silva stepped closer to Marcus. "I want her as my assistant trainer."

"Stealing her from Magda while you're in the barn next door? It could cause a lot of problems."

"I realize it could be an issue. Hopefully, Magda will go back to Russia when season is over." Silva went back to her barn.

Marcus waited at the edge of the arena while Dee dismounted. He considered taking her hand as they strolled next to each other but thought it wasn't a good idea in front of the others around the farm. Back in Dee's barn, he topped off the water buckets while she dumped grain. Working like this together felt so right. He could imagine doing this every day for the rest of his life.

"It's not a school night. Could I talk you into coming to my house, and I'll make us some dinner?" she asked.

"Even though it's not a school night, I'll need to get home before Kaitlyn goes to bed. But we could get take-out and go to your house. You've been working hard all day. I'm not asking you to cook for me."

"Spaghetti isn't all that hard, and it's quick."

"Spaghetti? How did you know I enjoy Italian?"

"Maybe since you said so the night we went to Aglioli's."

"Umm. You didn't tell me you cooked."

"Didn't I? Well, are you interested?"

"Lead the way."

Chapter Ten

After an excellent dinner, Marcus hadn't wanted to leave Dee's house. The two of them fit together like puzzle pieces. But unless he was on an emergency, he always put his daughter to bed. That came naturally. Sunday morning he'd taken his mother and Kaitlyn to lunch after church, then helped her with her homework before he left to see Dee at the stable. Now dinner with her and home to read a quick story to Kaitlyn before bed. A perfectly natural day.

He replayed their evening together in his mind as he got into his truck the next morning. Detective Brad Tyler pulled in and parked next to him.

"You're heading out for the day?" Brad asked as he exited his unmarked car.

"I was about to, what's up?"

"I wanted to pass along information. Forensics determined the same person murdered those two men."

"You thought so the other day."

"Well, now it's confirmed and there's more—the killer is female."

Marcus leaned on the patrol car. This was unexpected news. "What? Are they sure? How can they tell? From what the news said, the two men were in good condition. It's hard to imagine a woman taking them down easily. She would have to be an excellent fighter."

Brad sat back on the hood of the car next to Marcus. "Not when she uses drugs to subdue them. They found traces of Ketamine."

"Ah, also known as Special K. I've heard that men use pills like that to subdue young women."

"Instead of pills she used the injectable type. They found puncture marks."

Marcus shoved himself off the car and faced Brad. "What? How would someone get that who isn't a veterinarian? Injectable Ketamine is found in every animal clinic, but I haven't heard of any being broken into in Palm Beach County. Where did she get it? Surely, she's not a vet or technician."

"That's where it gets interesting." Brad crossed his arms and legs as he leaned back on the car. "Forensically, they can trace the drug to the manufacturer and lot number. We can find who bought them. Turns out, the clinic that purchased the lot number used in our crimes is yours. Do you carry it on your truck? Could someone get it without your knowledge?"

"I have it on the truck and in the clinic. No one has access inside other than my office manager, and I trust her implicitly. I used some a week or so ago. I'll check if the bottle is still here." Marcus stalked off to unlock the side compartment of his veterinary truck.

"Wait, don't touch it!" Brad shoved off the car and grabbed Marcus's arm before he could touch the truck. "I'll have the forensics team come dust for prints. We'll take yours and Margo's for comparison. Listen, Marcus, I'm aware that you and Margo have nothing to do with this. She's my mother's age. But it's possible you and the killer have crossed paths."

He slumped back against Brad's car. The weight of Brad's words hit like a baseball bat to the gut. Someone in his world was a murderer, or at the least, an accomplice.

"You weren't going on an emergency call, were you?" Brad asked.

"No, a soundness check," Marcus answered.

"Call 'em and tell them you'll be late."

Marcus did. He also called one of the other vets who helped him with calls during the winter months. If she took the second call of the morning, he wouldn't fall too far behind. Brad was on the phone at the same time calling for a forensics unit.

After the call, Marcus decided to check his drug supplies that were locked inside the clinic. There was no Ketamine missing there. Back outside, he observed as the police service aide dusted his truck for fingerprints. After lifting a couple of latent prints, they opened the compartment. The bottle stored in the truck was gone.

"Perhaps you can provide a list of farm calls you've been on over the past six weeks. It might give us some suspects," Brad said.

"Okay, but when I'm at a farm call, I'm not only with a horse's owner or groom. There are workers, feed store guys, and visitors at many of the stables. When I'm handling a horse, I can't always watch the truck. I trust no one will get into it. There are no hard drugs that addicts can use so basically I've thought it safe. I've never heard of injectable Ketamine being used on humans. I park the truck inside the clinic at night and it's locked if I leave it outside. Since I haven't noticed anything else missing, I assume whoever took the Ketamine was after that specifically."

"It's not your fault. But it worries me that they could try to use it on you. The victims worked in the horse world."

"How did you conclude the suspect is female?"

"Without being overly graphic, there were sexual secretions on the victims, and they verified the suspect to be female. They collected DNA, but it matches no one in the database so far."

"Well, if it's any consolation, I haven't been with a woman other than my ex-wife for a long time," Marcus said.

"Do you think she could do something like this and try to pin it on you?" Brad asked.

"Oh please. Unless the victims were doctors, lawyers, or bankers she wouldn't have anything to do with them. There's no way it involves her. She couldn't even draw a syringe, let alone give a shot."

"I had to ask, under the circumstances."

When the forensic techs finished with the truck, they rolled Marcus's fingerprints before going inside to do the same with Margo. After they released the truck, Marcus said goodbye to Brad and started out on his daily calls.

He mulled over who in his sphere of horse people could possibly have stolen drugs from his truck. He came up empty. Certainly, he wasn't acquainted with everyone in the barns he frequented. Yet he couldn't think of an owner or trainer who would hire someone who would steal, let alone commit a murder. As inconvenient as it would be, he would have to keep the truck locked up and pass the word along to the other vets to do the same.

~ * ~

On Monday, Dee wondered how Magda fared after her fall. Dee sent a text to ask, but of course, Magda didn't reply. She never did. Silva also took the day off, so when Dee arrived at work, she found only Gale and Julie in the first two barns. With so few people around, it was ghostly quiet, once Rocket Man had been fed. As soon as the morning cleaning and turnouts were done, Dee planned to leave and run errands.

She finished moments before Lily Stoneman, another trainer who worked at the farm, walked in. Lily lived in an apartment on the property so even on a day off, she often showed up to talk or hang around.

"Hey, how is that horse Magda was riding when she came off?" Lily asked. "I saw Marcus watching him move. He survived the ordeal?"

"He seems fine," Dee said. "Nothing visible."

"Have you heard from Magda? How's she feeling?"

"I sent her a text, but she didn't return it."

"She's strange. I can't put a finger on what is different about her, but there is something. One of my stall-cleaning guys, Pico, was catching a ride home with her for a while. They live near each other. A couple days ago he didn't show up for work. I asked her about it. All she said was he wasn't at the coffee shop where she picked him up. I get that sometimes these guys find a better job and just leave. When Miguel left, I figured he'd tired of her moods. But she had contact with Pico, and now he's up and gone without explanation. She puts me in mind of someone who would sabotage other people's affairs. Leaving me without stable help might be her idea of hurting my business."

"You think she deliberately didn't give Pico a ride to work?"

"I think she is purposely driving our workers away. They leave without a word after being around her. It sets my mind to wondering. Keep your wits about you when you are around her." Lily's cocked eyebrow gave her words a serious edge. "At times it sounds like she'd like to drive you away also."

"I'll keep my eye on her. She's different, and you're right, she can be volatile."

As Lily left the barn, Dee wondered if Lily's statements about Magda driving away grooms could be true. Was there more to Miguel and Pico leaving suddenly?

Dee checked all the horses before leaving the farm. As she opened the door to her truck, her phone rang with a call from Marcus.

"Hi, are you busy?" he asked.

"No, leaving to run errands."

"Do you have time to assist me on a call?"

"Where are you?"

He gave her the address and directions. She jumped into her truck and headed that way. Already there, he sat in his truck in front of the property, a large, fenced field with lots of grass and trees interspersed.

He got out of his truck and came to her. As soon she was out, he snatched her up for a quick kiss.

"Your clients will give you grief for doing personal things on their dime." She giggled. But she took his face in both hands to kiss him again. "There aren't any horses in this field, so what's up?"

"Juan wants to move his polo horses here. He wanted us to check it out for locoweed and nightshade before he brings them here. I'm still treating his horses, but they are recovering."

"He wanted *us* to check it out? Or you mean he wanted *you* to check it out. I'm along to keep you company."

"No, you're wrong. Juan asked for *you* to check the field. You made quite an impression on him. He wanted your phone number. I wouldn't give it to him."

"Why is that?" While glad he hadn't given out her number, she couldn't resist asking. She enjoyed the flirting.

"I didn't want to." He opened the gate for them. "Why? Did you want me to?"

Now whose is it turn to flirt? In all seriousness, she said, "This is a big field. How are we going to be sure we don't miss some?"

"You found it under the trees in thicker undergrowth. That's a good place to start."

They went to the far corner and started their search. She moved along the back fence where she could check both sides. About halfway through the field, she noticed some movement under the brush on the other side.

Curious, she climbed over the fence to inspect. She stopped. Whatever stirred was on the ground. She went nearer to take a closer look. A large black bird burst from the overgrowth, flapping its long wings, nearly flying into her face. Before she could draw a breath, two more of the same type birds flew out. The vultures landed above her in a tree, squawking loudly.

Marcus ran over to her, jumping the fence with ease. "What is it?"

"I don't know. A dead animal, I think. Those were vultures, right?"

"I think you disturbed them from their lunch. It looks big, whatever it is." He shifted the underbrush aside, allowing Dee to get a closer look at what lay underneath: the remnants of a man lay facing her.

She turned away. She took hold of the fence as her knees threatened to buckle. Marcus came to her side. The contents of her stomach churned into her throat, but she didn't vomit. Lightheaded and white-knuckled, she clutched the fence.

"Are you okay?" Marcus asked. He put an arm across her shoulders.

"I'm fine. It's… I expected a deer or something like that."

"You saw it? I hoped you hadn't."

"Oh, I saw it."

Marcus steadied her while he took out his cellphone. She

listened while he talked to someone on the other end who appeared be a friend and police officer. He gave the address before clicking off the call. His tight hug helped slow her beating pulse.

~ * ~

Marcus moved Dee away and settled her under a tree. Her skin had paled. When Brad and the deputies got there, Marcus took them over to where they could climb the fence to get to the body on the other side.

"How did you find it under there?" Brad asked.

"Dee found it. We were out here looking for toxic weeds. Ask her, but I think the vultures attracted her attention."

"Who's Dee?"

"The girl sitting over there under the tree. The sight of the dead body hit her hard." Marcus pointed over to Dee.

She had a deer-in-the-headlights look. Brad instructed one deputy to go talk to her. He handed Marcus a pair of latex gloves, which they donned before pulling the brush back to look at what lay underneath.

He maintained a hold of the brush so Brad and the deputy could view the body. Marcus glanced at Dee as she and the deputy walk away. The sight of a dead human shocked most people, but he hadn't expected Dee to nearly faint. He wondered if whatever frightened her and caused the shaking he'd observed on several occasions had anything to do with her reaction. Could it be related? Had she experienced a trauma that she couldn't confide?

He couldn't get the answers right now but made a mental note to ask at a more appropriate time.

"Brad, do I need to stay here with you? Dee may need medical attention."

Brad stared straight at Marcus. He must have given away more than simple concern for Dee's health. He drew Marcus aside and whispered so the deputy couldn't overhear. "You're in love with her, aren't you?"

"What? I'm concerned for my friend."

"*I'm* your friend. Would you be this concerned for me?"

Marcus waved his hand, batting the question away. "You've seen a few dead bodies. She said she hasn't."

"Who is she anyway? Why was she out here with you? When did you start dating again?" Brad crossed his arms and took a firm stance.

"Dee works for a trainer over at Everglades Equestrian. She's extremely good at identifying a specific weed that is toxic to horses. We were checking the field for it because a client asked us to."

"She's closer than an acquaintance. You're not fooling me."

Marcus stared hard at him. He seldom got anything over on Brad.

"Okay, let's go check on her. I'll send the rest of the team back." He gave instructions to the deputy before they started back to the cars.

"When did you meet her?" Brad asked.

"A while ago. She's helped me out with some cases."

"It's good to see you show some interest in a woman again."

~ * ~

Dee observed the deputy approached her. Decision time. Using her sister's name posed no harm. But disclosing a fake name to the police? They might not figure out her true identity right away but as this investigation went on? Two of her uncles were cops. Her family had discussed situations like this when she left. Basically, they'd told her to stay out of trouble so she wouldn't have to lie. But now trouble had found her.

The deputy stopped in front of her. She leaned against a tree. Her legs still felt wobbly.

"Hello, ma'am," the deputy said. "You found the body?"

"Yes, I saw something move under the bush. As I got closer to look a vulture flew out. Marcus came over and lifted the brush out of the way. That's…that's when…that's when I saw…a body." Her nails dug into the tree bark.

"Are you okay, miss?" The deputy asked.

"I've never seen a dead person before. Dead animals, yes, but never a… a human."

"That's understandable. Perhaps you should sit down."

Dee let go of the tree. "I'd like to go sit in my truck if that's all right."

"I think that would be okay," the deputy said. He grasped her elbow as they crossed the field.

They arrived back at the road. She took a seat in her truck. She gave the deputy her sister's name when he asked. After some follow-up questions, he went back to his patrol car. She could observe him typing on his computer through the rear-view mirror. Hopefully, she'd be out of there soon. Her nervousness had subsided but not by much.

When Marcus came out of the field, he strode straight to her. She leaned out of the truck into his arms and buried her head into his chest. Her shaking stopped as soon as his arms enveloped her.

"Dee," he whispered. "I want you to meet someone."

She lifted her head.

"This is Detective Brad Tyler. We've been friends for a long time. He'll be investigating the body we've found." He turned to Brad. "Brad, this is Dee Collins."

"I'm glad to meet you. I wish it were under better circumstances.

Are you feeling better? I understand seeing something like that is upsetting."

"I'd feel better if I could go home now."

"If Deputy Watson has your information, I don't see why not. I may want to talk to you later. We have your address and a phone number, right?"

"Yes, Detective."

When the forensics team arrived, Brad opened the gate for them to drive back to the crime scene. Marcus stood with Dee beside her truck.

"Are you sure you're all right?" he asked.

"I'll be fine. I wish I could unsee that body." Dee's voice faltered.

"I know, baby, I know." He crushed her to him again.

They stayed that way for several minutes. When she looked up again, a television van maneuvered behind the other vehicles. She tensed.

As he turned, she viewed the crew getting out to set up for a live shot. "Marcus, I've got to get out of here. I've got to get out of here *now*."

"I'll follow you home."

"No, I'll be fine. I don't want to see myself on the news. I can't do that."

"Okay, call me as soon as you're home. I'll come by later to check on you. Why don't you see if someone else can care for the horses this evening?"

She didn't answer him and instead slammed the door closed.

Marcus backed up as the truck started, and she drove away, leaving a wall of dust behind her. It might have been rude, but she wanted out of there before the camera caught a glimpse of her face.

Chapter Eleven

Dee didn't go home. She went back to the stable. The smells and sounds of horses comforted her like nothing else could. Her thoughts turned to how she finally found a place she felt safe. She enjoyed the riding and the horses. She'd made new friends. She'd made this her home.

But what did any of it matter? The story would soon be on the newscasts all over the state. What if her picture appeared as the woman who found the body? Could they, would they do that without her permission? If that happened her stalker would find her. Plus, she'd lied to the police. She contemplated the verse in the Bible that said, "Your lies will find you out."

She'd lied to all the new friends she made here. She'd lied to Marcus, even if they were lies of omission. Why hadn't she told him the truth? There'd been plenty of opportunity to tell him the real story.

Suddenly, another Bible verse came to mind. *One day God will make whatever has been lost up to you by giving you something greater in its place. Then you will understand why you have been given this trial.*

Certainly, this past year had been a trial. She'd survived, learned some things along the way, and found a new place she could call home. Perhaps God had more in store for her. *Forgive me, Lord Jesus, for my sin of lying. Please help me find a way to rectify this and keep me safe while I do. Amen.*

She buried herself in working with the horses. She turned off the phone so she wouldn't be distracted. Her thoughts turned to the *other thing*: she'd recognized the body under the bush. Miguel. The man she'd replaced when he didn't show up for work one fateful morning. As if lying to the police wasn't bad enough, she had to recognize the identity of the body.

She understood police investigations. She'd observed them in her own case. Cops were as relentless as a dog with a bone. They would come around asking questions. They would figure out she took Miguel's job. Would they conclude she killed Miguel for his job?

If she became a suspect, her picture would get out on the news. They'd discover her true identity and give the press her real name. No matter how much she had changed her looks, her name would bring the stalker back into her life.

The stalker. The police had surmised the stalker might be someone she'd dated or who'd been interested in her. She'd dated but nothing serious. With her rigorous schedule at the track, she never found time.

All of that had changed in the past weeks since meeting Marcus.

Marcus. She had to tell him the truth before he discovered it on his own. Could she wait until she was sure the press wouldn't splash her picture all over the news? Should she tell Marcus now and hope he would help keep her identity safe?

So many questions she didn't have the answers to. If only she could be sure the stalker wouldn't resurface, all of this could be easily rectified. *If only.*

~ * ~

Once Dee left, Marcus explained to Brad he still had an extensive list of calls to go on. After he finished up with the first one, he picked up his cellphone to call Dee, but it rang in his hand. It was an emergency—a ranch horse gored by a bull. As he hurried to the call, he called Margo to reschedule the rest of his day.

Hours later, he stood in the shower at the clinic, washing off blood and intestinal matter. He'd attempted to save the horse but the injury proved too massive. Sometimes the only humane thing was to put the animal down. Like Dee said that evening at the restaurant, it was the hardest thing a vet had to do. Even when it was the only solution, it still hurt. He let the water wash the bad feelings away.

He hopped out and dried off. He changed into spare clothes he kept at the clinic. It was getting late, but if he left now, he'd get home in time to tuck Kaitlyn into bed. He still hadn't called Dee. He punched her number from his contacts list.

"Hello," she answered.

"Hey, how are you feeling?"

"I'm better, thank you. I hope I didn't worry you. I turned the phone off earlier and forgot to turn it back on."

"It's been a day from hell for both of us. I didn't call earlier because I received an emergency call, a bad one. I had to put the horse down."

"Oh, Marcus, I'm sorry." The sincerity in her voice warmed him. "You sure have had a difficult day."

"I've had worse. I'm on my way home to put Kaitlyn to bed. Are you at home now? I could come by later." *Perhaps we could commiserate together?*

"No, I'm doing night check. I'm at the barn."

"It's early for night check, isn't it?"

"Yes, but after today, I thought I'd get it done so I could have some extra sleep. I expect tomorrow will not be any better when Magda gets there."

"Have you heard from her? She may not come in tomorrow after the spill she took." He made the turn into his driveway.

"That's a possibility. But I doubt it. I'll be prepared all the same."

"I'm sure you will be. Are you sure you wouldn't like me to come by your house later? I'd like to talk about what happened today."

There was a long pause. He thought perhaps the call had dropped until she spoke again.

"I think after the day we've both had, sleep is what we need."

Is she pushing me away? There must be more than she is telling me. "If you think that then I'll have to understand."

"Thank you, Marcus. This is a day I'd like to forget."

"I understand. I'll come by the stable in the morning."

"That sounds wonderful. I'll see you in the morning."

"Good night, Dee, I—" he faltered. Realizing what had almost slipped out of his mouth, he choked off the words. *Love you.*

"What was that, Marcus?" she asked.

"Sorry, dry throat. I'll see you in the morning."

"Good night."

Did those words almost slip out of my mouth?

No, Brad had to be wrong. Yet Marcus did sense...what? Certainly, his heart skipped beats at the sight of her. But the emotions went deeper than that. Belonging, maybe? Like a complete set? The evening the three of them had spent together seemed exactly that, a complete set. He believed she needed him as much as he wanted...okay, needed her.

If only he could find out what made her so evasive. But it wouldn't happen tonight because it seemed when he got too close, she shut him out. He sent a simple prayer heavenward. *Lord, help me to be there if she needs me and grant me the patience to know when the time is right.*

~ * ~

Despite only getting three hours sleep, Dee wished she'd asked Marcus to come by last night. She wasn't ready to tell him the truth but his presence might have kept her from jumping at every sound. His presence might have kept Miguel's face from appearing every time she closed her eyes. She even tried finding an old B-movie to take her mind off the day.

But the horrible sounds coming from the giant ants as they attacked the town only put her nerves on edge. Concern she might see herself on the news made that impossible to view. Then a tiny voice in her head reminded her she had an app on her phone that should help her get some sleep.

She opened the Pray.com app and selected a reading from the Bible. The soothing tone of the reader soon had her forgetting her day and drifting peacefully off to sleep.

Even with the lack of sleep, she had the first horse groomed and ready to saddle. She couldn't be sure Magda would ride Chanel first; she might demand a different horse. Magda might not even show up. Her heart skipped a few beats when the gate squealed and Marcus's truck pulled in the farm. Whatever the day brought, all would be better now.

He walked in with two cups of coffee and biscotti, handing one of each to Dee.

"Thank you," she said. "You're always welcome when you bring treats."

"You mean I'm not welcome if I don't bring treats?"

"No, you're not."

"See if I bring you biscotti next time."

The light-hearted banter happened easily between them. Even after yesterday and given the fact she needed to be straight with him, being free to tease came naturally. "There were days at the track when I wouldn't think of eating something this decadent. Now, I'm sure I can work it off. You can bring me coffee and biscotti anytime, Doctor Helton, or you can come visit without them."

"You hoped to be a jockey."

"Only for a brief time. Exercise riders do the real training of the horses while on their backs. My father was a good teacher."

"Was?"

"Is."

"Which track?"

Dee suddenly realized she'd said too much.

Silva breezing into the barn, saved Dee from answering. "Why, it's the good Doctor Helton. I hope this is a social call. Rocket Man is okay, isn't he?"

"He's fine. A bit sore yesterday, but back to his obnoxious self this morning," Dee answered.

"I see coffee cups in both your hands, so I guess it's a social call."

Marcus turned to Dee. "Rocket Man was sore yesterday?"

"Muscle soreness. I massaged the knots out," she said. "Besides, you had enough on your mind yesterday."

"What was going on with you yesterday?" Silva asked.

"He had an emergency call where he had to put a horse down," Dee answered for him.

"Oh, I'm sorry, Marcus."

"It's part of the job. And are you here socially, or do you have a sick horse?" He grinned over the top of his cup.

"Oh, socially. Dee, have you heard from Magda since her fall?" Silva asked.

"Not a peep. I texted and called but she never returns my calls. But I'm ready when she comes in."

"Did you listen to the news this morning?" Silva sought Dee's gaze. "They found another body not far from here. Lily's worried it's the guy who used to work for her."

Marcus and Dee stared at each other. Dee placed both hands around her cup to keep from spilling it.

"One of Lily's employees went missing?" he asked.

"Yes, Pico never come to work two mornings ago. She came over to tell me about the news story. She said they haven't identified the body, but she's scared it could be Pico."

"Why does she think it's her groom they found?" The image of Miguel's bloated face popped into Dee's mind. She slid onto a tack box in the aisle. How could this happen in the one place she felt comfortable?

"It's simply coincidence that two grooms have left mysteriously but it's got her scared."

"Lily and her husband live on the property," Marcus said. "Steffen hangs out here. There are men in the other barns. I don't think this killer is nabbing the victims in such a public place. At least not from what I've seen in the news reports."

"I think you're right. I hope the body they found isn't his," Silva said.

Dee said nothing. The body wasn't Pico, but she couldn't let on as to who it was. This necessitated a call to her uncle in the Hialeah

Police Department. She needed to tell him about her involvement in these murders in Palm Beach County.

"I have to go to work," Marcus said. "Dee, I'll see you later."

Silva waited until he drove out the gate before she pulled Dee aside.

"How's it going with you two?"

"Okay."

"Gee, that's all I get?"

"Well, there isn't any more to tell."

"Did he come by yesterday?"

"No. He had an emergency call." Dee left out the part about helping him yesterday.

"I was hoping you went on another date. You two seem to be all talk, no action."

Dee laughed. "Well, since you asked, and I didn't see you yesterday, I made dinner for him Sunday night at my place."

"Great, Dee. I told Steffan you two would hit it off. I'm happy about that."

"Thanks, Silva. We'll see how it goes. I like him a lot."

"What's not to like? I'll keep a couple horses for you to work when Magda leaves. Unless you have other plans."

"No, no plans. Magda just drove in so I gotta get to work."

"Okay, I'll see you later." Silva zipped out the side entrance.

Dee led Chanel out of her stall and tied her in the aisle.

"Horse isn't ready?" Magda demanded.

"I wasn't sure you wanted to ride in the regular schedule or not. I have her ready for the saddle."

"We do normal schedule today." Magda stood in front of Chanel while Dee put the saddle on. Suddenly Chanel snapped at Magda, getting skin between her teeth. Magda jumped back. "How dare you!" she yelled.

"Whoa, easy, Chanel," Dee said. She moved between Magda and Chanel so Magda couldn't hit her.

"What is wrong with this horse?" she yelled.

"Sometimes, horses get girthy when they have ulcers. I told you she needed to be checked."

"What are you, psychic? Horse has bad behavior and you pamper it. If you get out of the way, I'll show it who's boss."

"You won't hit her. It's not bad behavior. She's telling you she's uncomfortable in the only way you can understand."

"What makes you think so? You are only stable help. You don't train horses. I am the Olympic trainer. You barely care for them. I let you stay here only because I don't have time to look for someone better. You know nothing."

Dee bit her tongue. No reason to make the situation worse. Magda would only take it out on the horses. It wasn't the first time she had belittled her like this. Dee put on the bridle and handed the horse to Magda.

Next, Dee prepared Rocket Man. He tossed his head while she curried him. "Yes, big boy, I understand. You don't want to go out there with Magda."

When Magda returned with Chanel, sweat covered the horse's body, her nostrils flared, and her ribs heaved. Magda tossed the reins to Dee. "No, red horse," Magda said, refusing the reins for Rocket Man.

Dee led both horses away. When Magda was out of earshot, Dee said to Chanel, "Poor girl, this is abuse." To Rocket Man she said, "You get a reprieve today." She put both horses in their stalls, so she could get the next one ready.

After Magda left, Dee took extra care cooling out Chanel. Dee and Magda exchanged no words the rest of the day; they handed horses back and forth.

When she brought back the last horse, Dee seized on the moment to ask her a question she'd been debating, especially now since Rocket Man dumped Magda. "I'd like to buy Rocket Man. Do you own him, or could you tell me who does?"

Magda cackled so loudly Dee thought the entire farm could hear her. "You? Buy one of these horses? Stable help doesn't have money to buy horses. You have old broken-down race horse. You work a lifetime and not afford these horses. Where would you get money for one of these horses?"

"Roscoe is not broken down," Dee spat indignantly at Magda. "He may not be a Grand Prix dressage horse, but he is well bred."

She doubled over in hysterics. "Well bred? Like you are a horse breeders. Ha!" Still sniggering, she stumbled out to her car.

Dee wanted to slap Magda for the insults. Now would be the perfect time to quit. After all, she had other offers. But the welfare of the horses came first, not her pride. Still fuming over the conversation, she stomped over to Silva's stable.

As soon as she put her foot into the stirrup for the first lesson, all the irritation from Magda's comments left Dee's mind. Her riding this afternoon earned her compliments.

"Your timing with the cues were perfect on Musket," Silva said. "You two are in harmony with each other. I'd like to enter him in a show in a few weeks, and I'd like you to show him. Are you interested?"

"I'd love to, but how can I groom for Magda and go to a show?"

"The show I'm thinking about is here, next month. I'll work things out with the show secretary so your classes are the last of the day. By then Magda will be gone. It's hard to work non-showing horses while the show is happening. I doubt she'll hang around."

"You've been thinking hard on this, haven't you?"

"I have. You deserve a chance, and Magda sure won't give you one. I heard some of what she said this morning. I wasn't eavesdropping. It's hard not to hear when she yells like that. The bump on the head didn't help her attitude," Silva said. "I'm wondering why you stay."

"It's hard to explain. I'm concerned for the horses." Dee swung down from the horse's back.

"I understand an attachment to animals, but you could do so much more. Come over and train with me." Silva seized Dee's arm. "There's no future with Magda."

They walked toward the stable. *Time to put my plan into action.* "I asked Magda if she would sell Rocket Man to me. That's what she thought was so hilarious."

"Oh, Dee. Top horses like him are six figures. You couldn't afford him."

"What makes you say that?" Dee stopped in her tracks and glared at Silva.

"No offense, but you drive an old pickup truck and own a washed-up racehorse. You work as a groom. Surely you're aware of how much a horse like Rocket Man costs. How do you think you could afford him?"

Dee stared at her. Insulted like this twice in one day? Magda, she understood. But Silva? Her friend since coming here? Then Dee considered what Silva said. She'd purposely made herself appear simple and unassuming. *Pat yourself on the back for being a better actress than you thought.* Silva only recognized Dee as the person she portrayed herself to be, not who she truly was.

"I'm sorry, Dee, that sounded harsh. You will have exceptional horses in training in the future. You have the ability, and I want the best for you. That's why I am offering for you to show Musket. Leave Magda and come work for me."

Temptation fleeted through Dee's mind. She'd love to train with Silva. Yet something wouldn't let her leave these horses to Magda's bad care.

"I'm flattered, Silva. And there may come a time when I'll leave here and come work with you. But I seem to be called to be here right now. I'll be honest with you. I drive an old truck because someone keyed my car, slashed the tires, and vandalized it beyond use. When I left Hialeah, I took the truck so I could haul a trailer. As for Roscoe, he isn't a washed-up racehorse. He didn't have the heart to run and is better suited for other equine disciplines. In fact, he never ran a race. I taught him tricks and preliminary dressage so I could learn. I appreciate your offer, really I do. The funds to buy Rocket Man or any other horse I want are in the bank."

She left Silva sitting there with her mouth open.

Why is it so difficult telling the truth to people who want to help me? Dee could have easily told Silva the entire story. Dee portrayed herself as a simple groom so she could hide from someone who wanted to do her harm. She believed in the Golden Rule. Who could she have harmed in such a way that they would threaten to kill her? All her relationships had ended amicably. She treated everyone at the track with respect. Now she was tied up in all the lies. *How will I ever untangle this mess and get back to being the real me?*

Rocket Man, Chanel, Dancer, and Roscoe each nuzzled her as she put their feed in the stall. Comfort came in the form of equine slobber. When she finished, she called the Hialeah Police Department and left a message for her uncle to phone her as soon as possible.

When she walked out toward her truck. Silva sat on the bench in front of the barn.

"Dee." She stood grasped Dee's hand. "I'm sorry about what I said. It was wrong. I have always known there was more to you than stall mucker. Please forgive me. I think of you like a little sister and don't want to lose your friendship."

"Apology accepted, Silva. I think the same way about you. I'm sorry I haven't told you more about me, my family, and the reason I left Hialeah. I can't, at least not yet. I promise, as soon as I can, I will."

"Dee, I don't care if you are running from an abusive husband or from some religious cult. I stand by you. You tell me when you're ready. In the meantime, if you want Rocket Man, we'll figure out how to accomplish that. Magda will never sell him to you or me. She knows I'm working with you."

"Thank you, I appreciate your help. But so you know…" Dee chuckled. "I've never been married, so no abusive husband. Just saying."

They hugged. Truth was that Silva's support went a long way in healing her fears.

"That's good, especially since I'm hoping you and Marcus get together. You want to have a soda?"

"I can't. I have family business I need to take care of tonight."

"I'll do your night check tonight, so you don't have to come back. It's the least I can do." Silva held up her hand when Dee argued. "I'm doing it, don't argue. Go home, and I'll see you in the morning."

"Thank you, Silva." She got into her truck and headed home.

Chapter Twelve

"Daddy, Daddy, it's time to get up. Come on," said Kaitlyn as she shook Marcus.

He rolled over to look at the clock. Still ten minutes before the alarm went off. Kaitlyn out of bed early on a school day? The sky must be falling.

"Sweetness," he said with a groan, "we need to have a talk." He sat up and leaned back on the headboard. He patted the bed next to him.

She snuggled in.

"First, when a door is closed, especially a bedroom or bathroom door, knock first and don't enter until someone tells you to come in. Is that understood?" he asked.

"Yes, Daddy," she answered, dutifully.

"That goes for my door or Grandma's. No more running in and jumping on my bed. Now, second, why are you up so early?"

"I finished my science project last night, with your help. Thank you, Daddy. Since I did, I get to have a riding lesson after school today. I can't wait for school to be out, so I can go ride Roscoe and see Dee."

Wow. His talk last night while they worked on her homework took effect quick. If he'd known she'd get her homework done and clean her room without being asked a hundred times, he'd have signed her up for riding lessons sooner.

"How about you go get dressed for school? I'll see you downstairs for breakfast."

"Okay, Daddy." She scrambled off the bed. "Can I wear my new riding pants to school?"

"No, you wear your uniform like you're supposed to."

"Aww, can't I put them on under my uniform skirt?"

"When you get home from school you can change and put them on."

Kaitlyn ran out. When the alarm went off, he rolled across the bed to turn it off. He lay there a few minutes more before getting up to get dressed for the day.

Not that ten minutes made much of a difference in how much sleep he got, but he had been dreaming of Dee. He sighed.

They'd spent over an hour last night on the phone. They had so much in common and not only horses. They both liked old movies. They both hated cold weather and liked the heat, which was great since they lived in Florida. She had been open with him the entire time but he had stayed away from the questions he so wanted answers to. But it didn't seem right to question her over the phone. They'd get to it this weekend. Perhaps he'd bring her home to meet his mother.

Later that morning, he sat in his office updating case histories. His first farm call wasn't until ten.

"Sorry to bother you," Margo said with a knock on his open door. "But Lauren is on line two."

Marcus sat back in his chair and huffed out a breath. "Thanks, Margo."

She pulled his door closed. He took three deep breaths before picking up the phone. "Doctor Helton, how can I help you?" He hoped it would annoy her.

"Marcus, it's Lauren. Didn't Margo tell you? She never was much of a secretary."

"Did you call to berate my staff, or do you want something?"

"I called to ask if you had decided about Kaitlyn and Christmas vacation. I need to make arrangements for her, like a plane ticket."

He sat silent for a long minute mulling it around. All thoughts came to the same conclusion. "If you want to have Kaitlyn for a few days before Christmas at your home, I can live with that. I want her at my house Christmas morning. That's my offer."

"I've made my plans to go to Vail for Christmas vacation. I want to take Kaitlyn with me. You have her for the entire year. Why shouldn't I have her for one week?"

"Well, first of all, because you abandon her whenever one of your jet-setting friends calls. I can only imagine how Colorado will be if she goes with you. She'll be alone in a hotel room while you're out partying. For a curious eight-year-old, that can only lead to trouble. She won't stay where you put her like she did as a baby. Second, I have custody."

"Marcus, I have a right to time with my daughter."

"Actually, no, you don't. You gave all that up in a courtroom a year ago. I don't have a problem with Kaitlyn visiting you. I don't have a problem with her spending some of Christmas vacation with you. I might have considered letting her go with you if my mother went along. But I'm certain Mom won't go as being here with my sisters and their families for Christmas is her priority. That's what I want too. So, you can cancel your ski plans with your friends and stay here to spend Christmas with your daughter or not. It's up to you."

The phone slamming down shocked his eardrum. Lauren would go to Vail with her friends. She'd never cancel her plans. Moving up the society ladder meant more than her daughter.

Confident he'd made the right decision, he finished up the case file and left for farm calls.

~ * ~

When Dee arrived at the stable the next morning, it surprised her to see Silva feeding over in her barn.

Even with Rocket Man banging his door, Dee hoofed it over to Silva's barn. "Why are you here feeding? Did something happen to Julie?"

"No, Julie is fine. I felt so bad about what I said to you yesterday, I called both Julie and Gale last night and told them to take the day off, go to the beach or something. I can do my horse chores for one day. Sometimes we take our help for granted. I don't want to do that again."

"When I finish my feeding, I'll come help you."

"No, I'm good. Steffen's assisting me today. You have enough to do keeping up with Magda."

"Well, yell if you need anything."

"I will." She went back to work.

Dee trotted back to her own barn. She hadn't meant to cause any anguish yesterday. However, she hoped the girls would enjoy a day at the beach.

"Hold on, Rocket Man, I'm coming," she yelled at him.

She fed them all and started mucking the stalls. The sound of her phone ringing in the tack room sent her flying down the aisle to get it. "Hello?"

"Good morning, Ileana. It's Uncle Adolfo. Sorry, I didn't get your message until this morning. Are you all right? Your mama says hi, and she loves you."

Being called by her real name stunned Dee at first.

"Oh, Uncle, I'm so happy to hear your voice. I'll be so glad when this nightmare is over, and I can hear Mama say that to me in person.

Tell her I love her. Yes, I'm fine. I haven't checked in in a while. I'm sorry, I've been busy working."

"Does that mean you've settled in one place? It's been a year now. I think God has answered our prayers and the family can be reunited."

"I'm in Wellington. I'm working for a trainer here. There've been no calling cards from the stalker."

"Thank you, Lord Jesus, for watching over our Ileana," he said.

She pictured him crossing himself. She needed to thank God more.

"Your sister and her family are in for Christmas. We're hoping he's given up or left the area. If all goes well, you can come home soon."

"Yes. I miss everybody."

"The message said you needed me to contact you as soon as possible. If not the stalker, what's happened?"

Dee related the entire story about finding the dead body. She told him how she escaped the scene before the television station could get a picture of her.

"That's good you got out of there," Adolfo said.

"Yes, but I had to give a statement to the deputies." She hesitated before going on. "I was with someone else when we found the body. He knows me as Dee Collins. So, to keep my identity secure, I lied to the deputy. You said not to lie to the cops, but I didn't feel I could take the chance giving them my real name. It would be in police reports, and the press will get a copy. I'm sure the story has been on the news down there about the bodies found murdered in the fields of western Palm Beach County."

"Yes, it has. Do you think this is somehow connected to you?"

"I can't be sure. The problem is I recognized the face of the victim. He used to work where I am now. In fact, I got the job when he failed to show up for work."

"Oh, Ileana. This is not good. It's so close to you. Are you sure your stalker is not up there?"

"I don't think so. I watch around me all the time. There's a security gate here on the farm. And all the victims have been men."

"Someone murdered a man who you replaced on the job. The stalker means to kill you. He's not someone who wanted you romantically, never someone who thought, 'If I can't have you, no one can.' Whatever his reason for going after you, when he painted, "U R Dead" on the wall of your house then smashed the surveillance camera while shouting, "I'll use this on you next," he meant business. That's why we sent you away. Think about it, he could have killed someone around you to send a message. The other kills could be practice runs. I'm sorry, Ileana, to bring all that up. But I'm an old cop who thinks like a cop from years of experience."

"Now you're scaring me. Do you really think that's possible? He'd kill to send a message? But there has been nothing sent like before. No notes or roses. I've felt safe here. Safe enough that I've been seeing a guy. I trust him. You don't think he's at risk, do you?"

"You're at risk. The people around you, I'm not so sure. I'm surprised you're dating."

"I wasn't planning on it. It sort of happened. But the moment I met him I realized I could trust him. I don't know how or why. It's something I recognized in my heart."

"Love has no how or why. The spirit moves in strange ways. Take it from an old married man." Adolfo chuckled. "I think the best thing is for me to get in touch with the Palm Beach Sheriff's Department and see if they will keep you out of the reports. I'll fax them the case files and explain why it's important to keep your identity safe. I'll explain to them you can identify the body. From now on, you cooperate with them. If you need anything else, call immediately."

"I will, I promise. Tell Mama and Poppi I love them. And give a hug to my sister."

"Will do, little one, stay safe. I pray your ordeal is almost over. Read the story of Job again. Your trials are not so bad as his."

"I pray you're right. Thank you, Uncle."

After they hung up Dee couldn't decide if she should feel relieved or more frightened than ever. This situation might put Marcus, Silva, and the whole farm at risk. Dee sent a prayer heavenward to protect her new friends.

She strode out of the tack room where she'd hidden during the call. Behind on her work, she'd have to hurry to get the first horse ready for Magda. She thought about what her uncle said. Yes, some time reading scripture might soothe her soul.

Chanel stood saddled and ready. Magda arrived a half an hour later, all twitchy and distracted. Dirt covered her breeches. She didn't say a word to Dee. Clutching the reins, Magda stalked out of the barn.

"Dark red horse next," came a shout from outside.

At least, Magda ordered up her next horse ahead of time.

The gorgeous bay was ready when she returned. She took the horse and ordered Sprite next. They progressed through all the other horses except Rocket Man, who snorted when Magda came in with the last horse.

"No, not today," she said before getting into her car to leave.

"You get another reprieve today, big boy," Dee told him.

Rocket Man snorted and shook his head at her.

"You think she's afraid of you? You shouldn't have dumped her like that. She was wrong, yes, and she has a mean streak, no doubt."

"Are you and Rocket Man conversing?" Marcus ambled down the aisle.

"I didn't hear the truck come in."

"You were busy talking to the horse."

Dee laughed. "What are you doing here this early? Kaitlyn's lesson isn't until later."

"I'm on my way to pick her up. I wanted to come by to see how your day was. I saw Magda driving off, didn't I?"

"Yes."

"Good." He took Dee in his arms and planted a kiss on her lips.

They stood, locked in an embrace in the open door of Rocket Man's stall. The horse head-butted them, knocking them apart. Then he slid his head in between them.

Marcus rose on his toes to see Dee over the horse's neck, but the horse raised his head higher. So, Marcus knelt to look under, but the horse lowered his head.

"Is he trying to keep you separated from me?" he asked.

Dee giggled. "Looks like it. Get back inside, Rocket Man." She pushed him back and shut the door. "He might not be fond of it, but I'm glad you came by."

"I've never seen a horse do that. He must really adore you. Let's walk to the tack room." Marcus took her hand and drew her into the room. Taking her into his arms, he pressed his lips to hers again.

"Marcus, are you here?" Steffen yelled from the front of the stable.

Marcus broke the contact but held on. "In the tack room."

"Oh, there you are," Steffen said as he walked in. "Oh sorry, hi Dee. I didn't mean to intrude."

Marcus released her. "Well, you did. What are you doing hanging out here?" He sat on a tack box and grasped up his knee.

"I'm playing groom for Silva today. I saw your truck. I guess this isn't a farm call." Steffen glanced from one to the other.

"No, not a farm call. Playing groom? How did Silva talk you into that?"

"She wanted to give the girls a full day off after her tiff with Dee yesterday."

Marcus turned his gaze toward Dee. "What tiff?"

"No tiff. She insulted the intelligence of grooms. She took it back, and we hugged it out, a misunderstanding. She said it made her consider not taking advantage of her stable help, so she gave them the day off."

Steffen leaned out the tack room door and cocked his head. "Hey, gotta go. I hear Silva calling. Are you hanging out for a bit, Marcus?"

"I'm leaving now but I'll be back later with Kaitlyn. Dee's giving her a lesson."

"Good. I thought I'd get a minute to catch up since we haven't spoken in a while. I forgot how hard grooms work. We can talk when you get back." Steffen sprinted back to Silva's barn.

"I'll let you go back to work, so you're done when I get back with Kaitlyn." With a quick kiss Marcus bolted for his truck.

Dee lingered a minute to savor the taste of his lips before going back to her horses. After the phone call with her uncle, Marcus's sweet caresses eased all the bad thoughts out of her mind.

~ * ~

Marcus, Silva, and Steffen sat at the edge of the arena as Kaitlyn's laughter echoed around the arenas at Everglades Equestrian Center. The lesson over, she and Dee performed tricks with Roscoe.

"Dee should get the word out that she gives beginner lessons," Silva said. "They require a lot of patience not many adults have."

"I don't think Kaitlyn enjoyed it much," Steffen said sarcastically then smiled. "It's been a long time since I've heard that much laughter in a dressage ring."

"Yeah, you stuffy dressage queens aren't allowed to laugh." Marcus needled Silva.

"I'm not one of those queens. I respect the craft and abide by the rules handed down for centuries. Kaitlyn is reminding us how much we enjoyed it when we were younger."

Marcus enjoyed the sight of Kaitlyn and Roscoe playing tag.

"You gotta love how much they enjoy playing with that horse," Silva said.

"Yeah, Dee's paid more attention to Kaitlyn in the last hour than Kaitlyn's mother has in a year," Marcus said.

"That's a sad state of affairs," Steffen said.

Silva glanced at Marcus. "I hope you're kidding."

"Sadly, I'm not."

Dee ambled across the arena to where Marcus and the others sat. "Kaitlyn has great balance. I'm glad you let her take a lesson."

"Daddy, did you see?" Kaitlyn strutted to her audience.

Roscoe trailed behind, an invisible lead line connecting them.

His head down at her level, he acted like an obedient puppy.

"Roscoe plays tag, Daddy."

"I see that. I think he likes you," Marcus said.

"I like him too." She turned and hugged the horse's big head.

"Let's take him back to the barn, unsaddle him, and cool him out," Dee said.

"Come on, Roscoe." Kaitlyn reached for Dee's hand.

Rosco shadowed them obediently.

"That has got to be the cutest thing ever," Silva said.

"I can't believe that horse is so smart," Steffen said.

Marcus's eyes never left them. The sight of the two females walking hand in hand with their puppy dog of a horse trailing behind warmed his heart. The trio looked like a Norman Rockwell painting. He still didn't want to admit it but his heart tipped over the edge. He'd fallen in love.

~ * ~

In the stable, Dee and Kaitlyn bathed Roscoe. The conversation never stopped. Dee assisted but let Kaitlyn do as much of the feeding as possible. They broke down a bridle, cleaning and reassembling it. When they finished, they sauntered over to Silva's barn.

"I'm ready to go," she said. "It has been a long day."

"Do you want me to do your night check?" Dee asked.

"Thanks, but my wonderful husband volunteered so I can go home and put my feet up. I'm happy I gave the girls an entire day off, but I'm worn out. Julie will be here in the morning, Dee, to feed your horses and mine so you can sleep in tomorrow. I'm going to do the same, so don't look for me early."

Dee smiled. Trainers rarely groomed and saddled their own horses let alone fed and cleaned stalls. And grooms rarely rode multiple horses in a day like trainers did. Today Silva had performed all of those tasks.

Weariness sagged her body. However, Dee recognized Silva would have a renewed appreciation for what her girls did each day.

Dee and Marcus watched as Silva and Steffen drove way.

"I thought Kaitlyn and I could take you to dinner tonight," Marcus said.

"I'd like that. Do you want me to follow you?" she asked.

"I thought you'd ride with Kaitlyn and me. After dinner I'll bring you back before I take Kaitlyn home for bed."

"It's silly for you to have to run back here. I can drive." Dee reached for the door handle of her truck.

"I want to ride with Dee," Kaitlyn said.

"That works, then *you* can follow us." Dee grinned.

Marcus's raised eyebrow expressed dissatisfaction. "I'm not sure about letting Kaitlyn ride in that old truck."

Everything slid to a halt. Dee blinked. "Why does everyone think there's something wrong with my truck?"

"Well, it's old. It might break down."

"Okay, I get that it looks dinosaur old. It might look that way on the outside, but it's got a rebuilt engine, new tires, new brakes, and the transmission overhauled. It's next to new. I've driven it from South Florida to New York and back this past year. Who cares what the outside looks like?" Each sentence notched up in volume.

Kaitlyn's snickering brought Dee's attention to the young girl.

"I get it. I jumped to the wrong conclusion. I assumed it was an old work truck on its last legs," said Marcus.

"Everyone jumps to the same conclusion. There's a reason for the idiom 'You can't judge a book by its cover.' I needed safe transportation that could pull a horse trailer and travel with Roscoe."

The snickers soon became loud laughter. Kaitlyn doubled over, she laughed so hard.

"What's so funny?" Marcus asked.

"Dinosaur old. That's really old, isn't it?" Kaitlyn grasped Dee's hand then her father's as she chuckled. "I never heard of a truck being *that* old." Her laughter drifted back to snickers.

Dee looked at Marcus as the three of them stood holding hands. She couldn't help but grin.

"Yeah, that's pretty old, Kaitlyn, but I promise the truck isn't that ancient. Since it is old, I'm not worried about it being vand—" She halted.

"Why were you worried about vandalism to it?" he asked.

Dee opened then shut her mouth. The lies had to stop. Again, she'd been presented the perfect opportunity to tell Marcus the truth. Yet these tiny ears didn't need to hear it. The tale would have to wait. "It's nothing. Forget I said anything. My father made sure I could travel without worry. I'll ride with you. You're right." She slammed the door of her truck.

Marcus opened the passenger door of the Mustang. "Kaitlyn, get in the back."

Kaitlyn jumped in and slid to the center. Dee got in the front passenger seat, and Marcus closed the door.

Lord, please help me keep my mouth shut until the time is right. She hoped Marcus wouldn't ask any more questions tonight. She'd like to tell him the whole story of the past year. She wanted to discuss the events that happened in the field. But with Kaitlyn there, those conversations would wait until another time.

~ * ~

Dee had given Marcus the perfect opening to ask all the nagging questions that burned in his mind. But not with Kaitlyn in tow. He stored it away. Tomorrow, or the next day, he could ask Dee about all the different things that didn't add up.

Everyone sat silent for about ten seconds before Kaitlyn began asking questions about Roscoe and horses in general. Leave it to the curious mind of an eight-year-old. Marcus listened while the two girls chatted.

He pulled in to a burger joint in the shopping center on Royal Palm Beach Boulevard, one of Kaitlyn's favorites. Inside, she rattled off all the best selections. When the waitress arrived, Dee's lost look prompted Marcus to order for all of them. Kaitlyn talked non-stop about her science project until the food arrived.

Finally, the adults could get a word in.

"Silva told me Magda didn't ride Rocket Man. Is he okay? He's not sore or sprained somewhere, is he?" Marcus asked Dee.

"No ill effects from the other day. Silva and I think Magda is afraid of him now. I offered to buy him, but she shot me down."

"Did she give you a price?"

"No, only insults about how I could never afford a horse like him."

"Please don't take this the wrong way. I'm aware Silva said something about you being able to afford him that didn't come out the way she intended." He paused, thinking back to the conversation about her truck. "Do you have the money to buy him?"

"Yes, I do, Marcus."

The way she sat up straight and looked him the eye, he didn't question it. "I wonder if she'd sell him to me."

"Well, she knows you wouldn't be the rider. She'd assume you would put him in training, probably with Silva. I can't see her letting that happen. Silva told me she's working with someone Magda isn't familiar with to make an offer. So, we'll see."

"Does Magda own him?" he asked.

"Silva thinks so. She saw an article in *The Chronical* about Magda coming to the States to buy a horse for international competitions. There's a picture of her and Rocket Man. The others?" She shrugged. "I don't know who the owners are."

"Magda hasn't paid the bill on Chanel's colic yet." He thought it was information Dee should be made aware of.

"She probably won't. She didn't think I should have called you out. Since I did, give me the bill for it."

"Why should you pay for it?" He raised both brows. "The horse would have died a painful death if you hadn't."

"Because Magda isn't paying her bills. When I called in the feed order for the week, the manager told me they couldn't deliver without payment up front. I discovered she owes at least two different feed stores. I paid for last week's feed because they wouldn't deliver unless they got cash. I won't let them starve." She shoved a french fry around on her plate.

"She's paying you, isn't she?"

"It's one of the few conversations we've had. She asked if I could wait a few weeks until one of the owners paid her for training."

"Dee, you have been there for how long?" He reached for her hand. "How can you do that?"

"I didn't need the job for money. I took the job because I'd seen how she treated the horses. I'll make sure they're cared for. I'm keeping receipts."

"While that is very altruistic, you shouldn't have to do that. I won't let you pay the vet bill either. It's not like I can't be philanthropic as well. I wonder who paid the farm for the horse stalls," he speculated.

"I haven't a clue, but they haven't thrown her out yet."

"What's al…. altrui…. altruistic mean?" Kaitlyn stumbled out the pronunciation.

Marcus looked over at his daughter, then smiled at Dee. "It means the unselfish concern for others. A trait all humans should work toward, including you."

"Oh, I get it. Dee bought the horse feed so they wouldn't starve. It's like putting cat food out behind the clinic for the feral cats, right?"

"Yes, very good."

"I like being altruistic."

As he and Dee smiled and clasped hands, he noticed Kaitlyn's eyes droop and her head nod. Time to get her home before she fell asleep in her food.

He paid the bill and picked her up. She laid her head on his shoulder and went back to sleep.

"You wore her out," he whispered.

"I see that." Dee got the car door so he could lay Kaitlyn on the back seat. He drove back to the farm. Leaving the car running and the door open, he hugged Dee when she got out. Kisses became sweeter each time he held her close.

~ * ~

The fact the lights were on in the stable concerned Dee. She snuck in and found Magda in the tack room. The woman looked up in shock.

"What are you doing here?" Magda asked.

"I came back for night check. I'm shocked to find you here so late."

"My horses. I'll come to the stable any time I vant." Her accent took on a heavy tone.

"You're right. It's unexpected is all." Going over to the feed room, she prepared to give the horses hay for the night.

"What're you doing?" Magda asked.

"Giving them hay for the night, same as I do every night."

"No wonder there is never hay. You overfeed them. Cut them all in half. No hay tonight."

"Okay, if that's what you want."

Dee didn't want to argue with her. She would come back later and give them hay once Magda left. Dee walked over to Silva's barn and found Steffen doing the night check. "Need any help?"

"I'm filling the last bucket. Are you back from your dinner already?"

"Kaitlyn fell asleep at the table. I thought I'd do my night check and get home early. But Magda is over there. She told me I overfeed the horses. As soon as she leaves, I'll go back and give them their hay and fill the water buckets."

"There's something wrong with her. She's very strange. I'm glad you're here because I don't like being around her."

"There *is* something different about her. I think I'll drive around the block and see how long it takes before she leaves."

"I'm done, so I'm leaving with you."

Dee drove down a side street and turned her lights off as she turned around. She could see the farm drive but not into the barn. An hour later Magda left the farm. Dee drove back in.

Rocket Man didn't bang the door. His rear hoof slammed the back wall of the stall. Once all the other horses were munching hay, she let herself into his stall. He left his hay to rest his head on her shoulder.

She ran her hands down each side of his glossy black neck. Did Rocket Man have a dislike for Magda? Did he sense something about her? In Dee's experience the horses sensed more about their surroundings than humans understood.

Dee could tell Magda had been around horses, maybe grew up with them, but she didn't act like a knowledgeable equestrian competitor. The language of horses and riding continued through the millennia regardless of country or culture. Xenophon, the Spanish Riding School, the Federation of Equestrian International all taught the same principles.

Dee determined to discover all she could about Magda. Researching for articles written about her might be a good start.

Chapter Thirteen

For a second night, Dee hadn't slept well. This time she fretted not about dead bodies but about Magda rummaging in the tack room. Having checked the room after Magda left, she found nothing amiss. Magda didn't have a tack box, only a few cardboard boxes stacked in the corner. The saddles hung on racks; the leg wraps and horse blankets were on shelves. Dee's own boxes had padlocks on them which were still locked.

When she arrived at the stable in the morning, she picked up her muck bucket and went to work. Chanel stood ready for Magda whatever time she decided to show up. But she failed to arrive. By noon, Dee figured Magda wouldn't be there at all.

At one o'clock the gate out front squealed, announcing someone driving onto the farm. Dee glanced out of the tack room and recognized the man getting out of the car parked in front as detective Brad Tyler. Her throat went dry.

"Hello." Her voice squeaked as he strode in.

"Good afternoon. Dee, right? What're you doing here?" Brad asked.

"I work here."

"Oh, I thought this was Magda Jovanovich's barn." He glanced up and down the aisle.

"It is. I work for her."

"Is she here?"

"No. She should be, but she didn't come in today."

"Do you have her phone number?"

"I have one, but she never answers when I call. Maybe you'll have better luck." Dee gave him the phone number.

""Let me ask you, were you acquainted with Miguel Torres who worked for Magda a while back?" He reached inside a back pocket and removed a notepad.

"Y-yes." *Do I sound nervous? I hope not.*

"What can you tell me about him?"

"Not much. He took care of her horses. His English wasn't the best, so I helped him with translation."

"Where is he from?" He scribbled something on the pad.

"Ecuador is what he said."

"Ecuador? You must speak Spanish."

"I grew up in Hialeah. English is a second language when you live there." She waved a hand as if swatting the comment away. *He probably knows that.*

"So I've heard. I learned a few key phrases a cop might need. Otherwise, I hope I can get my point across. I'm surprised you speak Spanish since your name is Collins. That doesn't sound Hispanic."

Her heart rate escalated. "Collins is Anglo, that's true. Most of my friends growing up were of Hispanic heritage."

"That makes sense," he said in an offhanded way. He pulled a stack of business cards out of his pocket and gave her two. "Would you give one to Miss Jovanovich when she comes in? Tell her to call me."

"I'll do that."

"By any chance, did you recognize the body you found the other day?"

Dee swallowed, hard. Tickling sweat ran down her back and sprung from her brows. Taking the advice of her uncle, she said, "Detective, I can't lie. Yes, I recognized Miguel. I thought I must be wrong. Seeing something unexpected like that is disconcerting enough, let alone thinking you recognize the person."

"You weren't wrong. When was his last day here working?"

"The actual day? I don't recall. The days run together."

"Did he tell you why he might have left?"

"No. He was here one day and didn't come in the next." *How shallow could her breathing get?*

"Okay, if you think of anything else, call me."

"Yes, sir, I'll do that." Thinking him ready to leave, she relaxed and sat on the nearest tack box.

"Marcus told me you two were friends. He and I have been friends since Little League."

"He mentioned that."

"We both had scholarships for baseball. He went to vet school, and I came home to become a sheriff's deputy. We stayed friends, close friends, all these years. Since he's met you, he's the happiest I've seen him. I think he likes you a lot."

She took her first deep breath. "I care deeply about Marcus. I hope he feels the same. We haven't talked much about it."

"You know, I like you."

His friendly attitude put her at ease for the first time since he'd arrived. "Thank you, I think?"

"I'm glad we talked. Make sure you call me if you remember anything else that will help the investigation."

She raised her eyebrows at his comment. She found the conversation confusing. All cops held back information. *What isn't Brad sharing?*

As he backed out, Magda drove in. Dee ran out in an attempt to flag him down, but he drove past Magda and out the gate.

"Who was that? Your boyfriend?" she asked as she walked in. "I don't vant people around this barn. Tell him not to come around."

"No, he's not my boyfriend. His name is Detective Brad Tyler from the Palm Beach Sheriff's Department. He left this card for you. He wants you to call him."

"About vat?"

"They identified the body that was found not far from here. It was Miguel. I guess the detective wants to ask you about Miguel's employment here."

The blood drained from Magda's face. "Oh, poor Miguel. I vondered vat happened to him. Why he vant to talk to me about it?"

"He's looking for information to aid their investigation. He asked me questions about Miguel also. I wasn't that well acquainted with him. Do you want me to get a horse ready for you? I put Chanel back when you didn't come in earlier."

"No, not today. I think I go home and call detective." Magda ran to her car and sped off.

How interesting. She must be spooked by cops. Considering the work day to be over, Dee strolled out to the arena where several chairs awaited spectators. Silva rode Loxley in the arena.

Silva trotted Loxley over. "Hey, what's going on in your barn? Isn't Magda riding today?"

"I guess not. A detective from the sheriff's department came by looking for her earlier. I guess she's going home to call him."

"I wonder what he wants with her."

Dee's heart thumped against her chest. Should she tell Silva the cops had identified Miguel as the latest murder victim? Lily Stoneman was riding her horse in the second arena of the three that covered Everglades Equestrian Stables. She'd be glad to hear it wasn't Pico they'd found murdered.

"Well, if you're finished for the afternoon, do you want to ride my horses? I'm still exhausted from yesterday." Silva's face looked puffy and bags had collected under her eyes.

"Sure, I'll get my boots and helmet."

Dee rode three of Silva's horses that afternoon. Even Lily stopped in her arena to watch as Dee did tempi changes.

"Good riding, Dee," Lily yelled and gave her a thumbs up.

Later, Dee joined Silva on the bench in front of the barn. Here, in private, she informed Silva of Miguel's murder.

"Oh, no, he was a nice young man. Lily will be happy it's not Pico. I guess that's what the detective wanted to talk to Magda about. It's scary that two young men left the farm mysteriously and one of them has turned up dead. It's so close to home?" She swung down from her horse.

"I was thinking the same thing. I wish Miguel hadn't left. I wasn't looking for a job, but Magda needed someone to care for the horses. You'd think she'd find someone else since she considers my work no good."

"She probably thinks you'll quit." Silva slid the stirrups up the leathers and loosened the girth. "Then she'll tell everyone how horrible you are for leaving her and cry crocodile tears. That's what she said when Miguel left. I figured he had enough."

"I think he liked the job even with her mistreatment of him. He cared about the horses like I do."

They began the walk to the stable. "By the way, did you ever figure out why Magda was here last night? Steffen told me about it. He said he doesn't like being around her at all."

"She was in the tack room when I got here. I looked in there after she left but nothing appeared disturbed. That's the second time I've discovered her in there rooting through her boxes. I mean, it's her stuff but the timing is strange. She also told me I over feed the horses and not to give them hay at night. I came back later and hayed them anyway."

"Of course you did." She lightheartedly punched Dee's arm.

"Have you devised a plan for Rocket Man?"

"Yes, but she hasn't ridden him in the last few days. I plan to have a friend come by and see Magda riding Rocket Man. Then she can try to buy him. Magda won't be aware we're behind it."

Dee halted and placed her hand on Silva's forearm. "You told me you read an article in *The Chronicle* about her purchase of Rocket Man. Did it include any pictures?"

"Yes. I'll see if I can find it tonight. Why?"

"I'm wondering how much he has changed." They continued along the path.

"You like that horse a lot, don't you?"

"Yes, I do, and he deserves to have a better life than what Magda is giving him."

~ * ~

After a long day of farm calls, Marcus opened the computer in his office. He'd discharged his in-house patient, Yellow, earlier after he'd removed her stitches. Kaitlyn would be disappointed she didn't get to say goodbye.

One of his farm calls that day involved a thoroughbred recuperating from a racing injury. He dialed the number for the horse's regular vet, Dr. Sam Engle, a friend from his internship days.

"How have you been?" he said once Dr. Engle answered.

"Marcus! Great to hear from you. How are you?"

"Busy, and the season's gearing up. I visited a horse you treated previously at the racetrack. The caretaker told me you did a procedure on it two weeks ago. It's here on lay-up. One of Wayne Hughes's horses, a chestnut."

"Yes, I know which horse you're talking about. How's he healing?"

They discussed the case in detail. Marcus took notes while his friend talked. Tomorrow when he visited the horse again, he would do some additional treatment. "Thanks for filling me in, Sam. Hey, do you remember a woman who worked the tracks down there by the name of Dee Collins?"

"Dee? Sure, she moved to England a few years ago with her husband trainer. I heard she's back in town for the holidays. How'd you run into her?"

"I met her in one of the dressage barns here in Palm Beach. She told me she used to groom down there. Said her family frequented the Hialeah, Gulfstream, and Calder race tracks."

"Dee's father is Eddie Garcia, one of the top trainers down here. He trained at Hialeah until they closed it for thoroughbreds. He's here at Gulfstream now. You said she's up there? I can't imagine her training warmbloods."

"Yes, for several months now."

"Can't be the same Dee Collins. In fact, I see her right now. She's in front of her father's barn chasing her toddler and looks like she has a bun in the oven. It must be someone else by the name of Dee Collins."

Marcus sat back in his chair and rubbed the back of his neck. There could be two women with the same name. However, a lot of what Dee told him matched up. Sam was familiar with nearly everybody who worked the tracks in Miami. Was it possible there were two women by the same name, and Sam hadn't run into her?

"Could you describe what Dee Collins looks like?" Marcus asked.

"Short black hair, brown eyes, petite. She married Ian Collins, the steeplechase trainer in England. They usually come back to the states for Christmas vacations."

"Hmm, I'll ask the Dee Collins up here. She speaks Spanish and says she grew up in Hialeah. She didn't say her father was a big-name trainer, only that he worked at the track. Guess I'll do more digging."

"Both Delfina and her sister, Ileana, have worked around here. We all call Delfina "Dee" for short. She and her sister were exercise riders and assisted their father. Dee got married and moved to England but she always come home to visit in December. Ileana left a year ago, but I haven't heard anything about her. People leave here to work elsewhere all the time. If the woman up there is aware Dee Collins is out of the country eleven months out of the year, she might be using her name. Especially the shortened version if she didn't know the real one."

"Yeah, I'll remember that. If I need any more information, I'll call you."

Marcus sat there staring at the wall. Dee, or the woman calling herself Dee, avoided talking about her past. She scanned the crowds when out in public. She didn't want to be around the cops. Could she be pretending to be someone else? If she were acquainted with the real Dee Collins, she could be using her name. Could she be an illegal alien using someone's identity?

Marcus mulled all the details he'd learned about her.

He couldn't believe his Dee would lie to him. It seemed out of character for the woman he'd come to care about.

And if she was someone else? Kaitlyn loved Dee, or whatever her name was. She loved Roscoe. She loved taking riding lessons with Dee. He needed to discern if Dee had truly lied *before* Kaitlyn spent any more time with her.

Then a thought occurred to him; something Brad had said leaped into Marcus's mind. The woman behind the murders in Palm Beach County was someone of his acquaintance. Was that possible? Dee trembled so badly and wanted to be away from cops the other day. Could she be the killer and he the next victim? If so, she should be on stage as an actress and not grooming horses. He couldn't believe his mind went there.

No, Dee couldn't be a murderer. Even if she lied to him about other things, he couldn't be that off the mark. *Please, Lord, please let me be wrong. Please let there be another explanation.* He picked up the phone and called Brad.

When Brad answered, Marcus said, "I need some advice."

"Of the cop type or the personal type?"

"Cop type, I guess."

"Shoot."

"I think someone I've been around might not be who she says she is. How can I find out for sure?"

"Easy, ask her."

"Why didn't I think of that?" He rolled his eyes.

"You're not talking about Dee are you? You haven't known her long."

"Of course." Marcus could envision the gears rolling in Brad's mind.

"What brought you to that conclusion?"

Marcus told Brad about the conversation with Dr. Engle. "He is familiar with the track people. He was looking at the real Dee Collins at the same time the Dee Collins here was at the stable in Loxahatchee. Something else—he said someone from the track might use Dee Collins's name to get employment elsewhere. My thought was an illegal immigrant looking for legitimate employment."

"Man, I like her. I thought she'd be good for you. I even told her that."

"What? When did you do that?" Marcus stood and paced around his desk.

"Today. I went by Everglades Equestrian looking for Magda Jovanovich. We got the ID on the body. The guy worked for Magda. I went to talk to Jovanovich and found Dee. We talked for a while."

"Not about me, I hope." Marcus sat on the corner of the desk.

"Mostly about the case. We may have strayed a bit here and there. But looking back on it, she seemed nervous while we discussed Miguel. She trembled, I noticed, and her breathing seemed shallow, very evasive about herself."

"She's always evasive. Perhaps that's why. What else might she be hiding?" Now his foot began tapping the floor.

"Did she tell you she recognized the body in the woods?"

"No." He jumped back on both feet.

"She admitted it to me. Her reason for not saying anything seemed plausible. She said she didn't want to believe it was him."

"Something you said the morning you informed me the drugs in the murdered bodies came from my truck keeps coming back to me. You said I might have had contact with whoever committed the murders. Please tell me it's not Dee." Marcus slumped back onto the desk.

"Wow, that's a big jump."

"But the totality of circumstances, it can't be a coincidence."

"My gut doesn't go there. Her eyes don't have the look of a killer. Why would you think that?"

"I have personal feelings invested in this. It wouldn't be the first time I was wrong about a woman."

"Dee isn't Lauren. That, I'm sure of. Listen, we have DNA and fingerprints for this case. I can easily prove whether Dee is involved and possibly tell you who she really is. Do you have anything she may have touched?"

Marcus thought back to when she'd been in the clinic. "She wrapped a horse for me. She would have touched the bandage box and the stall door. My prints should be the only other ones on the bandage box."

"I can lift them for comparison."

"Do it," he said.

"I'll come by and put a rush on them. If you could get a sample of DNA, that would be helpful too. Hair, toothbrush, even clothing will do."

He stood and paced. "I haven't slept with her. Now you're fishing. I don't appreciate that."

"I wasn't, really. I'm thinking about items that would have DNA on them. Even a glass or tissue might carry it."

"She drives an old pickup truck. Couldn't you run the tag? That might reveal her real name." This conversation would be easier in person so he could punch Brad for his assumptions.

"I'll drive by her home. I have the address from the police report. Of course, the address could be false like her name. Have you been there? Do you have the address?"

Marcus told him the complex Dee lived in and it matched the address on the police report. Brad said he would run by. If the truck wasn't there, he'd try the stable.

Marcus took a deep breath after hanging up the phone. Normally he would call Dee to see how her day went, but not this time.

~ * ~

Dee hadn't heard from Marcus all day, not even a text. Could Brad have said something to him? Did he think she lied about knowing the identity of the body because it involved her? Had he said that to

Marcus? If not, then why hadn't he been in touch?

She sent a text to Marcus asking about his day. A friendly unassuming text. She picked up her worn, dog-eared Bible from her nightstand. She spent the time before night check reading Job. God had taken everything except Job's life, yet he never turned his back on God. Job realized God bore his destiny, and God knew what he was doing.

She'd left her family voluntarily, thinking time away would discourage the stalker. But now she'd been caught lying. Nothing good ever came from that. Forgiveness. God would do that. Belief. God had a plan so she must keep believing. Trust. Trust in God to continue to protect her and trust in His plan.

Her knees hit the floor and she prayed for continued safety and the strength to right her wrongs. If Marcus decided not to have any more to do with her once she told the truth, well, then he was not part of God's plan for her life.

Later, when she arrived at the stable, only the horses greeted her. At least Magda wasn't there. The horses munched their hay so Dee turned the lights out and left.

Her shoulders slumped as she drove home. Should she be disappointed Marcus hadn't come by? He might be doing an emergency operation. He could be at some event with his daughter. Still, not hearing his comforting voice ripped her heart. Then the words *trust, believe, and forgive* came to mind. Trust in the Lord, believe in His plan, and He will forgive all trespasses.

Chapter Fourteen

Magda didn't show up at the farm the next morning either. No call or text, not that Dee expected one. The horses were ready. Yet Dee couldn't turn them out because as soon as she did, Magda would arrive and scream her horses weren't ready.

Dee sent a text to Marcus, hoping she would catch him before he got busy. Once again, no reply. Why the sudden cold shoulder? Had she imagined his interest? Had he discovered she'd lied to him?

She stood cleaning saddles in the tack room when the sound of footsteps sent a shiver down her spine. She hadn't heard the gate open, and the footfalls were too heavy so it couldn't be Silva or one of her girls.

"Dee, are you here?" The voice sounded like Detective Tyler.

"I'm in the tack room," she said.

Walking to the doorway, she nearly collided with him.

"Sorry," both said at the same time.

Dee backed up allowing Brad to enter. "Have a seat." She directed him toward a chair against the wall. She sat on one of the tack boxes.

He laid a thick folder on his lap.

Her gaze locked onto it before she glanced up at Brad. "I'm guessing that's a stack of police reports from Hialeah Police Department."

"You're very perceptive. I'm surprised you never figured out who the stalker was."

"The person I suspected was in prison. That large folder tells me you've talked to my uncle."

"Good observation. Ever considered law enforcement as a

vocation?"

"Horses have always been my life. The cop side is my mother's."

"Have you spoken to Marcus?"

"No, not even a text. We send texts when the other is busy. When we don't get together, he always calls to say good night. There was no call last night. What did you say to him after you left?"

"Nothing." He stood up and shut the tack room door.

She immediately thought of the interrogation scenes from the old movies. She wished for a bottle of water to quench her parched throat.

Brad pulled the chair closer and sat back down. "Marcus had a conversation with a veterinarian at Gulfstream Race Track. The vet said he was looking at Dee Collins while he spoke to Marcus. That doesn't mean there couldn't be two Dee Collinses, but it planted a doubt."

"My sister is home for the holidays. I didn't expect Marcus to have contact with the vets at the tracks. I guess I should've considered that possibility." She laid a finger on her chin.

"Hindsight. I did speak with your uncle this morning. He said he'd warned you about trying to disguise yourself as your sister. You didn't think you were far enough removed from the track down south that you needed an alias?"

She shook her head. "Horse people travel between the worlds of racing and show horses. I took an extra precaution."

"Can I give you some advice?" He met and held her gaze. "Tell Marcus the truth. He deserves that much. He can keep the secret; I know that for a fact."

"I shouldn't have gotten involved with him. My heart should have listened to my brain. If the stalker finds me—well... Marcus doesn't deserve to fall in love with someone who might leave him." Looking down, she slid a foot across floor.

"Dee—or should I say Ileana—you're too late. Marcus is in love with you." He had her full attention now.

"What? How can you tell? He hasn't said those words to me."

"Look, I understand my friend sometimes better than he understands himself. He'll also take his time telling you because he hasn't realized it yet. His brain is outthinking his heart. But the heart will win. I'm sure you're in love with him. You haven't admitted it either."

She didn't offer an objection. How could a stranger perceive the emotions between her and Marcus? Yes, her heart skipped beats when she heard his voice. Yes, his kisses left her breathless. Yes, she felt like half of a set that needed the other half to be complete. Okay, yes, she fully, head over heels, loved Marcus and Kaitlyn. The realization washed over Dee like a warm soothing balm.

His learning she'd lied about her name might be why he hadn't returned her texts. Now, because of her inability to trust, she'd probably lost him. "What I feel makes no difference now." She stood and turned her back.

"Why? Because he discovered the ruse? If you tell him why, he'll forgive you. He'll understand."

"I'm possibly putting him and his daughter in danger. I shouldn't have gotten involved with Marcus. Now that I've found that body, I'm worried the press will hound me. Once my face is in the news, the stalker will find me. That means moving on to protect them."

"Dee, the sheriff's department will keep you out of the press. I promise you we'll do everything we can to keep the stalker from getting to you."

"My uncle and his whole department couldn't do that. Why do you think you can?"

"You need to tell Marcus about the stalker and who you really are. He can decide what he wants to do after that. You think you're protecting him. But how can he protect himself if he doesn't recognize there's a threat?"

She'd never thought of it that way. Let Marcus decide for himself. But how to tell him? He hadn't returned her calls or text. It seemed he'd already turned away. But if what Brad said was true, and Marcus did care deeply for her, shouldn't he at least come speak with her about it? The crushing weight of her inability to be honest planted a pain behind her eyes. *God, give me the wisdom to do the right thing.*

She turned and faced him. "You're right, Brad. I don't want to run again. I like it here. I've made good friends. I care deeply about Marcus, and I love Kaitlyn. I'm happy for the first time since this nightmare started. Please let me stay as Dee Collins for a while longer."

"You can keep your identity as Dee Collins where everyone else is concerned, but you have to tell Marcus the truth. I don't like lying to my best friend. He'll help keep you safe. I'll give you my cellphone number. If you need anything or suspect anything, call me. Also, since the person you replaced has been murdered, perhaps you should consider quitting this position. Marcus told me he offered you a job. Best to take him up on that offer. Working with him may be the thing to discourage the stalker."

She waggled her finger at him. "You're trying to push us together, aren't you? Just like my friend Silva. I stay here because of these horses. I put up with Magda because the horses need me."

"I'm telling you, watch out for her. She may be a more immediate threat to you than your stalker."

"I can handle what I can see. It's what I can't see that frightens me." *Why does he think Magda is more of a threat than the person who wants me dead?*

"Out of curiosity," Brad asked, "how much do you and your sister look alike? How did you and your family think you could pull this off."

"Right now, I look a lot different, thanks to hair dye and colored contacts." Dee pulled the ballcap off and tugged her ponytail. "Without that, we look alike. We're twins. She and her husband live in England. They come visit during the Christmas holidays. When he sees her, and I don't come around for the holidays, then we're ready to believe he's given up. At least that's the plan."

"You don't think he'll realize it's your sister and not you?" he asked.

"If he sees her and not me he'll think I'll be returning soon. She stays at my parents' home. He'll break into my old house looking for me. My uncle plans to trap him there. He's had this planned for a while."

"I hope he's right." Brad shook his head. "You plan to stay here after it's over and not go back to Hialeah?"

"I didn't plan on meeting Marcus and Kaitlyn when I moved here. They are the reason I want to stay. I'm praying it's over."

Brad tapped his pen on the closed file. He gazed off at something over her shoulder. Finally he looked back at her. "Okay, call if anything strange or unusual occurs. And make sure you tell Marcus the entire story."

Chapter Fifteen

His day couldn't get any worse. Marcus hadn't slept well the night before. His brain mulled over the possibility that Dee could be the murderer. He couldn't be that wrong, could he? But then who was she? Could she be using the Collins name and backstory?

He remembered her carefully observing a parking lot or going a different way home. He'd always meant to ask why. Well, he needed to forget her, except he wasn't sure he'd be able to get her out of his heart.

Throughout the day, when he didn't have a horse or human to deal with, his thoughts returned to her. Brad had called it. Marcus did have it bad for Dee, or whoever she was. By the end of his workday, he thought, surely he'd hear from Brad. Good or bad, Marcus had to hear what Brad had discovered.

He should confront her in person. He wanted answers. But talking to her at the stables seemed wrong. Everyone there was aware of everyone else's business. Many of them were his clients. He could go to her house but would he be able to pass through the guard gate?

Finally, Brad called him.

"Thank goodness," Marcus said. "I'm going crazy. Did you find out anything?"

"Yes, a lot. Dee's fingerprints don't belong to the killer. They aren't the ones found on your truck."

He took a deep breath of relief. "It's nice a killer hasn't duped me."

"People get duped by psychopaths all the time. I don't care how high your IQ is."

"So, who is she and why the ruse?"

"Delfina Collins owns the house where Dee lives according to County records. I guess Dee is short for Delfina."

"So how is she not the Dee Collins my friend down at Gulfstream Park knows?"

"You need to go ask her."

"Why can't you explain it to me?"

"Because it's not my story to tell. Go ask her, buddy. You owe her that much. Trust your own instincts. Believe in your feelings."

~ * ~

Dee still hadn't heard from Marcus. If he didn't care enough to inquire how Dee Collins could be in two places at once, then maybe he didn't care as much as Brad said. She would maintain her cover. If she could get through New Year's without an incident, she could continue her life. Sadly, that life would be less fulfilling if he didn't share it with her.

She'd have to think about it later. Magda had shown up today. She didn't ride Rocket Man. She said another trainer would.

She rode the other horses and left before Lily's working student, Jimmy, arrived. He would ride Rocket Man. Dee had kept her mouth shut while Magda was around, but she wondered if this was part of Silva's plan to help Dee buy Rocket Man.

"Why didn't Magda have you ride him?" Jimmy asked. "I've noticed you on Silva's horses. You're pretty good."

"Thanks, Jimmy. That's a nice compliment. Magda doesn't think I can ride. She's never seen me on any horse but Roscoe and I'm not sure she ever took notice."

"Roscoe's a cool horse. You gave Doctor Helton's little girl a lesson on him. A horse who can play tag is a keeper in my book."

"Thanks. He's special all right."

"What can you tell me about Rocket Man? I was in the other arena when he dumped Magda. She spurred and jerked the reins back at the same time. Looked like the horse simply had enough."

"He's a good horse. If you ask properly, he'll give it. You wouldn't have any problems riding him."

As they walked out to the arena, the horse nuzzled Dee.

She gave Jimmy a leg up. Silva and Lily came out to watch.

"Magda's afraid of that horse," Lily said. "That's why she's got Jimmy riding him."

"She should have asked Dee to ride him instead of going to another trainer's working student," Silva said.

"You'd do well with him," Lily said to Dee.

"We've become attached," Dee said.

"I heard she's having money troubles." Lili's gossip wasn't new to everyone around the farm.

"I asked her to sell him to me but she laughed in my face," Dee said.

"I've got an owner who could make Magda an offer. She'd be none the wiser. It's worth a try."

"That's a great idea, Lily," Silva said. "Lily can keep him in her barn, Dee. Then you can ride him after Magda leaves."

"I'll talk to the customer," said Lily. "Once she knows the circumstances, I think she'll agree. She liked the tricks you were performing with Roscoe, Dee."

"Remember that there are other trainers who would hire you in a heartbeat," Silva said.

"And that's very flattering. But something tells me to stay with these horses." Dee kicked at a stone embedded in the dirt.

After his ride, Jimmy returned with Rocket Man. Dee led the horse back to her stable to cool out. At feeding time, she took her time with each horse, giving it extra pats and rubs. These horses and her friends at this farm had become the family she missed in Miami.

Silva waited for her outside the barn on the bench. Dee sat down with her.

"What's up with you and Marcus? I haven't seen him around. Did something happen?" Silva asked.

"I don't know. He stopped calling and texting. Perhaps he met someone else."

"Marcus isn't that kind of guy. He went through hell with his ex-wife. He got custody of his daughter because of the things she did."

When she stopped talking, Dee glanced up.

Silva had a faraway look on her face. "It wasn't long ago he told Steffen he wanted nothing to do with any female other than his daughter, his mother, and his sisters. Since he's met you, I've seen a tremendous change. I'd say he's in love with you. Maybe that scares him. Some guys back off because that word paralyzes them. It took me a while to convince Steffen."

"How long?" Dee asked.

"Several months. He finally figured it out."

"I do hope things work between us. But who knows what will happen after the season ends?"

"You have many possibilities here or you may want to go north with a trainer."

"I want to stay here year-round. It's close to my family."

"You don't think you might go back to the race track once

dressage season ends?"

"Race track training is a good old boys club. Old-fashioned, staid, and not easily changed. Women have it tough in that environment. My father said when he retired I could have his stable. But I want the challenge of training dressage."

"All the more reason not to give up on Marcus. Give it some time. Let him miss you. He'll come around, just like Steffen did with me."

If what Silva and Brad said was true, and Marcus did care for her, then she would wait. But with her situation, she didn't blame him for walking away. One thing she did count on—God had a plan He would eventually reveal.

Chapter Sixteen

Magda ranted at Dee again on Sunday for overfeeding. She accused Dee of stealing feed for her "useless old horse." She bought her own feed for Roscoe. Her feet were ready to leave right then but Rocket Man snorted softly in her ear as he rested his head on her shoulder.

Soon after the argument about the feed, Lily came into the barn to talk to Magda. Dee hadn't thought Lily heard the argument, but it was fortuitous she showed up when she had. Dee stayed in the back of the barn while the two trainers talked. She witnessed the handshake between them. Magda's attitude improved drastically after Lily left.

When she came by on Monday morning, Lily told Dee Rocket Man would be vet-checked later that morning. If he passed, which Dee was sure he would, he'd be moved down to Lily's barn. Magda wouldn't be aware that Dee had purchased the horse until after the money and registration papers had been exchanged, and by then Magda couldn't back out of the deal.

Dee went to the feed store and picked up hay and grain for two days, using her own money. At least the horses wouldn't starve. When she arrived back, Magda was down at Lily's barn. Rocket Man's stall stood empty.

Roscoe missed his buddy. Dee took a carrot to his stall to calm him. "It's okay, my friend. He's over in the other barn. He's away from Magda, and someday you'll join him again. If only we could get the rest of them away from her." She rubbed the spot on his withers he enjoyed. His lips turned back in ecstasy.

After feeding time, Dee strolled down to Suzanna's barn to visit her new horse and pay for him. That last race one of her horses had won a year ago had given her the funds to buy Rocket Man and she hoped a few more.

~ * ~

Marcus couldn't get Dee out of his mind. After church on Sunday, he spent several hours in the batting cage hitting ball after ball. When he came out, his foul mood returned. Usually, smacking the ball around made him feel like Superman.

Monday didn't improve. A man showed up to serve Marcus with papers from his ex-wife's attorney. They commanded him to appear before the judge on Thursday at nine o'clock. Lauren wanted the judge to grant her custody of their daughter on all holidays, effective immediately.

There wasn't much about her that still shocked him, but he was surprised that she'd gone this far. He had always been willing to allow Kaitlyn to visit her mother if Lauren asked, which she never had. Why did she suddenly want to take Kaitlyn away for the entire Christmas vacation? And where was she getting the money to pay the attorney?

Marcus had paid for her divorce attorney back then when she cried she couldn't afford one. She didn't work, so where were the funds coming from now?

She was nothing but a lie. And now Dee had lied as well. The question was, why was she lying? He had to believe there was a complicated explanation.

Brad had told him to go talk to her. But why should Marcus beg for an explanation? He figured his friend regretted his comments about him being in love with Dee. In love? Never again. He would never trust another woman.

Unfortunately, the second call of the day was at Everglades Equestrian, for a pre-purchase exam. Someone wanted to buy a new horse. He called Dr. Skyler, who worked out of his clinic during the winter season, to see if he would take it. He said he could do it, sparing Marcus the pain of seeing Dee. The pain? The pain of hearing her voice? There shouldn't be pain in observing her glide down off a horse. He missed her. But the fact that she'd lied to him stung.

"God, I miss her, but I can't get over the fact she lied," he muttered again. In irritation, he pounded the steering wheel.

~ * ~

Tuesday, Magda was no worse than usual, but it was a relief when she left. Silva gave Dee her first lesson on Rocket Man. The two worked like they'd been training together for years.

Wednesday, Magda didn't show up. Dee rode two of Silva's horses before riding Rocket Man. She still hadn't heard from Marcus.

She figured Kaitlyn's lesson was canceled. Then a minivan drove in. Kaitlyn jumped out of the front seat and skipped to Dee.

"Dee, Dee," she squealed. "I'm ready for my lesson. Where's Roscoe?" she asked as she sprinted into the barn. She grasped Dee and gave her a big hug.

"Hello, Miss Collins. I'm Kaitlyn's grandmother, Judy Helton." An older woman ambled up to Dee and shook her hand. "Kaitlyn was so excited to get here. You and your horse have made a big impression on her. She's been doing her homework, practicing the piano, cleaning her room, and even helping in the kitchen. Thank you for that."

"A little incentive goes a long way, whether kids or horses." Dee laughed.

"Marcus was still out on calls, so he asked me to bring Kaitlyn. Neither one of us could disappoint her when she's being so good."

"I'm glad. I enjoy working with her. Roscoe was looking forward to seeing her too."

Judy laughed. "I'm sure the horse doesn't care. Kaitlyn drew several pictures of him. I put them on the refrigerator."

"They like each other. I know that much."

Dee pulled a tack box over next to Roscoe so Kaitlyn could stand on it while she brushed him. "Good boy," she said to him.

Dee set the saddle on his back and tightened the girth. Kaitlyn put her helmet on. Dee let her mount from the box and led Roscoe out of the barn to the arena.

Like the previous week, Kaitlyn had an audience. Her laughter and squeals of joy were infectious. The horse doing tricks entertained them all. While she enjoyed the horse and little girl playing, a nagging prickle of being watched crept up Dee's spine.

Where did that old feeling come from?

She scanned the farm with a worried gaze, but everyone she saw she recognized. As the lesson finished her eyes found the source. Parked out on the road beyond the gate sat a familiar veterinarian truck. Her heart rate quickened. She couldn't help but smile as she finished the lesson.

"Great lesson," Dee said, "but let's finish with a flourish. Take hold of the front of the saddle and sit very still."

Kaitlyn did as she said. Dee swung up behind Kaitlyn. "Don't make a sound. This will be fun," she whispered in Kaitlyn's ear. Taking the reins, she gave Roscoe the cue.

He stood up on his hind legs in his version of what the Spanish Riding School in Vienna called a levade. Kaitlyn leaned back against her.

"Now wave to your dad over there beyond the gate," she said.

Kaitlyn waved to her father. Marcus returned the gesture.

Dee cued the horse to set all four legs on the ground. She swung down then led Roscoe to the edge of the arena in front of Silva, Lily, and Judy Helton.

"Grandma, did you see that?" Kaitlyn beamed. "I hope Daddy saw me."

"Well, if he didn't, I took a picture with the cellphone. He can see it later."

"You taught Roscoe the levade?" Lily asked Dee. "You'll have no problems with Rocket Man."

"Thanks. It's another trick in his queue. Let's take Roscoe back and cool him out, Kaitlyn." Dee took the little girl by the hand.

Together, they walked to the barn. As they did, Marcus drove away. Her quickened heart rate turned to a stabbing pain as he drove out of sight.

~ * ~

Marcus hadn't realized Dee saw him until she'd vaulted onto the horse behind Kaitlyn. What a beautiful picture the horse, Kaitlyn, and Dee made as they waved at him. He'd loved the picture of Dee and his daughter together. He wished to be there at ringside applauding them.

But he couldn't drive through the gate. He longed to embrace Dee and seek her lips. He drove off thinking of all the unanswered questions he had. He should be furious with her. He tried, but he couldn't summon the emotion. Seeing her again, with Kaitlyn, cut through him. He desired Dee as he'd never desired another woman.

"Brad, you were right. You had to be right," Marcus said to no one. God help him, but he was in love. Now he only needed to get those answers.

~ * ~

Dee and Kaitlyn unsaddled and cooled Roscoe. Dee's heart hurt but Kaitlyn's enthusiasm took some of the pain away. She asked lots of questions. They were never the same ones and every answer led to another question. The girl was smart. She remembered everything from her previous lessons. Observing her around Roscoe gave Dee great joy. She hoped Marcus wouldn't take Kaitlyn to another trainer for lessons. Losing both would hurt too much.

When they finished with Roscoe, Kaitlyn helped Dee with the feeding. She would make a great assistant someday. They finished and walked outside where Silva and Judy sat on the bench.

"Are you coming with Grandma and me to dinner?" Kaitlyn asked Dee.

"I don't think so, Kaitlyn. I have things I need to do tonight."

"You're welcome to come along, Dee," Judy Helton said. "It's nothing special; I thought I'd take her to DQ this evening."

"I love Blizzards and hot dogs. Come with us, Dee, please?"

Kaitlyn's pleading eyes undid her. "That sounds tempting." Dee looked at Kaitlyn. Would it be presumptuous to go to dinner with them? If Marcus didn't want to see her, then she shouldn't hang around with the child. "I must pass on Blizzards tonight. Sorry, but I will remember you like them for the future."

Kaitlyn kicked the ground. "Okay, maybe the next time." She dragged her feet as she and her grandmother headed back to their car.

"You had nothing planned. Why not go with them?" Silva asked.

"You didn't see Marcus sitting out on the road observing Kaitlyn's lesson? He left instead of coming in. I couldn't go knowing he didn't want to see me."

"Oh, Dee. I think I'll find a different vet."

"No you won't. Like you told me before, he's the best. If I need a vet, he's the one I'll call first." She crossed her arms and stared out toward the road.

"Well, he could at least come say, 'Dee, I'm sorry, but I don't want see you anymore.'"

"Isn't that what he's saying?" Dee sat up and turned toward Silva.

"Yeah, but he's taking the coward's way out. I never thought he'd be like that."

"It doesn't matter now." She slumped back on the bench. "I have horses to ride and learn from. I don't need romantic entanglements."

"That's one way to put a positive spin on it."

Silva's sarcasm wasn't lost on Dee. "I'm going home. It's been a long day. I'll see you in the morning."

Silva gave her a hug. On the way home, Dee felt as if she were being followed. She glanced multiple times in the rearview mirror. She changed lanes as many times as possible without ticking off the other drivers around her. She breathed a sigh of relief when she reached her gated community. As the guard waved her through, she thanked God for keeping her safe. Within the high walls of the development, home became a sanctuary.

~ * ~

Marcus sat on the couch watching the news when Kaitlyn and his mother came in. Kaitlyn crawled in his lap. Good thing a commercial had come on, as the explanation of her lesson couldn't wait. She showed him the pictures of Dee, Roscoe, and her on her grandmother's phone.

His mother had snapped the picture at the exact moment Kaitlyn waved at him. He'd have that picture blown up to poster size for her bedroom. Except the picture also had Dee in it.

A pain stabbed through his heart, which he ignored. A good photo artist could probably crop her out but he didn't want her out of it. He loved the picture the way it was.

"Dee didn't come to dinner with us, Daddy," Kaitlyn said. "I think she was sad about something."

Very intuitive child. "Well, she looks happy in that picture. She must have enjoyed your lesson."

"I want to learn to swing up like Dee does. She mounted Roscoe like the cowboys do in the movies." Kaitlyn scrambled off his lap. She swung a leg over the ottoman to mount it like a horse.

"I think you'll need to grow up some, sweetness. Roscoe is pretty tall." He had to laugh at his daughter's antics.

"I want to learn how Dee makes him do what he did today. She told me she makes him do his tricks with cues."

"The standing on two hind feet is called a 'levade.' I think we need to see if we can find a DVD of *Miracle of the White Stallions*. You'll enjoy that. Do you think you can learn the cues?"

"She showed me how to make him bow today." She bent forward and t ouched the side of the ottoman. "I did it, Daddy, just like that. He bowed!"

"Good for you. Now isn't it getting close to bedtime? Head upstairs for a bath, and then I'll come tuck you in."

"Okay." She leaped off his lap and vaulted up the stairs.

His mother came in the room and took a chair across from him. "It surprised me Dee didn't come to dinner with us. I was looking forward to talking with her."

"She's very private, Mom. She doesn't share much about herself."

His thoughts went back to the first time they met. Dee would discuss herself up to a point, then clam up.

His mother brought him back to the present. "She's open with Kaitlyn. Dee's an enormous influence on her. They seem to almost belong together, two minds on the same page. Kaitlyn is gonna have more interest in horses than you or your sisters."

"Not more interested in horses than me. Simply more interest in riding them. I liked baseball more. Horses will become her sport, I have a notion."

"She'd be a lucky young lady to have a veterinarian for a father and a horse trainer for a mother."

"What did you say?" Marcus asked her incredulously.

"You heard me."

"I heard you all right. But why did you say it?"

"Marcus, you're so dense sometimes for a man with a DVM. But then I just said why—you're a very stubborn man."

"What's that supposed to mean?"

"It means you're in love with Dee and so pigheaded you can't admit it."

"How do you know that?"

"Mothers intuition. I've seen the look in your eyes since you met her. Some men are like that; it takes something knocking them upside the head before they see it. You're like your father. He took a while before it hit him."

"You didn't say that before I married Lauren."

"Because my intuition told me you weren't really in love with her. I kept my mouth shut because of the baby. I'm glad you married her because now we have Kaitlyn. Lauren could have taken the other route and had an abortion. So, wake up. Kaitlyn deserves a nice woman in her life instead of that sorry excuse of a birth mother."

"Now you sound like Brad."

"What does he have to do with any of this?"

"He's been telling me the same thing. But there are complications."

"There always are, in any relationship. She looked devastated when you drove away instead of pulling into the stable. Whatever it is, work it out and quit making both of you miserable."

Marcus stood and went over to his mother. He bent and kissed her on the forehead. "I'm going up to tuck Kaitlyn in bed. I'll think about what you said. Oh, and what knocked Dad in the head?"

"A baseball bat."

Chapter Seventeen

Marcus strode out of the courthouse, jubilant. Worry had furrowed his brow when he went in but now he stood on top of the world. The emergency hearing for Lauren to have Kaitlyn for the vacations was over. The judge had sided with Marcus. When he had pointed out that Lauren spent only a few hours with Kaitlyn in the last year, the judge grimaced and groaned.

Lauren hadn't even visited on Kaitlyn's birthday.

The real reason Lauren wanted Kaitlyn back in her life had been revealed. Lauren had remarried. She'd married the attorney who represented her in the custody case. That explained how she'd paid for the emergency hearing. She and new husband thought they would be going on a Christmas vacation like a nice respectable family. Her new husband must like kids.

It didn't improve Marcus's opinion of Lauren. Sure, there'd be future custody battles, but at least for this Christmas Kaitlyn would be with him. A question that popped into his mind: Would Dee be a part of this Christmas celebration? He needed to confront her about who she was. But right now, he needed to get to work. He drove to the clinic, parked his truck, then went inside.

"Wow, don't you clean up nice," Margo said as he strode in.

"Thanks, but I'm much more comfortable in my work clothes," he said as he jerked off his tie. "No emergencies came in?"

"Two routine calls. I added them to the end of your day like you asked."

"Good, thank you." He started toward the locker room to change when Brad came into the office.

"Hey, look at you, all spiffed up. Are suits the new work attire?" he asked.

"Ha, you're funny. What are you doing here this morning?"

"I can't come for a friendly visit?"

"No, you came to find out how my court appearance went."

"Guilty as charged."

"Have a seat in my office. I'll be right back."

Marcus changed into his khaki pants and blue cotton shirt. Suits were for church and other special occasions, nothing more. He went to his office and sat down behind his desk. Brad was sitting on the corner.

"We have chairs," Marcus said.

"I see them. So, what happened?"

He summarized the court hearing in about three sentences.

"She's a piece of work." Brad laughed. "None of my exes even come close. But it may get harder to fight her in the future now that she remarried."

"I thought about that. I'll deal with it when the time comes. I figure the pending alimony cancelation hearing will prevent that."

"Which you should get automatically since she remarried."

"So, now you have the skinny, I've got calls to go on."

"Have you talked to Dee yet?" Brad asked.

"No, I wanted the hearing over first. I need to find the right place and moment."

"Do it sooner rather than later."

"Why? Is something up? Do you have more information?"

"Nothing I can share. But I'm concerned for her. That woman Dee works for is trying to implicate her in the murders. Dee's clear of any involvement, but I've had two more voice mails from Jovanovich demanding answers as to why I haven't arrested her."

"Why should I get involved?" Marcus asked.

"Because the two of you to need to wake up and admit your feelings. You're the most obstinate couple I ever saw. You won't go ask what's after her. She's afraid you'll run away when she tells you."

"Brad, what are you talking about? What's after her?"

Brad shook his head and held up his hand. "I've gotta go." He said nothing else.

"You have information, don't you? And not what Magda is claiming. Spill the beans."

"I can't."

"You've shared other aspects of this murder investigation. Things no one outside law enforcement knows. Why won't you share this?"

"I shared information with you because you're in the community where all the victims came from. You could, conceivably, also fall victim to this killer. Therefore, I shared that information. As far as Dee goes, I'm under orders to keep her identity confidential. It's up to you two to figure things out for yourselves."

Marcus put his elbows on the armrests and steepled his fingers together. Could this be as simple as two people unable to trust each other? He'd admitted his feelings to himself. He didn't want to express them to Dee until he knew what secrets she hid. "Can't you tell me anything? What could be so bad she won't tell me, and you have orders to keep to yourself?"

"If you ask her, she'll probably tell you." Brad slid off his perch on the end of the desk. "Talk to Dee. And get her out of that stable before I have a female to add to my pile of dead bodies." He left the clinic.

Marcus clenched his jaw in frustration. Nothing in life came easy. Well, falling in love with Dee came easily. Telling her, however, might be difficult without the words sticking in his throat.

~ * ~

Thursday morning Magda arrived at the stable almost an hour earlier than usual. Dee still had four stalls to clean. Magda berated her for not having Chanel saddled. Dee stopped mucking and hurried to get Chanel.

The unsettling sensation from the night before set her teeth on edge. She worked through the horses and stayed inside the barn. The one time she had to go out the back toward the paddocks, she sensed eyes boring into her.

She glanced around the farm. At that moment, she couldn't see anyone. Trotting out the front toward the road, she hoped Marcus had parked out on the road like the evening before. But he wasn't there. She tried not to let her disappointment cloud her mind.

When Magda finished riding the last horse, she sauntered off to one of the other barns. Dee watched her as long as she could, but when Magda turned the corner she couldn't see which stable she visited. Since she came in early and had one less horse to ride, Dee would have extra time to ride. But first, Magda needed to leave.

Into which of the other four barns had she gone? And more importantly, why? None of the other trainers wanted her around. Surely they'd chase her off. The minutes dragged by before Magda reappeared and peeled out of the drive with one of the stable boys.

Dee ran over to Silva's barn. She plucked her aside before going out to ride.

"I thought you'd like to know, Magda's spreading a rumor you killed Miguel to take his job." Silva's eyes burned with outrage. "She even told Lily you murdered *her* stable boy. We're all aware of the truth, but I'd still like to stuff something down her throat for spreading such lies. She's alienated everyone here. We're all behind you."

The news shook Dee. Why would Magda say something so outrageous? Brad's warning flashed into her mind. Perhaps his cop instinct made him suspicious of her. Dee couldn't imagine that Magda was the person she said she was. She'd have to prove it herself.

Silva hugged her hard. "Hey, pay no attention to her. She's trying to make trouble."

"I don't understand. She's said nothing like that to me. She accuses me of overfeeding the horses and being slow getting my work done. She treats them like she does me."

"I know, honey." Silva released her. "Just quit! Between Suzanna, Lily, and me there are enough horses for you to ride. It will really frost Magda if we hire you as an assistant trainer. You can still watch out for the horses and keep checking on them when she isn't around. You have the one you love the most out of there and Roscoe can move into my barn. If the Russian Equestrian Federation hadn't paid for the stalls up front, I'd kick her out of here."

"Oh, Silva, is Magda going to say I schemed to get Rocket Man? Is she going to say I threatened to harm her if she didn't sell him? If she can spin my taking the job from Miguel, what else can she lie about?"

"Quit thinking like that. All of us worked on that deal. Magda is none the wiser. You can do so much better. Come on, get on Musket and let's go ride. You need an endorphin rush."

The offer to go to work with Silva sorely tempted Dee. Like most other times in her life when things went bad, her gut told her to turn to the horses.

Musket, at first, trotted tensely under her seat. The longer she rode, the more her shoulders and hands relaxed. As she relaxed, he did also. Soon they were in harmony. By the time she mounted the second horse, the monkey had leaped off her back. Even the sensation of being watched dissipated. But the synchronization between Dee and Rocket Man amazed her the most. Silva and Lily agreed they were a perfect match.

Dee took Rocket Man back to unsaddle and cool in Lily's barn. Dee wanted to care for the horse herself. When he was bedded in his new stall, she left to feed Magda's other horses. Once back in her barn, the spied-on feeling returned as intensely as it had before she left Hialeah. She tottered out of the barn. Fear knotted inside her.

"What's wrong?" Silva asked.

"Nothing." Dee's voice quivered.

"You're white as a ghost and shaking, so don't tell me nothing. Steffen, do you care if Dee and I go to dinner together? It's time she and I had a private talk."

"No, go," he answered.

"I'll call later so you can meet us back here for night check. Dee, you're driving."

Silva took Dee's arm then they headed to the truck.

~ * ~

Marcus finished his last call of the day not far from Everglades Equestrian Center. Since it was around feeding time, he hoped Dee would be there. He decided it was as good a time as any to seek the answers to his many questions.

As he drove through the gate, he didn't see her truck. Disappointment washed over him. Steffen's Mercedes sat alone in the parking lot. Well, he could visit his friend for a few minutes. It surprised him to see Steffen sitting in front of Dee's barn on the bench by himself.

"What are you doing sitting all alone?" Marcus asked. "Where's Silva?"

"Silva left with Dee. You missed them by only a few minutes."

"Where did the two of them go without you?"

"Something bad spooked Dee. She came out of the barn all pale and shaking like a leaf. Silva scooped her up, and they left."

Marcus sat next to his friend on the bench.

"Magda is spreading rumors that Dee killed Miguel and Pico," Steffen added. "Everyone wants to get together and throw Magda off the property. I don't know if that's what's bothering Dee or not. Probably is, though."

Marcus had observed Dee tremble like that. Why hadn't he been here for her? Brad had warned him about Magda. Marcus wanted to comfort her. They should face whatever frightened her together.

"I haven't seen you around the farm for quite a while. Where have you been?" Steffen asked. "I heard your daughter had another good lesson."

"I've been busy. Between Christmas and all the new people coming into town, it's been hectic. Kaitlyn regaled me about her lesson. Were you here?"

"No, Silva related the events. Dee has that horse of hers doing some amazing tricks."

"My mother took a picture of Dee and Kaitlyn. She sent it to my phone." Marcus withdrew the phone and scrolled through to find the photo. He showed it to Steffen.

"How cool is that? I bet it thrilled Kaitlyn."

"She tells me about it every day. She says she'll get her own horse and train it to do that movement."

"Don't you have something to look forward to?" Steffen laughed.

"Yeah, don't I?"

The horses stirred behind them in the barn. One whinnied and kicked the wall. Marcus stood and walked inside. A man Marcus didn't recognize stood in the aisle. Steffen ambled up beside Marcus. The man froze when he saw them.

"Can I help you?" Marcus asked.

"I'm looking for a friend of mine. I thought he worked at this barn," the stranger said with a slight Hispanic accent.

"Who are you looking for?" Steffen asked.

"I'm looking for Jaime Garza."

"There's no one by that name on this farm." Steffen said.

"Oh, sorry. I must have the wrong farm. I'll check the next one over."

The man marched out of the barn and vaulted the fence out front. Marcus and Steffen sat back down on the bench. They watched the man trot down the road until they lost sight of him in the dark.

"That was strange," Marcus said.

"Yes, it was. He must have come in the back or we'd have seen him. Good thing we were here. He's probably looking to steal something."

"Better yet that it wasn't Dee or Silva sitting here when he came through." An uneasy feeling settled in Marcus's gut.

A car drove in the front gate a moment later. Magda slid out and raced by Marcus and Steffen. She didn't say a word, going straight to the tack room. She unlocked it and went inside.

He and Steffen looked at each other and didn't say a thing as rummaging sounds came from the room. Shortly after, she walked out with a stuffed plastic bag.

"I forgot to take these saddle pads home to wash," she explained as she passed them. "Good night."

"Good night," they both said. She slowed only long enough for the gate to open.

"Is it a full moon tonight?" Steffen asked.

"Sure feels like one."

Steffen whistled and shook his head. "Something is going on here today. Bad karma, full moon, but definitely something strange."

"Tell me about what Magda said about Dee," Marcus said.

"This is all third hand," he said before relating what Silva and Lily had told him that afternoon. "Silva and Suzanna are trying to get Dee to come be their assistant."

"That would be the smartest thing Dee could do."

"I suspect that's part of Dee and Silva's talk tonight. I think I'll hang out until they come back for night check. Things are too bizarre tonight."

"I'd stay but I need to get home and put my kid to bed. Next week she'll be out of school, so I'll be able to stay out later."

"We should plan to do something. Maybe hit some baseballs?"

They said good night and Marcus got into his truck. As he pulled down the drive his scalp prickled. An intuitive gnawing persisted that something bad lay on the horizon.

~ * ~

"Nice apartment, Dee," Silva said.

"Thanks. I had it designed so I could rent the house out. I didn't need much room since I'm always at the stable."

"Smart," Silva said as she took a seat on the sofa. "Now, are you going to tell me what upset you earlier? It's not the first time I've seen you like that. But tonight it was the most severe."

Dee had purposely kept the conversation in the car away from the obvious. She couldn't concentrate on the rearview mirror and think how to explain her situation. "I can't answer why it was so intense tonight. I've had a tingling like someone is staring at me all day today. It's unnerving."

"I've never pushed the issue, but it seems pretty clear that something has bothered you since you came to the farm."

Dee decided to confide in her friend. Maybe unloading the burden would help her tell Marcus the whole truth. "I worked as an assistant trainer with my father down at the race tracks in Miami. Then someone began stalking me," she said. "The first time, the tires on my car were slashed and a note left on it that said, 'You will pay'. There were times I sensed I was being watched anytime I left the race track. Then my house was broken into three times. I got a security camera but when the stalker broke in again, he smashed the camera and left a death threat painted on the wall. I moved in with my parents and someone tried to break in there. I became scared for my family, so I left Hialeah and moved from racetrack to racetrack starting in New York and coming south as the horses traveled this way. Over the summer I decided not to go back into training race horses and follow my true passion, dressage. So I settled here."

"Oh, my God, Dee." Silva grabbed both shoulders. "I was sure it was something bad, but I never expected that. Now I understand." She released her.

"When I'm shaking like tonight, it's because something reminds me of the time before I left. It's probably nothing, but tonight I thought I was being watched again. I felt it yesterday when I was in the arena with Kaitlyn. Then I saw Marcus's truck by the gate. He was watching Kaitlyn's lesson. That's what prompted me to swing up behind her and cue the levade. Showing off since he hadn't been around lately. Then he drove away, and it was like someone stabbed me in the heart."

"I wish you'd told me sooner." Silva reached over and took Dee's hand.

"I couldn't. If the stalker found me again, I might put everyone around me at risk, and probably flee again. But I don't want to run anymore. I love it here and want to make this my home. I want to train dressage horses and give lessons. I've found what I've missed this past year."

"I feel even worse about what I said last week. I had no idea you were a racehorse trainer. You sure fooled us all with the humble stable-hand persona."

"Well, I've performed all the tasks at the track. My father said it would make us appreciate the people who work for us, and he's right."

"I agree." Silva sat back in her chair. "Perhaps I'll get to meet the rest of your family. They sound like good people."

"They are. If there are no more incidents during the holiday season then we pray he's given up or perhaps tip his hand and the police can finally arrest him."

"You have a lot of faith, and for the sake of everyone, I hope you're right."

"I can't believe it's time to go back for night check, but I'm glad I told you everything."

"You must tell Marcus. His ex-wife did some serious lying to him. He probably backed off because he could sense there was more than you were letting on. You have to talk to him."

Dee took a deep breath before saying, "Well, you've given me the courage to do that."

"Good. Let's head back. Is it okay if I tell Steffen? I hate keeping secrets from him."

"Yes, I understand, but no one else."

They hugged each other tightly. Silva's friendship replaced at least some of Dee's fear with a new-found confidence.

Back at the stables, Steffen had night check done for Silva. Dee went into her barn but stopped at the tack room.

"What is it?" Silva asked when she came in and Dee was staring at the open door.

"I know I locked this door before we left."

"Oh, Magda came back to the barn," Steffen said. "She must have forgotten to lock it when she left. She said she was picking up saddle pads that needed to be washed."

"That's strange," Dee said. "I do that once a week for her. They didn't need washing today."

"She's been acting strange all week." Silva waved her hand as if batting away a bug. "Let me help you get these guys hayed and watered then we can all get out of here. Why don't you come home with us for tonight? You might be more at ease."

"Thanks, Silva, but I'm safe there. You saw the guarded gate and high walls around my complex. I prefer to sleep in my own bed."

"I understand. We're all here for you if you need us. But to be sure, call me when you get home."

"Mother Hen, I'll do that." Dee laughed before hugging her friend.

Chapter Eighteen

After her talk with Silva, the weight on her shoulders that she'd carried for the last year eased up. Dee wished she'd confided in her sooner. Now the question was how to tell Marcus when he didn't seem to want to talk to her. Dee said a quick prayer for guidance.

When she arrived at the stable the next morning, she sat in the truck looking toward the barn. Would she have the same watched feeling as yesterday? Could it all be in her head because of the events since she found Miguel's body in the field? It could be residual anxiety from the chills she'd felt before realizing it was Marcus who watched her.

Those months before she left Hialeah, dealing with being scrutinized by the stalker, wouldn't magically go away now that she'd confided in Silva. Dee found it difficult to enter the stable until someone else arrived.

She waited until Gale drove in. With a wave of hello, Dee climbed out of the truck. As she passed the tack room, she stopped short. The door stood ajar. She locked it when she left last night, she'd double checked it. Yes, Magda could've come back later and left it open.

Dee held her breath as she stared. *Did Magda carelessly leave it open? Did someone else break in? Could the stalker be inside or had he left one of his creepy messages? If so, what should she do?*

Frozen in place, Dee contemplated her options. *Grab a pitch fork? Lace her keys between her fingers like her cousin had instructed her to defend herself? Yell for Gale to come be with her?*

Roscoe kicking his stall door brought her back to reality. She should call the police but later. Six AM was much too early to call Brad. She'd call him later. 9-1-1. Her hand quivered so violently she almost couldn't hit the numbers 911. *Deep breath, get a grip on yourself.*

Roscoe's incessant battering made it difficult to speak with the 9-1-1 dispatcher. The dispatcher even asked about the noise. Once she had a police officer on the way, she began feeding. Her sweaty fingers slipped on the stall door latches. Her hands quaked, spilling feed on the floor. She warily kept an eye on the tack room door. Finally, the gate squealed and a sheriff's deputy drove through. She huffed out a sigh of relief.

"I'm the one who called," Dee said to him. "Oh, Deputy Watson, right? You're the one who took all my information on the crime scene the other day."

"Yes, I remember you. What's happening here this morning?"

"Someone broke into my tack room last night." She moved closer and whispered, "I'm scared to check if they're still inside."

"Show me where."

They moved to the door. In a hushed voice she said, "It's locked when I'm not here. I came in last night about nine o'clock to check the horses. I locked it before I left. This morning, it's exactly as you see it now. I listened in case someone was inside, but I heard nothing."

"Are you the only one who has a key?"

"No, I share it with the trainer I work for and the trainer next door."

The deputy put on gloves before touching the door. He used his pen to push the door open with his left hand while the other rested on his gun. With a slow, measured gait, he entered the room. Dee could see that only the ambient light from outside illuminated the inside.

The deputy leaned back. "Where's the light switch?"

"Inside on the right."

He turned on the lights then scanned the room. Exiting the room, he said, "You can go inside now. Let me know if you're missing anything."

Dee walked in. Her gaze settled on her tack box with a broken lock. She glanced toward the boxes where Magda kept her personal stuff. Several were open and things askew. The tack hung neatly on hooks or folded on shelves.

"My tack box has been broken into. These other boxes belong to the trainer I work for, and they don't contain anything I use daily."

"I'll go get my print kit. Hopefully, I can get a few good prints off the door and the box. After I collect any prints, you may check for missing items," Deputy Watson said. "I'll be several minutes."

Dee began picking the stall nearest the tack room. Between forkfuls of manure, she glanced at the deputy brushing black powder around the door lock and handle. Rolling her shoulders, she patted Dancer on his neck. He caressed her cheek with his soft nose. Unable to wait any longer she called the number on Brad's card and left a message.

Silva came into the barn as soon as she arrived. "What happened?"

"I found the tack room door open when I came in."

"Is anything missing?"

"They broke into my tack box." Closing the stall door, she glanced toward the deputy as he placed tape on several areas of the door. She'd seen enough fingerprint tape to last a lifetime.

"What did they take?"

"I haven't gotten to look yet. It appears he's found some prints."

"Last night after we went to your place, Steffen told me Marcus stopped by." Silva tugged Dee down the aisle away from the tack room. "They were sitting out front when they heard the horses kick the walls, so they came in to check. Some guy they didn't know was standing in the aisle. He said he was looking for someone and that he must have the wrong farm. That was before Magda came back."

"I wish I'd known that last night." Dee laid a hand on Silva's arm.

"Well, no one thought much about it. I guess in hindsight, after what you told me last night, I should have."

Deputy Watson came down the aisle to where Dee and Silva stood. "I got several prints off the box. The door only had smudges. Whoever picked the door lock wore gloves but must have taken them off to break into the box."

Dee and Silva looked at each other. Silva's expression mirrored Dee's thoughts: *Why use gloves to pick the lock and not use gloves to break into the tack box?* Plus Magda had a key, why pick the lock on the door?

"You can check the box now," the deputy said.

She and Silva entered the tack room. Dee carefully opened the tack box. At first glance it didn't appear they took anything. Dee moved a few blankets. She removed the lid from a cardboard box on the bottom. The box contained a few family photos and some pictures from the winner's circle at the racetrack.

Dee rummaged through the box. There were some personal items gone, horse mementos and ribbons. Mostly items that held value only to her. The stalker had never removed any of her personal belongings before and left his dead roses and threatening words written on the walls. Nothing like that appeared here. She gave the deputy a list of the absent items.

"When Magda gets here, she can tell you what's not here from her stuff," Dee told him.

"When does she come in?" he asked.

"About nine o'clock."

"I can hang out until then. I'll be in my car working on the report."

"Thanks, Deputy."

"I'm going back to my barn," Silva said. "It can't be what we talked about last night."

"I hope you're right," Dee said.

Silva gave her a quick hug. "Would you prefer I stay here with you?"

Dee considered the offer. "No, I'll be fine. Besides, there's a cop sitting right out front."

Before nine her cellphone rang.

"Dee, what's up?" Brad asked.

"Someone broke into my tack room last night."

"Call it in and have a deputy take prints." His instructions sounded serious.

"I already did. He said they used gloves to pick the lock. They also broke into my personal tack box. The deputy got prints off that. Some pictures and personal things are missing. This is how the stalker started."

"Are there people around? You shouldn't be alone."

"Yes, and Magda will be here soon. The deputy is out front waiting on her."

"Which deputy responded?"

"Deputy Watson."

"Thanks. I'll call you back after I speak to him"

She bit at her cuticles. After all this time, the thought of her stalker having found her, and his ability to come and go at a place she felt secure, brought those helpless feelings back again.

A few minutes later the phone rang.

"Yes, Detective?"

"Stay around people. I'm on a crime scene right now. I'll come check on you as soon as I can. Have you talked to Marcus yet?"

"No. He stopped by last night, but I had gone to dinner with Silva. Marcus and her husband Steffen are friends. They were here last night when a stranger came through the barn. They told him to leave, and he took off."

"I'll talk to Marcus and get a description. I've instructed the deputy to put a rush on those prints. I don't think the person who broke into your tack box is your stalker."

"How can you be sure of that?"

"Call it a hunch."

"That's not much to go on but I hope you're right."

His *hunch* didn't give her any reassurance. She'd been down this road with the police before.

Dee checked the time. Magda was late, again. Dee groomed three of the horses to have them ready for a saddle when Magda arrived. Lately, Dee had given up trying to figure out which horse Magda would ride first.

Deputy Watson walked in the barn. "I can't hang out any longer as there are calls holding. Do you think your employer will be here soon?"

"Honestly, I can't say. There are days she's early and days she's late. And sometimes she doesn't show up at all."

"Here's a case card. If you find anything else missing, you can call me. I've got to get going."

"Thank you, Deputy Watson. I appreciate your help."

"I hope we find who did this. I'm sorry it happened."

"Thank you again."

After he left, Dee went back in the tack room to look through the box again. It occurred to her she hadn't seen her old cellphone. She'd locked it in the tack box along with other personal items. She had separated the phone and battery so no one could track her through it.

Dee didn't know if they could really do that like in the movies, but she didn't want to take any chances. The phone she carried now had been purchased by her sister and given to her on the day she left home. Dee went through all the items three times—but no phone. The burglar had it. Why had he, or she, taken her phone and her pictures? One other item was missing: a lead rope and halter from her childhood pony. She phoned Deputy Watson to add the additional items.

She headed over to Silva's barn. If Magda came in, she could yell at Dee for not sitting there waiting. Perhaps Magda really thought Dee was a murderer and wasn't coming in until she was arrested. Wouldn't that be a real turn of events?

Brad drove into the farm a few minutes past noon. She waved at him from the front of Silva's barn.

"You're staying around people, that's good," he said.

"I'm keeping busy, trying to strengthen my resolve. That way I won't think about the possibilities. Otherwise, I might get into my truck and run."

"Don't do that, Dee. We'll get your stalker. I feel it in my gut.

Magda didn't come around today?"

"No."

"Interesting. She is elusive."

"She seems to have her own agenda."

"I've got some things I'm working on involving your cases. As I get more, I'll keep you informed. Stay around people."

She watched him leave. What was it about cops with their hunches and cryptic warnings?

~ * ~

"Hey, Brad," Marcus answered his cellphone.

"What're you up to this morning?" Brad asked.

"Watching cartoons. How about you?"

Brad hesitated a second or two. "Oh, with Kaitlyn." He snorted. "Listen, I heard you were at Everglades Equestrian last night."

"Yes, I stopped by, talked to Steffen for a while. I didn't see Dee if that's what you're fishing for."

"I'm not fishing. I'm aware you didn't see Dee. What can you tell me about the man you confronted in her barn?"

"How did you...Why? What happened?" He left the living room and marched out into the hallway.

"Someone broke into Dee's tack room last night."

"What? When? Is she all right?" Marcus glanced around the corner to make sure Kaitlyn still watched her cartoons.

"Tell me everything from beginning to end."

"One of the horses kicked a wall and snorted so we went to check it out." He paced down the hall toward his study. "A man with a Hispanic accent was standing in the aisle. He said he was looking for someone and thought this was his barn. We had been sitting out front so he had to have come in from the back. He left out the front gate."

"You never saw him before?"

"No. Steffen told him the person he was looking for didn't work on that property."

"What did he look like?" Brad asked.

Marcus closed the door to his study. "Late fifties. Long, stringy, dark hair shot with gray. About five eight or nine. He was wearing dirty faded jeans and a black T-shirt."

"Who did he ask for?"

"Someone by the name of Jaime Garza."

"Did you see where he went after he went out the gate?"

He sat in his office chair. "He disappeared into the dark. What happened at Everglades after I left?" Marcus placed both elbows on the desk. Worry inched up his spine.

"Dee came in this morning and found the door ajar. She called the police. The deputy attempted to lift prints from the door but had someone picked the lock, skillfully, and used gloves or wiped it down, so no prints."

"Anything taken?"

"Personal things out of Dee's tack box. They broke the lock. We lifted prints from it."

"How's Dee?"

"If you're interested in how she is, go see her."

"Brad." He could hear the irritation in Brad's voice, and it ratcheted up the irritation in Marcus's own.

"What? I'm tired of this game. Dee isn't Lauren. You need to get over your trust issues. Sometimes things aren't what they seem."

"Fine," Marcus said. "Is there anything new in your murder investigations?"

"Yes, there is. I've been on a crime scene all morning. But there's nothing I can share right now."

"Since you haven't made an arrest, I guess that means she's not a suspect?"

"Dee *never* was a suspect. I told you that before. If that's what you're using for an excuse, it's a thin one. Now get out of the house and go talk to Dee!"

Brad hung up on him.

As deep as Marcus's feelings for Dee were, he couldn't let go of thinking of her as a liar like his ex-wife. He scrubbed his face with his hands. Confrontations with women were not his strong suit.

Chapter Nineteen

Shortly after coming to Palm Beach, Dee had found a small group of caretakers, riders, and owners who met at the show grounds at sunrise on Sunday mornings for church services. She hadn't attended before, but she needed the spiritual guidance this morning. She fed early and went to the service. Later, she'd clean stalls as time permitted while grooming the horses for Magda, if she came in on time.

This morning's sermon hit a nerve: *Light will always be shone on your lies.* Dee heard God's message loud and clear. She'd devised a plan to escape the stalker, but her lies had caught up with her. From God she could ask forgiveness. But would Marcus forgive her? As soon as possible, she needed to confess.

Back at the stable, she glanced out of the stall at the sound of the gate. Silva drove through and parked between the barns. If Magda were on time, she would be coming in soon. Dee abandoned the stall she'd been working on and decided to saddle the first horse.

Silva rushed in to the barn. "I found that article you asked about with Magda and Rocket Man. He is one beautiful horse in these pictures." She placed the magazine into Dee's hands with the page opened to a color photo of Rocket Man trotting with Magda.

"You're right he's magnificent. He didn't look like that when she rode him here."

"Well, he looks like the picture when you're riding him."

"Thanks." Warmth flowed through Dee.

"I'll let you finish getting the horse ready for Magda. See you later for your lesson."

"Thank you for the magazine. I can't wait to ride."

Dee tucked the magazine under her arm as she finished brushing Chanel. Then she ran to the tack room and shoved the magazine under some saddle pads. She'd look at it more closely later. A thought occurred to her as she picked up Magda's saddle.

As she set the saddle on the horse, she noticed it differed from the one in the photo. The stirrups were shorter, which meant the rider in the picture had shorter legs than Magda. It couldn't be her in the picture. Before Dee could verify her observation with the photo, Magda drove in. Dee would have to investigate later.

Fortunately, Magda moved through the horses without her snide comments about lazy stable help. She also didn't act like someone who seemed concerned about working around a person she'd called a murderer. Although her behavior was unsettling, Dee put it out of her mind and concentrated on her job during Magda's time in the barn.

Once she'd finished the evening feeding, she took the magazine out and studied the picture, confirming her thoughts from the morning. The woman in the picture appeared shorter than Magda and much younger. To prove her theory, Dee brought Rocket Man over from his stall in the other barn.

As she stood looking at him with Magda's saddle on, the gate squealed. She watched as one of the other grooms left and an unmarked police car drove in. Brad.

"What brings you out on a Sunday evening?" she asked.

"I hoped I might find Miss Jovanovich here. Is she around?" Brad scanned the aisle.

"Left hours ago. Is there anything I can help you with?" Her curiosity piqued.

"Actually, yes. Do you know where she lives or have another phone number for her?"

"Sorry, no. She doesn't answer her phone, am I right?" She cocked a brow.

"No. I'd hoped to find her here. Nice-looking horse you have here." Brad's gaze perused the horse.

"Thanks, I like him. While you're here, can I ask your professional opinion about something?"

"I'm not an expert on horses like Marcus, but professionally, what ya got?" He sat on the tack box and crossed a knee over his other leg.

She handed him the magazine with the picture. "This photo is of Magda sitting on this horse. This is the saddle she last rode him in. See the length of the stirrups? Does this picture appear to have a shorter stirrup, thus a shorter leg which would belong to a shorter person?"

"You're telling me you think this saddle would hold a taller person than the picture?" He looked from the photo to the saddle and back several times. "Yes, I suppose that could be the case. What are you getting at?"

She vaulted into the saddle in one smooth, fluid motion. Landing lightly, her legs hung down yet the stirrup extended about six inches below her boot. "In order for me to ride this horse, the stirrup needs to be much shorter. Let me place it where I would ride it." She adjusted the stirrup up. "Now it looks more like the picture, do you agree?"

"Yes. I do. Great reasoning."

"I wish there were pictures of Magda standing on the ground for comparison, but I believe the person in the picture is closer to my height than Magda is."

"Since I haven't seen her, I don't understand what you mean."

"I'm five foot one. She's seven inches taller than me. The person in the photo isn't Magda. Which would explain why no one around here believes she could be on the Russian Olympic Team."

He looked at her, at the photo, then back to the horse. Did he see the same things she did? Could Magda be an imposter?

"I think you're on to something." He smacked his hand on the page. "I've been running searches for Magda Jovanovich in our national system. Nothing comes back. I'll expand the search to Interpol. I should have thought of that. Good work, Dee. I'm glad you brought this to my attention."

"Now if I could only identify my stalker as easily." She took the magazine he handed her.

"You did all you could. I read in the reports that he'd smash the cameras installed in your house. By the way, are there any installed around here?" He glanced toward the four corners of the roof.

"No, why do you ask?"

"I'd like to get a look at Magda and the person who came through the barn the other night."

"What person?" Her gaze became laser-focused on Brad.

"Marcus told me a strange guy entered through the back asking for someone named Jaime Garza. When he and Steffen told him there was no one on this farm by that name, he left. I'm wondering if he could be connected to Magda since she came in not long afterwards."

"Jai…Jaime Garza?" Terror ran up her spine. She sat heavily on the tack box when her legs gave out.

"Are you okay?" He grabbed her shoulders to steady her.

"Yeah, let me catch my breath."

He released her. "Do you recognize that name?"

"You read the reports. He's the man I suspected of being the stalker, but he was in prison when these attacks started."

"I didn't put the names together." He stepped back. "Now that you bring it to my attention, it can't be coincidence."

"He must be here. Now I understand why I've had the sensation of eyes boring into me every time I go out the back of the barn. I've felt watched for several days. I thought it was my imagination." She bounced up and paced the aisle. "He's found me. I should have known."

"What's in back of the property here? I can see the white boundary fence but it looks grown up beyond." He marched out the back of the stable.

She followed but stayed behind him to be out of sight of anyone watching. "I've been told the property behind here is in foreclosure. No one is supposed to be living there. Is there any way to check?"

"I can have our aviation unit fly the helicopter over it while they are up tonight. I'd need a warrant otherwise. I'll also check with DOC and see if Jaime Garza is still in prison. Until I find out, I suggest you avoid being here by yourself." He turned to face her. "Have you spoken to Marcus recently?"

"I tried, but he didn't answer any of my texts. I guess he's lost interest."

Brad shook his head as if exasperated. "I don't know what he's thinking, but it doesn't change anything. You should be around people at all times, including your home in case that man followed you."

"Here is the only place I've gotten that spied-upon sensation. My apartment has no windows. But I'll see if I can arrange for others to be with me."

"Good. I'll also arrange some extra protection here and at your home. And call me the next time you see Magda. I'm gonna run a check on her now. I'll wait until you're ready to leave and shadow you home."

"Silva and her grooms are next door. I'll leave when they do and I'll stay around the front of the stables."

"No, I'm trailing you home. I'll be out front when you're ready." He marched out to his car.

She'd always suspected Garza but prison was a good alibi. But how had he found her? Could he really be out there observing her now?

Dear Lord Jesus, please protect me. Help me to end this nightmare, help the police to find the person responsible. Grant me guidance to know what to do next. Do I leave this place and hide again, or do I to stay and fight? I need your help, no matter what path I chose. Please help me choose wisely. Amen.

Calmness settled over her. It seemed God had led her here for a reason, so she would wait for Him to show her His will.

~ * ~

"Daddy, why don't we go see Dee and the horses this afternoon?" Kaitlyn asked as they got into the car after church.

Marcus didn't have an excuse handy, so he took some time to mull over the question. He desired to speak with Dee. Should he go? Kaitlyn wishing to visit the horses provided a good reason to stop by. But something held him back.

"If you two go to the stable, we can have dinner later and you can bring Dee over to enjoy it with us," his mother said.

"Actually, I'm hungry and I'm on call today. I'd hate to get called out while Kaitlyn is at the barn. You'll have all week to visit the horses. Let's you and I draw some horses at home instead."

"Aww, but I can draw them while I look at them."

"Yes, but Dee is working. The lady she grooms for doesn't like people around while the horses are being trained. We can go another time."

He hated the sad look in his daughter's eyes as she buckled herself into the back seat. His mother didn't say anything but he saw the disapproving look she gave him.

After dinner he kept an eye on Kaitlyn as she drew and colored good likenesses of Roscoe and Dee. The little girl had some talent here. She sure didn't get that from him. On the other hand, she did get her love of horses from him. He'd let her explore it. She'd developed a fondness for Dee, and the two bonded together. Everything in his world led to Dee.

"So tomorrow I can visit Dee and the horses? I really like her. I wish she could be my mommy."

She hadn't looked up while making the comment. Kept coloring in one of the outlines of the horse she'd drawn. How perceptive. "You're right, sweetness. I really like Dee as much as you do."

"Then why isn't she here with us?

Why did children ask such difficult questions? She'd never asked why her mother wasn't here. He thought of a Bible verse that had something to do with, "Out of the mouth of babes." Perhaps God used his daughter's words to get him to listen? And the sermon this morning had been about forgiveness.

Okay, okay, he heard the message loud and clear now; it didn't take a baseball bat to knock the sense into him. He did love Dee and it was time to find out what prevented her from sharing everything about her life.

Why not do a computer search to check her story? He went to his home office and typed her name in the search engine. He'd never done this before and something akin to shame washed over him. He should be asking her in person.

Several articles came up for Dee Collins. The first a recent news clip, only two weeks old, about a horse owned by Dee Collins winning a steeplechase event in England. He continued to scroll. Further down, he found a wedding announcement in the *Miami Herald*. Delfina Garcia, daughter of Eduardo and Maria Garcia, of Hialeah, Florida, to marry Scott Collins of London, England. A photo accompanied the article. The woman's facial features looked similar to the Dee he knew but with dark hair. Could this be his Dee? Anyone could dye their hair, after all.

He scrolled to the next item, a news article about the trial of a horse trainer in Miami charged with animal cruelty and insurance fraud. The names of two sisters, Ileana and Delfina Garcia, made him lean in closer. He remembered the incident. They had testified against the suspect, Jaime Garza. Jaime Garza?

Wasn't that the name the stranger asked about in the stables the other night? No way it could be coincidence. He hadn't followed the trial closely when it happened. But as he read the article, he remembered bits of what Dee had told him that night at the restaurant. All of it came together. But the woman here in Palm Beach, was she Dee or the sister Ileana? He searched the name Ileana Garcia.

The same article came up first. Then a couple of news items about vandalism to her car and home. Older articles about her winning horses at the track. Finally, one with a photo. Yes, it looked like Dee but with long dark hair. Could she be Ileana and using her sister's name? But why? And did her doing so somehow connect to Jaime Garza? Only she could answer these questions.

He thought about the subtle warning from Brad. Whichever one of the Garcia sisters worked at that stable, perhaps she was in danger. What if there were extenuating circumstances that made being honest with him impossible?

If he'd never been called by God to act before in his life, he did at that moment. God spoke to his soul: Time to go ask questions and get the answers from the woman who had stolen his heart.

Chapter Twenty

Dee arrived at the stable before nine. Traffic had been light, so watching the rearview mirror became easier. She'd rather enjoy the Christmas lights on the surrounding farms than worry about being stalked. Gale would arrive soon to do night check so Dee waited in the truck. When her phone rang, she flinched, then grabbed it off the console. Detective Tyler.

"Why are you at the barn without anyone else there?" he asked.

"How do you...?" She looked side to side and twisted around to see behind her.

"I'm in the tractor shed doing surveillance."

"Oh. I'm waiting on one of the other girls before I come in. You're keeping an eye on the farm? I'd have liked a heads up on that plan."

"Don't get upset or scared, but someone is squatting on the farm you showed me yesterday. There are car tracks in and a foot path to the fence between the properties. It's in foreclosure and the bank says it's unoccupied. I can't be sure who it is. Perhaps your stalker or perhaps the woman who has been murdering men here in the County. It may also be none of the above. Either way, I'm watching the property."

Tremors wracked her whole body. Her mind seized on something else he said. The serial murderer was a woman? How could he tell her that? Could that be why he'd questioned her? Was that Marcus's reason for backing off? The detective and Marcus were good friends so perhaps he'd told Marcus she was a suspect. Any and all of those scenarios would certainly make her back away from someone.

"Dee? Dee, are you still there?"

She gulped. *Breathe, breathe, calm your thoughts, breathe long and deep.* "Yes, I'm still here. Sorry... well, you understand."

"I do. I'm here, there's another deputy in the farthest barn, and K-9 is standing by. Go ahead in and go about your regular routine. I'd like to catch this person."

"What about my friend from the other barn I planned to meet here?"

"She drove up a few minutes ago. I explained to her that we had the farm under surveillance and you'd call her when she could come back onto the property."

"You want to use me as bait? Are you crazy?" Her voice rose several octaves.

"You'll be safe, I promise. You want this over, don't you?"

Of course she did. But to actually confront her stalker? If that was who hid over there. Could she do that?

Amazingly, peace settled though her body. *A peace that passes all understanding.* The shaking stopped. Confidence flowed through her. God brought her to this moment and she could do it. *Thank you, Lord, for answered prayers. Keep me safe and please may the police get these criminals so it will all be over.*

She punched in the code and drove through the gate.

~ * ~

Roscoe kicked his stall door as soon as she entered the stable. She picked up flakes of hay and doled them out. As she passed the tack box sitting next to Roscoe's stall, she observed a small brooch in the shape of a Christmas wreath and a handwritten note. Closer examination showed a note from Brad.

Pin this to your shirt, it read. *If Garza shows up, get him talking about his previous stalking episodes. This will record his confession. Good luck and remember we are here and will help as soon as needed.*

She wasn't sure if that made her feel secure or not but hopefully it would end this nightmare, and life could go back to normal. Placing the tiny brooch on the lapel of her shirt, she sat on the tack box. Her legs swung back and forth with impatience. Sitting and waiting wouldn't help.

Jumping up, she went to Roscoe's stall. After haltering him she tied the horse in the wash rack at the very end of the barn. Now in full view of the back property, she stood on a short stool and began grooming.

Less than a minute later, tingling sensations crawled up her back. The hair on her neck stood up. The sensations intensified. Roscoe pinned his ears and snorted. Turning her head, a face she hoped never to see again came into view.

The man didn't look the way she remembered; he'd aged. His long hair was shot with gray, tied back into a ponytail, and thinner on top. She remembered him as clean-cut, with black hair and a stout build. But when he smiled, memories of that snarly grin rushed back, and a cold chill ran through her veins.

"Hello, Ileana. Remember me?" he asked.

The voice turned her blood to ice. "You've changed, Jaime Garza." Her voice didn't sound like her own.

"Prison will do that to you."

She didn't respond. Roscoe's ears remained flattened on his head. The stale, sour smell of an unwashed body hit her nostrils, sickening her. Roscoe fidgeted and snorted in the cross ties.

"Well, well, how far you've fallen. Mucking stalls and caring for someone else's horses. You're not so high and mighty now, are you?" He snarled the words.

"I've never been above anyone else. I believe the content of a person's character should speak to who they are." She spat the next words at him, "You're a corrupt and abusive trainer. I avoided you whenever I could."

"Your opinion. I had a job to do and clients who paid me well to do what needed to be done." He shrugged as if what he said was a natural thing to do.

"By destroying animals for the insurance money? That's not how the racing business should be conducted." Her first desire was to punch his face in, but she remembered the words on Brad's note. She needed to keep him talking.

"Again, your opinion. If you'd gotten acquainted with me better, you'd have seen it my way. Instead you threw my roses in the trash." Bitterness rolled off him. "I wanted to congratulate you for winning that big race. How could you do that? Then your father banned me from coming around his stable."

"My father didn't want a corrupt cheater like you hanging around his stable. As for me, I never had any interest in you. You just never got the message," she snorted.

"You testified against me at the Jockey Club tribunal, and I lost my trainers license. I went to prison. Everything that happened to me is because of you. Now I'm here to return the favor."

Her thoughts revisited those six months before he'd gone to prison. He'd always made her feel uncomfortable with the way he leered at her. She'd never given him any indication of *liking* him. Why had he fixated on her?

"Like vandalizing my car and house? Breaking in and tearing up my belongings? I heard the threat loud and clear. So I left. How did you manage to find me in Palm Beach?" The butterflies in her stomach threatened to erupt from her throat.

"I heard you went to England with your sister after the holidays. So I waited. You and your sister would come home for Christmas. So I hung around the track."

Bile rose in her throat at the lewd gleam in his eyes. She considered throwing the brush in her hand to hit him in the face. *Keep your cool, remember what Brad said in the note.* Instead she flicked the brush roughly over Roscoe's coat, hoping some of the dust would fly into Garza's eyes.

"I got lucky last week. One of the vets was talking on the phone to a vet up here. I heard your sister's name so I listened in. The vet asked about your sister, who was standing right around the corner. It didn't take much to put two and two together. I followed the local vet until I discovered where you were. I recognized your cursed horse and even with blonde hair, I could pick you out anywhere. You've haunted my dreams. I've waited and planned all these years exactly what I'd do once I had you cornered."

"You were still in prison when the stalking and vandalism started, so how could that have been you?"

"Well, I do admit, I had some help. I met some people in prison who gave me the idea. When they got out they started the work for me. I guess they got you stirred up real good. But it was me who smashed that camera in your house. The police thought they were so smart and it couldn't be me because I was in prison. They never checked to see that I got out the day I wrote that message on your wall. You left the next day so I had to wait. Now that I've found you, I won't need to dream about what I'm going to do. I'm gonna have the real thing. You're all alone here now and there's no one to help you."

He grinned maniacally as he closed the gap between them. Roscoe snapped his teeth to bite Garza. The cross tie snapped taut as the horse lunged, preventing her escape. If only it had been longer, Roscoe would have gotten a hold of Garza. The squeal of the gate out front distracted her. *Who is coming in? Where is Brad and the other cops?*

Garza darted at her, snatching her arm then jerking her off the stool. Something cold and sharp pressed against her ribs. *Does he have a knife?* Bile burned the back of her throat at the stagnant body odor emanating off him as he clamped one arm around her neck. The knife pressed harder against her flesh. *Where is my help?*

She glanced toward the other end of the stable, hoping to see Brad coming to her aid. What she saw was Marcus standing at the entrance to the stable. She froze. Would he attempt to save her and get hurt himself? Garza jerked her back into the darkness. She lost sight of Marcus. Her brain tried to formulate a plan. Kick, bite, or finger in the eye, she could do this.

Lord, now is when I really need your strength and guidance. I refuse to be a victim any longer.

~ * ~

Seeing Dee with another man at the other end of the stable sent a stab through Marcus's heart. *Is that the same guy I saw in the barn the other night? Something isn't adding up here. Wait, he's dragging her against her will. She needs help!* Marcus sprinted down the aisle just as Roscoe jumped forward. The horse's lunging and rearing caused Marcus to stop. The cross ties strained then broke. He glanced beyond the horse to see Dee disappear into the night.

"Whoa, Roscoe. Whoa, easy boy." He grabbed the halter and led the trembling, wild-eyed horse to its stall.

At the sound of the gate opening again, he looked back toward the front of the barn. *Perhaps whoever is coming in can help me locate Dee.* Magda drove in. He closed the stall door as she approached.

"Oh, Doctor Helton, how wonderful to see you again," she cooed. "I never got to thank you for taking such good care when that horrible horse threw me the other day. Let me thank you properly." She slipped her arms around his neck, drawing him against her.

He pushed and pried, attempting to get out of her grasp. The more they grappled, the tighter she clenched. The woman was stronger than she looked. When her mouth came down on his, he turned his face away. "Magda, stop. I'm here to see Dee."

"Stupid stable girl no good." She let go with one hand and swatted the air as if swatting at Dee. "You need better than lazy girl. Come home with me. I show you a real woman."

She leaped and wrapped her legs around him. With her legs hooked at the ankles, she squeezed. The death grip took the air out of his lungs. Together they tumbled to the ground but she never loosened her grip. The arm around his neck squashed his windpipe. She'd smother him if he didn't get her off soon.

The harder he fought, the tighter she squeezed. Finally, he got an arm out of her grasp. Then he did something he'd been taught never to do—he plowed his fist right into her face. She loosened her grip as blood poured from her nose. He slid out from under her and stood up so fast he wobbled and went down on one knee. The world spun around him for several minutes before coming back into focus. *Dee is in trouble!*

He looked across the barn where he'd last seen her. He staggered before he got his legs under himself. Too late he realized Magda was jabbing something into his arm. The pinch of the needle came before a warm sensation spread throughout his body. He swatted at the needle and shoved her away, then ran to the other end of the stable where Dee had disappeared.

~ * ~

Garza dragged Dee toward the back of the property. *Where's Brad and his help? Doesn't he have enough of a confession?* They'd probably gone only about twenty feet when she deliberately collapsed, becoming dead weight on Garza's one arm. The knife grazed her ribs as she slipped out of his grasp. Warm, wet, sticky blood seeped from the cut, but she ignored it.

Once free of him, she stood up and drove her left foot into his right knee, forcing it sideways. Garza yelped in pain. Dee turned and sprinted back toward the stable just as Brad appeared and tackled Garza. The sound of the handcuffs snapping brought joy to her heart.

She galloped into the barn at the same moment Marcus ran out. He stumbled right into Dee's arms. Her nightmare appeared to be over yet another was about to begin.

Over Marcus's shoulder, Dee saw Magda coming toward them. *Is that a syringe in her hand?* Magda raised her arm ready to jam it into Marcus's back. Dee shoved him away. Face to face with Magda, Dee saw the blood dripping from her nose.

Still, her fury at the mistreatment she and the horses had endured bubbled to the surface. Dee cocked her right arm and caught Magda square on the chin. The woman went down in a heap, unconscious. Dee turned back to Marcus, who swayed, looking woozy.

It took all her strength to hold him upright. "Marcus, are you okay?"

"I saw that guy grab you, then Magda came in and jumped me. Did you knock her out? That's a wicked right hook you have there." His words slurred and his head wobbled. "I think she stabbed me with something. I need to sit down."

She slung his arm over her shoulder and supported him to the tack box. As he crumpled onto it, Brad came into the barn, propelling the now-handcuffed Garza ahead of him.

"Marcus, you okay? What happened in here? Who's the woman on the floor?" Brad asked.

"Magda." They both answered at the same time.

"Here, snap these cuffs on her. She's under arrest too." Brad pulled a second set of handcuffs out of his pocket and tossed them to Dee. "Let me get this one into a patrol car, and I'll come back for her."

He dragged a limping Garza toward the parking lot in front of the stable.

"Is he arresting Magda for jumping on me? How did he know I was struggling with her? And who's the guy in cuffs?" Marcus's words slurred.

"I'm not sure about Magda, but the guy is Jaime Garza." Now that she had the opportunity to relieve herself of the lies, she blurted out everything without taking a breath. "Garza has been stalking me, and I've been running for the past year. I'm sorry I didn't tell you the truth. I was afraid I might need to run again and didn't want to get you and Kaitlyn involved in this mess. Please forgive me for not telling you sooner."

"Something told me I needed to come help you, but Magda got in the way. I'm glad Brad was here." His head drooped forward. A few seconds later he glanced at Dee. "Wait, why is he he...he...here?" He slurred the words.

Dee place both hands on his shoulders. *He sounds intoxicated.* "Are you okay?"

"Yes, she knocked the wind out of me. Tell, tell me what is going on."

"Brad discovered Garza has been watching me from the property behind this farm. He set this whole thing in motion so he could catch Garza. I was wired, so we got the whole confession on tape." She slid onto the tack box next to Marcus. The adrenaline had finally fizzled out.

"Good for that. But I still don't understand about, about, about Magda."

"She isn't really Magda." Brad returned and knelt next to the unconscious woman on the ground. "Her real name is Svetlana Jovanovich, Magda's cousin. She's the killer of the men here in Palm Beach, and she's wanted in Russia and several other countries in Europe. She's suspected of killing her cousin and using her passport and credentials to come the U.S. to escape authorities over there. She planned to frame you for the murders, but she didn't count on me running her DNA so fast. She stole the Ketamine from your truck, Marcus. Her prints were all over it. Speaking of which, is that a syringe there on the floor? She didn't get any into you, did she?"

"She hit me with something. It's probably why the barn is spinning."

"Ketamine? Horse tranquilizer?" Dee asked. "No wonder you sound drunk. How much would it take to harm a human? Call an ambulance, Brad. They need to check him out."

"It's on the way," Brad assured her.

"I don't feel so good." Marcus sunk forward, collapsing toward the floor.

Both Dee and Brad caught him before he tumbled off the tack box. Dee wrapped her arm around him, holding him upright.

"You need the ambulance, Dee. There's blood on your shirt. Did he stab you out there?" Brad asked.

"He might have nicked me but in the heat of the moment I put it out of my mind. It seems to have stopped bleeding."

"Still, you both need the paramedics. My prisoners will also. You must have a wicked right hook to keep her out so long," Brad said to Dee.

"Stuff I learned from my cop cousins. When the stalking started, I took a few self-defense classes."

"Here come the paramedics. Can you hold Marcus up while I deal with the prisoners?"

"I've got him." *And please, God, take care of him. I don't want to lose him now that You've helped me find him.*

One of the paramedics attended to Marcus and Dee while another one placed an ammonia inhalant under Svetlana's nose. She sat up coughing and spitting. They strapped her on a gurney, and Brad cuffed her to the rail. She muttered something that sounded Russian, as they wheeled her away.

Another gurney came for Marcus. Dee grasped his hand as the paramedics wheeled him outside to a second ambulance. He hovered between coherence and sleep. They cleaned and bandaged up Dee's side, saying the wound was superficial.

Protocol would not allow her to ride in the ambulance with Marcus so she followed them to the hospital in her truck.

Chapter Twenty-One

The next morning Dee drove Marcus home from the hospital. Her ribs were sore but she didn't feel the pain because of her happiness to have her stalker nightmare behind her. She'd called Silva to tell her about the events of the night before and ask her to feed the horses. Dee now had responsibility for the entire stable.

She sighed heavily. The sooner she went through the boxes in the tack room the sooner she could locate the owners of the horses. Calling them to explain the circumstances of "Magda's" departure and asking if they would like them to remain in training with Dee would have to start this afternoon.

Marcus drew her close as they walked toward the house. His arm draped over her shoulders. She glanced up at him. A sly smile crossed his lips. They hadn't spoken of anything other than the events of the previous night so she questioned the silly look.

As they neared the front door, she heard the running patter of feet down the hallway. *That explains the smile.*

"Daddy! Daddy, you're home. Did you have an emergency last night?"

Marcus knelt and caught the little girl in his arms for a big hug. "Yes, an emergency. I've brought Dee home with me."

"Oh, Dee!" Kaitlyn turned and hugged her around the waist. "Can we go ride today?"

"Perhaps later," he said. "I have some things to discuss with Dee first. Why don't you put a video in, and we'll come watch it with you when we're done?"

"Okay, but then I want to go to the barn." She scrambled off.

"Girls and their horses." Dee looked up at Marcus.

"Yeah, girls and their horses." He led her to his home office.

The screen of his computer still displayed the article he'd found about her before he'd bolted out the door the night before. "Should I continue to call you Dee, or Ileana?"

She gave him a big grin. "I've answered to both my entire life. Even my mother often didn't call us by the right names."

"I guess that made it easier to assume your sister's identity. I wish you'd confided in me."

"I wanted to. I planned to, but you quit taking my calls and texts."

"I always meant to ask you questions, but the time never seemed right. I'm sorry I didn't give you a chance to explain things but it wouldn't have made a difference."

She cast her gaze to the floor. So he really didn't care about her the way she cared about him. Brad must have been wrong. Still, she thought from the way Marcus had clung to her hand last night and kept her close to him this morning that he did care for her. "Well, I guess I should be going. I have a stable of horses that need attending. I'd love for you to bring Kaitlyn to the barn to ride. In fact, anytime she wants to come out while she's off for Christmas vacation it's fine with me."

"Dee—I mean, *Ileana*. I'm gonna have to get used to that name." He drew her into an embrace. "It wouldn't have made a difference if you had told me or not. I think I fell in love with you that first night while we doctored the horse. If I'd known, I could have protected you. Of course, as you made quite clear last night, you didn't need my protection. Instead you protected me from that woman. Thank you for that, by the way."

"You're welcome. Something in the back of my mind told me she was bad news, but I never suspected her as a killer." She snuggled in closer before glancing up into his eyes. "And I should have trusted you. You never gave me a reason that I couldn't... Wait, what did you say about that first night?"

"I fell in love with you. I didn't want to acknowledge it even when everyone around me could see how I felt. And Kailyn sure is in love with you."

"I love her so much."

"We go together. We're a set, and my mother is part of the set, if you'll have us."

"*Have* you?"

"I love you. I thought I'd lost you when that man grabbed you. I didn't know if you had moved on because of my stupidity or if you needed my help. But God knew and He told me as clearly as if He'd hit me with a baseball bat. I never want to lose you. I want you by my side, and I want you to help me raise Kaitlyn. Do you think you could do that?"

"Oh, Marcus! I've loved you since that first night, and every minute we've spent together made my love grow stronger. I'd love nothing more than to be with you."

"Come with me." He tugged her out of the room and waltzed her down the hall.

At the entrance to the living room, he stopped and hugged her close. Kaitlyn sat on the couch watching a movie.

He bent to whisper in Ileana's ear. "I love you, and I want to marry you." His words tickled her ear and her heart threatened to jump out of her chest.

"Oh, Marcus," she whispered back.

He pointed up to lintel of the doorway. A sprig of mistletoe hung there. He gathered her up into his arms and the kiss went straight to her toes. She'd never look at mistletoe the same way again.

Epilogue

Dee, now happy to be called by her real name, Ileana, admired the illustration of Roscoe and Rocket Man that Kaitlyn had sketched for her. From there her gaze traveled to the diamond that graced her left ring finger. Marcus had slid it on the night before.

He'd taken a few days off work after being released from the hospital. They'd spent every one of them together with Kaitlyn enjoying horses and each other.

Ileana kept an eye on Kaitlyn as she rode Roscoe in the arena. She really loved that little girl. Kaitlyn had been so happy when they told her the news. Now Ileana had a family and a stable of horses to train. Ileana's mother and father sat nearby enjoying the view of girl and horse. God had blessed her richly after the trials of the last year.

Thank you, Lord Jesus, for watching out for me this past year. Thank you for bringing me here and finding Marcus and Kaitlyn. Thank you for my family and all the rich blessings You bestow upon us. Continue keeping us safe in your arms. Amen.

Marcus put his arm around her shoulders. "Feeling good about being able to have your family here?"

"I feel wonderful. Garza is going back to prison, and Svetlana will soon be on her way back to Russia to stand trial for the crimes she committed there. I still can't believe she's a serial killer."

"I feel wonderful. Garza is going back to prison, and Svetlana will soon be on her way back to Russia to stand trial for the crimes she committed there. I still can't believe she's a serial killer."

"Right? Sounds like a movie plot."

"One I'd never want to see," she muttered.

"I'm glad the owners of the other horses decided to leave them with you. You have a whole barn full of talented dressage mounts."

"Thanks to you." She pressed a kiss to his cheek. "I'm glad we found the true owners."

"Now I have to pin you down on a wedding date." He wiggled his eye brows, causing her to giggle.

"How about New Year's Day? My family is all here in the States, so no extra travel. I bet my father can pull some strings and get Hialeah Race Course Pavilion for a venue." She caught the sound of his elevated heartbeat against her ear. She snuggled in closer.

"Are you sure? You don't want to wait until you can plan a big wedding?" With his finger, he tilted her head up to gaze into her eyes.

"I've waited long enough to find you. I don't need a big fancy wedding either. I couldn't have imagined when I came here that God had a plan in mind, but I'm sure of it now. God sent his Son on Christmas Day and He sent you to become my new family. New Year's Day will be the start of a new year and a whole new life for both of us. I think it's part of His plan."

"Oh, Ileana, I do love the way you think." He peered skyward and whispered, "Thank you, Lord, for these blessings."

"Yes, Lord," she said in her own prayer. "Thank you for your protection. Thank you for my finding this place and thank you for this wonderful man. Amen."

Acknowledgements

I cannot thank enough the amazing staff at Champagne Book Group. Everyone is so helpful in putting these books together. Thank you, Cassie Knight, for enjoying the book enough to offer to publish it. Thank you to my editor, Nikki Andrews, for your exceptional advice and 'picking my brain' to get the most out our work together.

Thank you to my beta readers, Craig Hastings, KC Gallagher, Diane Carlson, Nancy Weider, Steve Grossman, and Jamie Lynn Boothe. Each of you gave a great critic that helped make each page better.

Over the years I've had some wonderful horses and instructors who shaped my horsemanship skills. Each of you provided a little real life into the personality of the characters and horses in this book.

About the Author

Horses have been a part of Kat Canfield's life since childhood. She has been riding and competing in the Dressage ring for more years than she wants to admit. Now competing in the upper levels, she would be the first to tell you it is a long journey.

To help pay for her horse obsession, she worked as a police officer in South Florida and retired several years ago. And as expected, she rode on the Mounted Patrol. She plans to include some of those heartwarming experiences of working with a horse partner in upcoming novels.

Kat lives in the heart of the winter equestrian world, Wellington, Florida with her husband, horses, and cats. If you ever visit, you may see her go down centerline at a local horse show.

Kat loves to hear from her readers. You can find and connect with her at the links below.

Website/Blog: https://www.katcanfield.com
Facebook: https://www.facebook.com/authorKatCanfield
Twitter: @KatCanfield and @CanfieldKat

~ * ~

Thank you for taking the time to read *Running with Horses*. We hope you enjoyed this delightful story as much as we did. If you did, please tell your friends, and leave a review. Reviews support authors and ensure they continue to bring readers books to love and enjoy.

Turn the page for a peek inside *Moose Ridge: Ending to Beginning*.

All beginnings lead to endings, but some endings bring beginnings.

Attending Harvard was the first positive thing in Jazmine's life in a long time. While a member of an affluent New York family, her mother died when she was five and her father went to jail when she was twelve. She lost everything leaving her a ward of the state and a foster child. Meeting Michael, a medical student was the second positive thing.

Now she's looking forward to the perfect life she dreamed about. Leaving Boston and New York behind, the only cities she's ever known, she's on her way to join Michael and start their new life together in Wyoming where he will complete his neurosurgical residency. She's had a lot of hard blows, but now all her hard work and dedication are going to pay off.

The day has arrived for her and Michael to start the beginning of their future life together. Jazmine just knows, for once, everything is going to be exactly how she always dreamed it could be.

Then she's handed the letter.

Chapter One

My excitement builds as I rush down the jetway, trying not to bump into anyone. The four-hour flight from Boston was bad enough, but now everyone seems determined to get in my way. I struggle to remain calm but knowing this is the start of the next chapter in Michael's and my life together doesn't help. It will be perfect, and I can't wait.

Michael moved here three months ago. After medical school, he accepted a neurosurgical residency in Wyoming. I stayed behind in Boston while he got things organized out here. We'd been inseparable for close to six years so it was a long three months, but I knew it would be worth it. This move is the start of something big.

As I reach the main terminal, I check my phone for the text Michael said he'd send telling me where to meet him. My heart flips as

I see his message:

Can't be there to pick you up so sent Rick. He'll meet you at baggage claim. He's tall and should have a dark cowboy hat on.

I freeze and read it again. What could have happened? I push this thought aside realizing Michael's no doubt tied up at the hospital. I'll need to get used to the demanding life of a doctor. Now I only need to find a tall man in a dark cowboy hat. How difficult can that be? I race through the terminal, not really taking notice of the many people I dodge around.

At baggage claim, I find the carousel my bags should be at and, while waiting, I search for a tall man in a cowboy hat. This can't be right. Almost every man is wearing a cowboy hat, and most of them are dark. Right then, I hear a voice behind me. "Are you Miss Strake? Miss Jazmine Strake?"

I turn to find a tall, slender man, about mid-twenties, wearing the prescribed dark cowboy hat. "Yes, I am. Are you Rick, my ride?"

"Yes, ma'am. Are your bags here yet?"

Ma'am? I doubt I'm even a few years older than him. "Please, call me Jazmine. They should be coming soon." The carousel starts and bags are moving along in front of us. I spot one of mine and reach for it, pulling it off.

"I'll take that, ma'am," Rick says, taking it from my grasp. "Are there any more?"

"Just one more, and really, you can call me Jazmine." I spot my other bag and point to it. "Here it comes."

Before I can, he grabs it and, with my two bags in tow, turns and motions to the exits. "I'm parked across the way. It's not far."

We exit the terminal, and the cold hits me as he leads me across a large parking lot. I thought he said it wasn't far? After a long trek to the middle of the lot, he stops at a pickup parked among the rows of pickups. I stifle a laugh. I'm definitely not in Boston anymore.

He stows my bags as I climb into the passenger side. Not a simple task given my short dress. I saw it in a store window last week and knew it'd be perfect for seeing Michael for the first time in months. For reminding him what he'd been missing.

Once inside, the warmth from the truck's heater helps thaw out my legs. Maybe the dress is not the best for Wyoming? As Rick drives away from the airport, I watch the views passing, which further solidifies we're not in Boston anymore. That's okay. I'm here to start my new life with Michael.

As we park in the drive, I see the house for the first time. Depression threatens to overcome me, but I fight it back. Michael found this meager house in the country, wanting a place to relax from what promised to be grueling days ahead. I remind myself this is temporary. We will make do.

Rick helps me inside and sets my bags by the sofa as I scan the room. It's modest and contains a few pieces of drab furniture arranged on the speckled gray linoleum covered floor. There is a gray couch, a small, scarred coffee table, and an old chrome and Formica dinette table with two vinyl cushioned chairs.

On the far wall is an open metal cabinet which appears to have woodgrain contact paper covering it. Two more chairs are on each side, and an old TV is on top. A gray metal wardrobe sits by the front door in place of a closet. The room's distinct lack of color, thanks to the dull beige paint, and the musty smell speak volumes on its lack of attraction. The gray curtains covering the windows and a single frameless mirror above the TV are the extent of the decorations.

"It's not the Taj Mahal, but it should work for now," Rick says.

"It is rather basic," I agree while surveying the minute room.

He interrupts before more dread appears. "Dr. Stenson said your boxes are in the back bedroom."

"Oh, perfect. Did Michael say how long he'd be?" The title of doctor makes me smile, which helps since I'm seeing little reason to be positive.

"Ah, no, ma'am." Something in his voice causes me to break off my survey of the room and turn in his direction. He's holding out an envelope. "Dr. Stenson said to give you this. He said it will explain things."

"Explain what things?" Negative thoughts flood my brain.

"I'm not sure. He said to give it to you when we got here. I'm sorry, but I'm on the late shift and need to go to make it in time."

The sound of the door closing behind Rick intensifies my sensation of being alone. I stand in what they call a great room, but it doesn't appear great to me. I fight to keep the overwhelming dread from consuming me, trying to concentrate on the positive. I can do this. We can do this. It's temporary. The means to our future. All our hard work and sacrifice for his schooling is about to pay off. Yet here I stand, and no Michael.

The envelope Rick gave me doesn't help my thoughts to remain positive and magnifies the silence closing in around me. Jazmine is written in bold letters on the front, mocking me. Fearing what it might hold, I'm reluctant to open it and eliminate any chance I'm wrong. Why do I jump to the negative? This could be anything. Maybe my worst fears are nothing but that. However, with my past life and its disappointments,

I always expect my worst fears to come true. He could be working the late shift at the hospital? But why wouldn't he call? If there was an emergency and he's assisting surgery, he couldn't call. But a letter?

My pulse races as I stare at the envelope in my shaking hand. I know I must open it. Breathing is hard, and I'm sure I hear my heart pounding over the whooshing sound in my ears.

With a diminishing thread of hope, I open the envelope and remove the pages. I focus on the words while fighting to stay positive. As I read, tears fill my eyes.

Dear Jazmine,

I trust Rick found you. I'm sure you might be a little shocked and I'm sorry, but I have thrilling news.

About a month ago, the head surgeon, Dr. Williams, wanted to see me. He said he was impressed with me and that he'd been talking with a colleague about me.

To cut to the chase, there was a position for me in the residency program at UCLA Medical Center. He explained my talents demanded more than they could provide here and told me all about the program there. I couldn't let this pass.

The next few weeks were a blur. I wanted to tell you but didn't want to jinx it. Last week, all the details were finalized. The one issue was I needed to be there before you arrived. Not my choice, but I couldn't say no.

It was obvious this was fate since everything just fell into place. I have a place to live with Dr. Williams' daughter, Felicia, who is also going to UCLA for her psychiatric residency. We hit it off right away.

I needed to be there by Thursday, meaning yesterday, and it being a two-day drive, Felicia and I left Tuesday. Sorry I couldn't let you know sooner, but things snowballed and before I knew it, I had to leave. You'd already sent back the signed lease for the house, so I left it in your name. Now you're set. It's not much, but a year will go fast. You can find another place then. I was going to call to tell you not to come, but I knew how much you wanted to get out of Boston. Now you are. I used part of the money you sent for the first and last month's rent and to get the utilities started. The boxes are in the back bedroom, and I stocked a few groceries.

Jazmine, it's incredible how everything worked out for us. We're away from Boston and able to start our new lives. I appreciate all you've done and know you're thrilled with this fantastic opportunity for me. You're a special friend.

Now I leave you to start your quest for the perfect life. You deserve it. Take care, and with any luck, we'll meet down the road.

Michael

My heart creeps into my throat and warm, salty droplets spill down my cheeks. My legs weaken, and my knees buckle. The couch breaks my fall as I land on it. My eyes blur from tears as I read the letter over and over, hoping I'm missing something, but deep down I know I'm not. I thought ours was a close relationship, I thought we were about to start our perfect life. He makes it sound like this was nothing more than one friend helping another. I left everything behind in Boston to be with him, and now he wants me to start my quest? What happened to our quest?

My sobs rack my body, and while I wipe my eyes yet again with my already damp palms, I consider the possibility I'll never recover from this dark, desolate place.

The pages fall from my shaking hands, floating to the floor. I can't handle this. I've never felt so abandoned, so hopeless, so alone. Unable to stop, I slump to the side and end up lying on the couch in a ball. My arms hold on tight to everything I have, which is me, nothing but me.

~ * ~

I wake in a dark room. Somehow, I found my way to a bedroom. My coat is over me but being cold and seeing my boxes in the moonlight, I stumble to reach them. After rummaging through, I drag out a blanket and wrap it around me, tumbling back on the bed. Once again, I'm all alone.

My head knows he's gone, but something has pulverized my insides. There's nothing left. How could he think we were nothing but friends hanging out? I thought what we shared was real. How did I not see this coming? The tears continue as my mind searches for answers. Was he biding time until a better offer came along? Someone he could upgrade to, like Felicia?

There's been a lot of sorrow in my life, but nothing like this. The pain in my chest is excruciating, and I hope it's a heart attack and I'm never able to leave this bed.

I wake again with the blanket wrapped around me, but it's little comfort. It's a struggle to rise, but I make my way out to the front room. In the pale moonlight it's even more depressing, and my gaze lights on the pages of Michael's letter spread out on the floor. My legs give way and I drop, but there's no couch to land on this time, nothing but the floor.

With my legs against my chest, I pull the blanket tight. I should get up, but I have no energy.

While I lie, the tears flow again as thoughts of Michael fill my mind. The joy he brought back to my life. How he helped me to open myself to someone else. To concentrate on the positives. The fun we shared shopping for bargains and adding our own touches to our apartment. How for the first time since my father, I felt someone deeply cared about me. We shared everything and spent every moment together. Even when buried in our own school work we were together, across the table from each other. There was a home and someone to share it with, and that was all we needed. Now, there's no Michael. I'm alone.

I must have dozed off again, because the cold seeping through the blanket from the hard, worn linoleum wakes me. I struggle to get up, my stiff body refusing to cooperate. The realization there's dim light coming through the dingy windows gets through my stupor. Crawling to the couch, I gather my strength to stand behind it and gaze about the room. The dull light of the breaking morning does nothing to improve what is around me.

Not knowing where to go but needing to move, I take the few steps to walk past the couch. I trip on my bags and grab the couch to stay upright. My gaze again finds the pages of Michael's letter spread across the floor. Tears fill my eyes, and knowing I'm losing it, I stumble back to the bedroom, toppling into the bed.

~ * ~

When I wake again, sunlight fills the room. My phone shows it's close to noon, but the shock is it's Sunday. My flight here was on Friday, which means I slept through Saturday and most of this morning. I can't remember ever feeling like this, not when my mother died, or when my father left. Not even when I lost everything and moved into a foster home. This pain will never end.

It's not far, but stumbling to the meager bathroom adds to my misery. The hideous image in the flaking mirror startles me. My makeup is smeared, my hair's a mess, and my eyes are red and puffy. The revolting reflection matches how I feel.

There isn't much here. The small, worn sink below the mirror has visible cracks and two tatty faucets. The toilet crammed beside it has a seat but no lid, and there's a large tank mounted above it with a hanging chain. Across from these is what you could call a bathtub. It's miniscule, and there's not even a shower.

Maybe a bath will help? After turning on the water, I stagger to the bedroom to collect what's needed and return.

The water is getting warm, but I can't find the switch to shut the drain. There's a rubber stopper on a chain attached to the faucet. How old is this place? After plugging the drain, I undress. As I slip my dress off, I remember how excited I was seeing it in the store window, thinking Michael would be even more excited when he saw it on me. Now he never will. Not that he would care what I wore. It's only me, after all. The loser who sacrificed so much for him. The naïve little girl whose dreams will never be real. I want to toss the dress aside, but it's not its fault I can't attract anyone. That's all on me. I'm the one no one can stand to be around.

In the bedroom, I slide the thin, gray curtain covering the small closet open and hang the dress. It's a good thing I don't have a lot of clothes. Back in the bathroom, I step into the bath. While trying to lie back and let the heat soak into my body, its minute size becomes painfully obvious. As soon as I contort my body into a semi-comfortable position, I need to sit up to turn off the water. At least it's not a long reach.

I try not to think about my dismal life. My attempt fails and soon I'm crying again. Maybe I should end it all, let myself sink below the water and let go. No, that's not me.

The water is cooling, so I drain some and add more. The water coming out is colder than what is in the tub so I shut it off. With hardly any water left and my body shivering, I know my bath is over.

While drying off, I catch my reflection again. At least my face is no longer smeared with makeup. I brush my auburn hair the best I can, which takes time since it's well down my back. Michael bugged me about the time I wasted on my hair, but I prefer it long.

After returning to the bedroom, I put on cut-offs and my favorite shirt. It was my father's and all I have left of his. It's old and several buttons are missing so it might reveal more than it should. Not that anyone is here to see. I could parade around nude.

Might have to, since my budget didn't allow much for clothes. While packing, I'd thought this would change since Michael would have an income here. Now, though, what I have must last even longer.

My suitcase is open where I left it, with the boxes from Boston off to the side. They contain everything I own. Might as well sort out my meager belongings. It's all on me and will be from now on. What else do I have to fill my time? The tears start again.

Since there isn't much, it doesn't take long to unpack. It's a good thing I have so few clothes since there isn't much in the way of drawer space in the four-drawer scarred wooden dresser. In the kitchen, I find the basics, but knowing how to cook would help. Three frozen dinners are in the freezer, so I won't starve right away. When I discover there's coffee, I get my old coffee maker going and soon have a cup poured. I amble through to the living room, desperate not to let the drabness affect me.

With few choices, I flop on the musty couch and contemplate what is next. Michael's letter on the floor in front of me doesn't help. The tears are stinging my eyes again when I hear a knock. Before I can get up, there's another. After setting my cup on the bare coffee table, I hurry to the front door and open it. A man stands outside the porch door. He waves, smiling. The icy air making itself known makes me conscious of my missing buttons.

I grab my coat and open the porch door, finding to my amazement a cowboy, complete with hat, boots, and a heavy coat I think they call a duster. I didn't know cowboys still exist.

I motion him into the enclosed porch and he steps in, removing his hat and releasing his mid-length light brown hair with its lighter blond highlights. He's standing much taller than my five-six, and even though he's wearing a heavy coat, appears more than fit. "Afternoon. I'm Jason Withers. My grandmother sent brownies to welcome you to the neighborhood."

"Neighborhood? I have neighbors?"

He chuckles. "She's the closest and lives over the hill. She wanted to welcome you, but she's not real mobile and asked me to bring these by," he says, holding out a covered plate.

"Oh! Well, thank you. I'm Jazmine. Jazmine Strake," I tell him, taking the plate. "You say your grandmother lives nearby? Do you live with her?"

He smiles. "No! She'd think I was trying to take care of her."

"Well, it was nice of you to bring this by. I'll return the plate as soon as I can." That is a farewell. I'm hoping he'll leave.

"No hurry, take your time. I understand you're here alone?"

I'm not sure if he's trying to make conversation or what, but he seems nice. "Yes, the original plans didn't work out."

"I heard they offered your friend a better position."

How small is this community? Does everyone know? "Would you like some coffee and brownies?" Why did I ask that?

"No, I shouldn't come in, but thank you, I enjoyed meeting you. Let me give you this. It's my number, in case you need anything."

As I glance at the card, I'm startled by his title. "Doctor? You're a doctor?" I pause, appalled at my tone. "I'm sorry, I didn't mean it like it sounded."

"No problem. I'm not the type of doctor you're thinking. I'm a DVM, Doctor of Veterinarian Medicine. A large animal vet. You can still call me though, if you need something."

"Well, thank you. I might take you up on it."

"You should. Again, welcome."

He turns to leave and I half expect a horse to be close by, but no. Instead, there's a monstrosity of a truck out front. I've never seen a pickup that big. Not that I've seen that many. His name on the door with the words "Veterinarian Services" along with his phone number makes me snicker. I guess everyone has his number. He backs out and gives a wave before making the turn onto the road.

Not knowing why, I watch him disappear down the road toward who knows what. Fingers of depression crawl across my skin once again. Here I am, in the middle of nowhere, and I don't know which direction to go if I needed to go somewhere. Besides, I have no way to get there even if I did. How much more pathetic can my life be?

Back inside, I slip a brownie off the plate. It's rich and chewy and oh so tasty. I cram the entire thing in my mouth. Once in the kitchen, I set them on the worn, gray counter and leave before eating them all. Quite possible, considering my current mood. After taking the three steps to get to the living room, I stand still, thinking what to do. My image in the wall mirror is a fright as I realize my shirt reveals more than I thought. Why didn't I close my coat?

No wonder he didn't want to come inside the house. There's little left to the imagination. Might as well not even be wearing a shirt. I'm sure word will spread far and wide. In no time it'll be everywhere—how the big city harlot moved to town and flashed the local vet. Perfect, just what I need. As I collapse on the couch, the tears pooling behind my eyes pour unabated down my cheeks.

After more time wallowing in self-pity than I want known, I must do something. What is there to do? The memory of the brownies has me heading for the kitchen. Now I'm not a cook in any way, shape, or form, but I can make one thing well. Chocolate chip cookies are my forte. They were Michael's favorite, and I discover he bought everything I need to make them

While starting on the dough, my pathetic brain reminds me how he would sneak a cookie when they came out of the oven and was always asking for more. I tell myself to stop thinking about him, but I can't help thinking my life is over. I shake my head, trying to clear my thoughts, and concentrate on the cookies.

Not impressed by the grungy appearance of the old kitchen sink, I try scrubbing it while the cookies are in the archaic oven but find what I thought was grime and dirt are marks of wear. Knowing the stains are permanent helps me feel better, and I decide the sink should work for washing my hair. After retrieving my shampoo and a towel from the bathroom, I do the best I can with what I have to work with while monitoring the cookies. Once they are done, and with my hair in a towel, I head for the bedroom and my hair dryer.

With the cookies finished and my hair dry, it's time to do something, anything. After removing the brownies and washing the plate, I place a generous portion of cookies on it and wrap it in foil. In the bedroom to change, I remember how cold my legs were when I arrived in the short dress. This time I opt for a cute pair of jeans, a nice blouse, and one of my favorite sweaters. Knowing boots will work best, I put on my knee-high black leather ones with the four-inch heels. It's time to venture out.

My mind screams: What are you thinking? Where will you go? Why even try? Just stay here in your miserable existence. But that's not me. I must move forward. I must push through this. Regardless of how pitiful I am.

My first adventure outside will be to meet my neighbor.

Once I leave the house, it's obvious my Boston coat might not be enough for the weather around here. Even being October, the cold is noticeable. While it's more for fashion than function, my coat has a hood of sorts and my scarf helps a little. I forge ahead, determined to accomplish my task.

At the road, I pause, not sure in which direction to turn. The road goes over a hill to my left and levels out to my right. Left it must be since Jason said it was over the hill. I start with a purposeful stride. He said she's my neighbor. How far can it be?

After what feels like miles, I reach a driveway. Like in western movies, there's a sign stretching across above it is reading "MOOSE RIDGE" and a sizeable house set back from the road with two large barns visible in the distance. It's a large, rustic, western-style house built with stone and timber. This must be it, since there's no other house in sight. Pushed on by the cold, I hurry along the long driveway.

At the top of the porch steps, I can't find a doorbell so I knock on the frame. After a few moments, there's movement behind the curtained window, and the inside wooden door opens to reveal a mature lady. Once she sees me, she hurries out and ushers me into the enclosed porch. "Well, where did you come from?" Her cheery voice brings a smile.

"I'm Jazmine, your neighbor. Jason dropped off the brownies, and I wanted to return your plate."

"Oh, my dear, you didn't have to so soon." She takes the plate while glancing out toward the driveway. "Where's your vehicle? You didn't walk here, did you?"

"It's okay, I'm used to walking."

"Come inside, and we'll see what's on this plate." She heads in without giving me a chance to say I should leave. Tentative at first, I follow her through the front door, thinking it's a splendid idea to get warm before heading back. She calls out, "These cookies smell magnificent. We must try them. Would you like something to drink? Coffee or tea?"

"I should go," I say, walking the direction she went. As I walk through the front room, I notice how homey it feels. The braided rugs spread across the shiny wood floor have similar colors to the elegant drapes covering the many windows. The style carries on as I walk past the wide staircase and across the dining room with its massive two column dark wood dining table surrounded by matching chairs and a huge hutch filled with delicate china and crystal.

"Why? You have a hot date?" Right, like that will ever happen. "You can't leave until we sample these cookies. Did you make them?"

I find her in the large kitchen where she's setting the plate of cookies on the wooden table. "Well, yes. I didn't want to return an empty plate."

"Then your mother taught you proper. Many seem to overlook it nowadays. Which do you prefer? Coffee or tea?"

"Coffee is fine."

"Have a seat and I'll get it." She indicates a chair by the table and walks to the counter where a coffee maker sits.

The warmth of the room provides a cozy and comfortable atmosphere. I drape my coat on the back of the chair before sitting.

She returns to the table with the pot and two mugs. "I like your sweater. Did you make it?"

I chuckle. "No. I'm afraid the cookies are the total of my homemaking skills."

While pouring our coffee, she glances my way. "Well, the rosy color is picture-perfect for you. Highlights your blue eyes. Now, I must apologize for not introducing myself. Guess my manners are slacking. I'm Sadie, or Conswella Sandra Stephenson, but I prefer Sadie. Jazmine's a pleasant name. Is it a family name?"

"No, it was my mother's favorite flower. She used the z instead of the s."

"Well, it suits you. You're as pretty as any flower I've ever seen."

"Thank you." Not liking the subjects of my mother or me, I need to find another. "Is Conswella a family name?"

"No, it was the name of my mother's childhood friend. She vowed to use it for her first-born daughter. Sandra was my grandmother's name. I'm sure you don't want to hear all this."

"Honest, I don't mind. You were the first child, then?"

"Heavens, no. There were four boys before me." She places a mug in front of me. "I was the only girl, though. After me were three more boys. Do you want sugar or milk?"

"Sugar will work. My, eight children? Must have made for interesting times."

"Yes, we had our moments. However, my mother wished I was more like the original Conswella. I was too much of a tomboy. What did she expect? I grew up with seven boys on a ranch," she says, chuckling. "Glad you chose coffee. Afraid you'd be a tea drinker when I heard you were from Boston." Grinning, she slides the sugar my way.

"No, not me. Mind you, I didn't always live in Boston. I'm from New York City." Why do I feel so comfortable talking with her? "The coffee is delicious. Seems to have a pinch of something."

"A little cinnamon makes it special," she says, and I notice a slightly mischievous expression as she takes a bite of cookie.

"It does. I'll have to try it."

"A hint is all you need. I'm sure you'll get it right. Anyone who can make cookies like these will have no problem."

"Thank you, but these are the full extent of my baking expertise."

"I doubt that. These are excellent. Did your mother teach you to make them?"

"No, it was trial and error." I don't want to get into my past.

"Well, you hit on a winner. I hope I'm able to make them last. I might eat them all tonight."

"You go right ahead. There's more where these came from."

"If you're from New York City, why did you move to Boston?"

"I went to college there."

"There are fine schools in Boston. Which did you attend?"

"Harvard."

"Harvard's a wonderful school. Were you an undergrad?" I'm sure she's doesn't mean to be nosy.

"Yes and continued to get my MBA and MSF." I enjoy sharing this, even if it may sound like bragging.

"An MBA is impressive, but what's an MSF?"

"It's a Master of Science in Finance. It complements my MBA."

While we chat, I glance around. It's such a sizeable house, I can't believe she lives here alone. I wonder if she gets lonesome in such an enormous place. Even in my matchbox of a house, I feel alone.

"This was my parents' home," she says.

"It's nice. Large enough for eight children, for sure. Do your brothers live close by?"

"No. I'm the last of the family remaining. My two oldest brothers never came back from the war. One died at Pearl Harbor and the other in Europe during the Battle of the Bulge. Two other brothers died while serving. One in Korea, and the youngest in Vietnam."

"I'm sorry, I didn't mean to pry. That must have been heartbreaking to lose so many to war."

"They happened years apart, and war didn't take them all. Another died of influenza, the same as our mother, and another in a car accident. The brother before me died of cancer five years ago."

Knowing her thoughts are on her many losses, I feel the need to say something. "I'm sorry to cause you to remember them. I didn't realize."

"No, it's fine. I think of them often. They played an enormous part in making me who I am, and I'm ever so grateful they were in my life, even if for nothing more than a brief time."

She's a resilient woman. I wonder what her secret is?

We sit for a while before she asks what I'm sure she's been wanting to since I arrived. "Now, why are you here living down the road from me? Not the dream location for such a beautiful girl, not to mention a Harvard grad. Why Wyoming and why Cole Creek Road?"

"Not my first choice," I say with a giggle. "Things didn't follow the plan."

"I know part of the story. Not much goes unnoticed around here. I'm sorry things didn't work out. Remember, when one door closes, God opens another. It's what I've found. You wait. There is something delightful coming for you. Mark my words. In less than a year, you won't even recognize your old life."

"Well, I'll agree my old life didn't turn out how I thought it would."

"Don't worry, dear. God has a plan. You need to allow Him to work things out. You'll see." I guess she's one of those who believe in a god. With living all her life in such a rural area, I doubt there was much opportunity for an education or experience with the actual world. I'll overlook it. She's a sweet lady, and I don't want to offend her.

We sit, and she describes the surrounding area. It's obvious I'll need to figure out how I'll get places. With my cup empty, I let her know I should get back. It's getting dark out. She walks with me to the front and helps me with my coat. I thank her again for the brownies, coffee, and the visit.

Just before I leave, she hands me a flashlight. "Here, you'll need this. Don't want you wandering around in this cold. Now you be careful!"

"I can't take this," I say, holding it out.

"It's a loan. You'll bring it back tomorrow."

This catches me by surprise. "I'm coming back tomorrow?"

"Of course. You need to go shopping and don't know your way. In the morning we'll go shopping."

It's not a request per se, more an order, but in a nice way. She's lost me. "How? I don't have a car."

"Not a problem. You'll take my truck tonight. It's parked on the side. Keys are in it."

"What? I can't do that." Why would she do this for someone she just met?

"Why not? You drive, don't you? Now, you need a vehicle, and my old pickup is sitting there doing nothing. You take it tonight, be back in the morning at nine, and we'll have a beautiful day. Now drive careful."

Seems I have no choice in the matter. "Okay. I guess."

To my amazement, she hugs me. I've not gotten many hugs in my life and never one like she gives. It feels so enjoyable I'm close to tears. I'm quick to say thank you again and head out to find her old truck. She watches me through the bright gingham draped windows surrounding the porch as I walk to the driveway and give her a slight wave.

The pickup concerns me. My sum total of rides in a truck is one, and it was last Friday. There's one parked near the back of the house, but it doesn't appear old. Climbing in, one concern vanishes seeing it's an automatic. The keys are in the ignition, like she said, and I try it.

It starts right away. Why does this surprise me? The heater is on max, and the windshield is clear. Here goes nothing. Once it's in reverse, I back out with care.

The drive to my place is shorter than expected. Guess I didn't walk miles after all. I bundle tight and climb out, taking the keys. Once inside, I put the flashlight where I'll remember it. Not wanting to lie in bed letting my mind remind me of my pitiful state, I check out the TV.

There are more channels than expected. I come across the Hallmark Movie channel, which will do. I'm thrilled to find the small microwave on the kitchen counter works and put in one of my frozen dinners. One down, two to go. Maybe shopping tomorrow isn't a bad idea.

After the second movie finishes, I shut off the TV. Another day in my catastrophe of a life is complete. As my eyes close to sleep, I must admit there were delightful times today. Maybe tomorrow will be even better. Yeah, right. What are the odds?

Chapter Two

It's early when I wake, and I blame it on the time change, overlooking how much I slept this weekend. Why did I agree to go with Sadie? I lie staring at the ceiling, but I must be honest. What else is there to do? Plus, I need groceries.

While my gigantic washbasin of a tub fills, I select my clothes. An outfit appropriate for being in public. My one pair of designer jeans, a blouse and sweater, along with a cute pair of heels should work. Don't want a repeat of yesterday. I bathe fast since there's no point in stretching it out.

I was going to have the cereal Michael bought, but he failed to buy milk. Plus, corn flakes were his favorite, not mine. Especially not dry ones. I settle for coffee. I'm reminded of Sadie being glad I wasn't a tea drinker. Michael preferred tea and never drank coffee. Maybe that should have been a sign. Although I doubt coffee was to blame for his leaving. Did I drive him away? Did I not make him want to stay? This brings up the inevitable question: why didn't I see this coming?

The waterworks start again. I must get past this, must let Michael go and move on with my life. Of course, my mind has its say. Get past the man of your dreams tossing you away like day-old garbage? Sure, let him go. The man you sacrificed so much to help. Go ahead. Move on with your life. That's a nice one since he is your life.

Thankful it's time to leave, I redo my makeup, which was ruined during my self-pity session, and check the upper half of my appearance in the mirror. It will do. With my coat, scarf, and the flashlight, I head outside, not believing I'm driving a pickup.

It's one and a half miles to Sadie's driveway. My closest neighbor is more than a mile away. This makes me snicker. How many people lived within a mile of me in Boston? I already know Sadie better than any of the people there. I never even knew the names of the people next door.

After parking by the walkway, I make my way to the enclosed porch, knocking on the frame. Sadie hurries to open the door. I can't believe how cold I am after my brief time outside. "Come inside, coffee and rolls are ready. I hope you like pecans," Sadie says and heads to the back.

"I love pecans, but I thought we were going shopping?" I say, following her and the aroma of caramel and pecans into the kitchen.

"We are, but you don't want to go out without fortification. Have a seat, and I'll bring it to you."

"I can help."

"You can get our coffee, and I'll bring the rest," she says, motioning to the mugs beside the coffee maker. I fill two and go with her to the table. She sets the plates down, each containing a sticky pecan bun. They smell delicious.

We add sugar to our coffee, and after making sure it's right, I take a bite of the sticky bun. "These are fantastic, Sadie. Where did you get them?"

"Get them? Dear, I made them this morning."

"You're kidding. I've never known someone to make them from scratch."

"We always have around here. My mother taught me how. My husband used to joke these were the reason he married me."

"They are so delicious, I can believe it," I say, taking another bite.

"I enjoy cooking and baking, but I get little opportunity now. Jason and Tyler come for Sunday lunches and Wednesday dinners, so I get a chance then. Now with you nearby, maybe I'll have more."

"You'll have to watch it. If it's all this delightful, I might visit all the time," I say, holding out my roll.

"Wouldn't mind the company," she says, taking a sip of coffee.

"I met Jason, but who's Tyler?" I take a sip of my own.

"Tyler is Jason's son. He's four going on thirty," she says, chuckling.

"Son? I didn't realize he has a son. They visit, but not Tyler's mother?" I can't believe I asked that. "I...I'm sorry. It's none of my business."

"Not a problem. Carin, Jason's wife, passed away from cancer two years ago." Again, the hurt crosses her face. "She was a marvelous mother to Tyler and wife to Jason. It hit him hard."

"I can understand. Was it a lengthy illness?"

"No, the cancer was aggressive. Carin didn't live six months after the diagnosis."

I kick myself for mentioning that. We sit in silence, finishing our coffee and rolls. While Sadie stacks the dishes, I collect the cups and carry them to the sink.

"Let me get my things, and we'll get this show on the road. I'm sure you don't want to spend your entire day escorting me. Why don't you wait in the front room? I'll be right out." She leaves while I head for the front.

The room is neat and cozy, with carved wood and leather couches, matching chairs with cushions of brocade upholstery. There's a matching loveseat filling the area facing the enormous stone fireplace stretching across one wall. The furniture surrounds a large center rug in style with the house and the walls, mantle, and tables display many pictures. I recognize Jason in several. In a few, there's a woman with him. She must have been his wife. In one, she seems pregnant but appears to be outside in a rough setting.

"That picture was taken two months before Tyler was born," Sadie says, coming up behind me.

"It's a rugged area for someone seven months pregnant."

"They were on a rescue mission."

"A rescue mission? You mean overseas?"

"No, they were north of here rescuing trapped horses."

I'm not sure I understand. "Horses?"

"They'd gotten a call there were wild horses in trouble and worked with others to bring them to safety. Carin was a veterinarian too."

"Seems like an enormous risk for the sake of a few horses." I try not to sound harsh. We are talking horses.

"Yes, a few might agree, but if we can, we must help God's creatures when they need it." Her answer reminds me of her belief in this god. "Jason tried talking her out of it because of her being pregnant, but she'd have none of it. She was a strong, determined person and put others first."

A plaque gets my attention, and I move closer to read it. It's for a Doctor C. S. Stephenson for forty years of pediatric service. "Your husband was a pediatric doctor?"

"No, he was a banker. The plaque is mine."

"You were a doctor?" Too late I realize how bad that sounds.

"Still am. A pediatric cardiologist," she says with a slight smile.

I read where it's from. "You were at UCLA Medical Center?"

"Yes, was in the pediatric unit after med school at Stanford. Chief of pediatrics my last ten years."

I try to hide the surprise at this mild woman being a big city doctor. "You haven't always lived here?"

"Heavens no, I left for college. Then came medical school, where I met my husband. The Medical Center offered me a position, and he joined a bank in L.A. Now, we need to get going. We have a drive ahead of us," she says, turning for the doorway.

I hold her purse and help get her coat on. I do the same, and we're ready to head out to a place unknown to me.

Still not comfortable driving a pickup, I follow her directions and head south on Cole Creek Road. We stay on it for a distance. After crossing the North Platte River, we come to a crossroads, Highway 87. Sadie explains to the right is Casper and left is Glenrock.

As directed, I turn left, and Sadie guides me to the grocery store. Here, I get frozen dinners and other supplies. From her expression, I can tell Sadie doesn't like my selections, but I have no choice. I'm not a cook.

We stop for lunch at a small diner which provides an enjoyable meal. Sadie knows everyone, but most know of me too. There are a few inquisitive glances my way, but no mention of the big city hussy, to my relief.

As we return, I tell Sadie I'll stop and unload at my place before I take her home and walk back. She makes it clear that will not happen and tells me I'll need the truck for our trip to Casper tomorrow. This catches me off guard, but it seems I have no choice.

I help carry her items in and find out this means I must stay for coffee. I mention my groceries, but she chortles. "My dear, with the number of preservatives in frozen dinners and the cold outdoors, there's no problem leaving them in the truck. They'll be fine." Not able to argue, I help get the coffee on and put her groceries away. Afterward, we sit and chat.

She's a remarkable lady, and I enjoy talking with her, but I don't want to take up all her time. With my coffee finished, I thank her for the day and get ready to leave. She escorts me to the door and bids me goodbye, but that's not all.

"Now drive careful and mind the slick patches walking. Don't carry too much at a time."

"Okay, I'll try. Don't worry." I turn, but she catches me in another enormous hug.

"Tomorrow, we'll go to Casper and get you a warm coat and boots. Those high heels aren't suitable, and you'll freeze in this thin thing. Here we dress for function, not fashion."

I smile, knowing how out of fashion this coat is. "I'm okay."

"See, the cold is already impacting your thinking. We'll take care of it tomorrow. Now, be here at nine, and we'll have coffee first "

"Okay, I'll be here, but I'm not agreeing to the shopping."

"Nonsense. You need warmer clothing, and I know where to get it. It's simple logic. Tomorrow at nine, and you can bring more of your cookies." She checks that my scarf is tight to my chin. I guess I'm going to Casper tomorrow.

When I open my front door, I'm reminded how dreary my place is, but it's all I have for now. After putting my groceries away, which doesn't take long, I stand in the compact kitchen wondering what now.

In the past, I've been so busy with school and work, but now I have neither, and I feel lost. Then I remember Sadie mentioned cookies and occupy myself with those.

After dinner and with the cookies cooled and wrapped for tomorrow, I pass on TV and head for my minute bedroom. I'm picking out clothes for tomorrow when it hits me. There's no washing machine or dryer. I'm okay for a few more days, but I will need something soon. I'll ask Sadie tomorrow where to find the nearest laundromat.

With clothes laid out for the morning, I'm back to square one and at a loss for what is next. It's too soon for bed. I'd lie there, and the tears would flow again. The sight of my laptop bag gives me an idea, and I open it on the small table.

I'm not sure what I plan to accomplish since I don't have an internet connection. That will have to wait for an income. Which means I need to find a job first—that will be interesting, finding something fitting my MBA/MSF. As I stare at the blank screen, an idea pops into my head, and I grab my phone. I still have my unlimited data plan.

Now, my phone is not best for surfing, but I remember in college there was a shop favored for providing two things budget-weary students desired: bottomless cups of coffee and free Wi-Fi. One guy there would connect his laptop to his phone to access the internet. He said it was more secure and isolated him from everyone else. A total geek, but he knew computers. He told me once that to get to sleep he counted prime numbers backward from a thousand.

I search "How to use a smartphone to connect your laptop." A page appears with full instructions. It calls for a USB cord, which I plug in, and follow the steps. In no time, my laptop shows a connection, and my home page appears. I'm online.

With the browser window open, I wonder, now what? With limited free time in my previous life, I was never big on social networks. With plenty of time now, I search through several and create a login for one.

After filling in my details, I'm ready to go. The number of groups, blogs, and pages covering many topics amazes me. On a lark, I type in "broken-hearted ladies," and an extensive list appears. I didn't realize there were so many of us. I wonder if any of them know Michael? Next, for fun, I search "broken-hearted men," but find no groups.

Figures. I go back to the list of ladies' groups and select one claiming to be for women helping each other to heal their broken hearts.

The title page opens with a big red banner displayed at the top. The description says it's a group for women having difficulty dealing with the end of a relationship. Perfect for me. I click the "Join Group" button, and a notice shows for me to click another button to gain access. I follow the instructions and posts from women who seem to share in what I'm enduring appear.

The posts are compelling, with advice and comfort. I stay with my kindred spirits until the taskbar shows near midnight. Since I'm to be at Sadie's by nine, I tell my new friends I need to go but assure them I'll be back.

After changing into my nighttime attire and setting my alarm, I turn off the lamp on the minuscule nightstand and lie back. For the first time since I arrived, I feel ready to enjoy a decent night's rest. Of course, that does not happen. When my eyes close all I see is Michael, and when they're open all I do is cry. I don't know how much longer I can take this.

~ * ~

When my alarm sounds, I've been awake crying for a while. I pull on my old robe and force myself to get moving.

I arrive at Sadie's on time and she lets me in, leading me back to the kitchen. I'm carrying my offering of cookies, but I'm confused, sensing the aroma of cinnamon filling the house. The coffee is ready, and she's made a fresh batch of cinnamon rolls.

Setting my plate of cookies on the table, I turn to her. "What about the cookies I brought?"

"They're for later. Now have a seat," she says.

After fixing my coffee, I take a bite of my roll. "Sadie, these are something else. I don't think I've ever tasted anything like them."

"Thank you. These were another of my husband's favorites. I got the recipe from my grandmother."

"Was she a baker?"

"No, dear. She was a rancher," she says with pride.

"A rancher?"

"Yes, she came here with my grandfather in the mid-eighteen hundreds. The plan was to go further west, but when they saw this area, they stayed. The first morning they woke up, my grandfather pointed out a large moose standing on a ridge not far away. That was the start of Moose Ridge Ranch. They built it to be an enormous success. Others joined them and before long the town of Glenrock was born. Later rustlers killed my grandfather and, from then on, she managed it herself, right until the day she died."

"Wow, she must have been one resilient woman," I say, continuing to enjoy my roll.

"She was. She was also the local doctor. Her father was a doctor, and she worked with him before she married," she says, while taking a bite of hers.

"Your grandmother was a rancher and doctor, and you're a pediatrician. How about your parents?"

"My mother worked in the medical practice, which she took over. She met my father when he came to work on Moose Ridge. He became a veterinarian. They were happy here. Oh, look at the time. We best be getting on our way," she says, standing.

As she heads for the front door, she calls out, "Don't forget the cookies."

"You want me to bring them with us?"

"I have the perfect place for them." She's off before I can ask her to explain.

In the truck, Sadie tells me to take the right turn toward Casper. She has several places she wants to go and is insisting on my buying winter clothing. She doesn't direct me to the mall, but to several discount clothing stores instead. We find a nice parka and insulated boots at reasonable prices, so I get them.

We pop into another diner for lunch, and again, most know Sadie. She introduces me as her new neighbor. I follow her suggestion and order the vegetable soup. It's delicious and comes with fresh crusty bread. After lunch, Sadie says she needs to stop at a place in Glenrock. While making our way there, I mention my dilemma of needing a laundromat.

"Why would you need one of those?"

"I don't have a washer at home, and I'll need clean clothes before long."

"You'll use mine. Not a problem." She makes it sound like a foregone conclusion.

"No, Sadie, I couldn't use—"

"Why not? You need clean clothes, and I have the machines. Why wouldn't you use them? You can come Thursday. I do laundry on Wednesdays. Turn right at the next driveway."

It's not far, so I concentrate on slowing and making the turn into a parking lot without sliding. There's a sign saying, "Community Center" and several parked vehicles. All seem to be trucks or large SUVs. Are there any actual cars here? I park where Sadie tells me. "What are we doing here?"

"It's my Women's Auxiliary Committee meeting. Bring the cookies." She's out the door before I can say anything.

"Sadie," I call, but she's walking away. With no choice, I grab my bag and the cookies and hurry to catch her as she disappears inside the building. "Sadie? The Women's Auxiliary? Are you sure?"

"Yes. It will be a chance to meet the ladies." She enters a sizeable room with chairs around several tables. Near one table, a group of ladies are talking and glance our way when we enter.

"Sadie, I wasn't expecting you with Jason busy today," one lady says, coming over to us.

"My new neighbor was kind enough to drive me. Jazmine, Jill Carmine, our chairperson. Jill, meet Jazmine. She makes delicious cookies."

"Welcome to our little group. We're glad to have you here, Jaycee." I'm not sure she is. "We appreciate you bringing Sadie."

"Thank you, and it's Jazmine," I say, setting my cookies with the other snacks.

"Sadie, you know where the drinks are. Be a dear and show Joyce. Then we'll get things going."

I doubt she heard anything I said.

I follow Sadie to get a drink and notice several women glancing our way, talking in hushed tones. When we return, everyone takes a seat, and Jill starts the meeting.

"Welcome, everyone, and thank you for coming. Let me introduce Sadie's new neighbor, Janice. She's the one who moved here from back East. Guess she realizes she's not in the Big Apple anymore." Jill chuckles.

Sadie speaks before I can. "Jazmine; her name is Jazmine. She arrived here last Friday from Boston, is a delightful neighbor, and has an MBA from Harvard. She's perfect for here. Nice to have someone with class."

This shocks Jill into several moments of silence before she speaks again. "Well, welcome. Anyway, ladies, we have serious work this afternoon. Sarah, the financial report, please?" It's obvious Jill enjoys being in charge.

When they take a break to get more drinks and snacks. Sadie announces, "Ladies, try the cookies Jazmine made. They are beyond delicious."

Several try them, and most have something nice to say. Jill, however, shrugs after taking a bite and puts the rest on her plate. Does she have a problem with me?

After a short break, the meeting continues. It ends with Jill making sure everyone has their assignments. Afterward, several welcome me, mentioning the cookies as an icebreaker. I'm sure they're being polite. Sadie visits while I get our coats and watch Jill put treats on a plate. About half of my cookies remain, so I wrap them and wait.

As the group breaks up, Sadie spots Jill with the plate of treats and motions to it. "Are you taking something home for later?"

"No, thought I'd take these by Jason's. I'm sure he skipped lunch," she says while slipping on a mink coat.

"I believe he's busy with a foal's birth. He's expecting it to be a difficult one. Best to leave him alone," Sadie says as we make our way to the parking lot.

"Oh? Too busy for even me?" Jill says as though that's impossible.

"Plus, I believe he's on a cleansing diet. I wouldn't take him anything," Sadie says with a shake of her head.

Jill stops by a Lexus, the lone actual car here. It's also taking two parking spaces. "I didn't know. How long is the diet for?"

"I believe a full week. It was in a magazine. You know how Jason is. You want us to drop them by the fire station? I know they'll appreciate them."

"Well, since Jason can't have them. Are you sure it's not too much trouble?"

"Not at all. We're going right past it."

"Well, it will help. The girls have choir practice after school then their dance class later. Never a moment to myself. Now you take care Sadie, and it was nice meeting you Jackie." Once in her Lexus, she's quick to leave.

We climb into Sadie's truck, and I turn her way. "Which way to the fire station?"

"Make your way back to the eighty-seven and toward home. It's right before we leave town."

"We can add the cookies so there's enough for the entire station."

"No, the cookies are for Jason. Don't worry, there's enough on Jill's plate. It's a volunteer station, so no more than two men are on duty."

I'm confused. "Isn't Jason on a cleansing diet?"

"Don't think so. Where did you hear that?" She's displaying an amazing act of innocence.

"Didn't you tell Jill he was?"

"Didn't want her bothering him. Jason would never try one of those new-fangled diets."

I give her a questioning glare. "Sadie, what are you up to?"

"Why would I be up to something? It's the next block on the right. Stop at the door and honk. One of them will come out."

I follow her directions. Soon the side door opens, and a man hurries out. Sadie lowers her window and holds out the plate. "Hey, George, meet my neighbor Jazmine. We had these left after our meeting and thought of you."

"Nice to meet you, miss. Miss Sadie, you are too nice. You tell the ladies thank you," he says, taking the plate. "Now drive careful and watch for ice."

"We will. Get inside before you catch cold. I can't believe you didn't put on a jacket."

"Yes, ma'am. I should have, but seeing it was you, I wanted to get here quick. Anyway, thanks again, and have a nice day, ladies."

Once on the street, we're on our way. "Head for home?"

"Of course not. We need to drop your cookies at Jason's."

"I thought you said he was too busy?"

"What? Where do you get these notions? He'll be fine with us stopping by. It's not like he's having the foal."

I take a quick peek her way. She seems innocent enough, but her looks might be deceiving. "And?"

"What?" she asks in the same innocent voice she used with Jill.

"What do you think will happen when we get there?"

"We'll say hi and drop off the cookies. Why, what do you want to happen?"

I can't believe this. "What? I didn't say I wanted anything to happen."

"Fine, then. We'll drop off the cookies and be on our way."

"If you say so, but I think you're up to something. Where should I go?"

"Stay on eighty-seven and take our normal turn. It's on the left after the river."

Out Now!

What's next on your reading list?

Champagne Book Group promises to bring to readers fiction at its finest.

Discover your next
fine read!
http://www.champagnebooks.com/

We are delighted to invite you to receive exclusive rewards. Join our Facebook group for VIP savings, bonus content, early access to new ideas we've cooked up, learn about special events for our readers, and sneak peeks at our fabulous titles.

Join now.
https://www.facebook.com/groups/ChampagneBookClub/

www.ingramcontent.com/pod-product-compliance
Lightning Source LLC
Chambersburg PA
CBHW031124210626
46816CB00016B/2284